continued . . .

Also by Nancy A. Collins

The Novels of Golgotham
Right Hand Magic

NANCY A.
COLLINS

Left Hand Magic

A Novel of
GOLGOTHAM

A ROC BOOK

ROC
Published by New American Library, a division of
Penguin Group (USA) Inc., 375 Hudson Street,
New York, New York 10014, USA
Penguin Group (Canada), 90 Eglinton Avenue East, Suite 700, Toronto,
Ontario M4P 2Y3, Canada (a division of Pearson Penguin Canada Inc.)
Penguin Books Ltd., 80 Strand, London WC2R 0RL, England
Penguin Ireland, 25 St. Stephen's Green, Dublin 2,
Ireland (a division of Penguin Books Ltd.)
Penguin Group (Australia), 250 Camberwell Road, Camberwell, Victoria 3124,
Australia (a division of Pearson Australia Group Pty. Ltd.)
Penguin Books India Pvt. Ltd., 11 Community Centre, Panchsheel Park,
New Delhi - 110 017, India
Penguin Group (NZ), 67 Apollo Drive, Rosedale, Auckland 0632,
New Zealand (a division of Pearson New Zealand Ltd.)
Penguin Books (South Africa) (Pty.) Ltd., 24 Sturdee Avenue,
Rosebank, Johannesburg 2196, South Africa

Penguin Books Ltd., Registered Offices:
80 Strand, London WC2R 0RL, England

First published by Roc, an imprint of New American Library,
a division of Penguin Group (USA) Inc.

First Printing, December 2011
10 9 8 7 6 5 4 3 2 1

Dedicated to the memory of Janie Wester Thompson
1940–2010

Home is a name, a word, it is a strong one; stronger than magician ever spoke, or spirit ever answered to, in the strongest conjuration.

—Charles Dickens

Chapter 1

I woke up to find a dragon hovering over me.

The great beast's head was drawn back, its jaws agape as it prepared to spew its burning venom. It was so close I could see the veins running through the membranes of its unfurled wings and the iridescent scales that covered its underbelly. I was about to scream, but then I remembered where I was.

Waking up in my boyfriend's room can be disorienting at times, especially since there is a monster painted on the ceiling in photographic detail. Although I grew up in an apartment filled with works of art, the ceiling mural was freaking me out. It wasn't the dragon so much, though, as the chain of Kymeran maidens that danced around the big lizard. I had the strangest feeling that they were watching me when I wasn't looking.

Then again, that might have been the bedposts.

The carved owls perched atop Hexe's four-poster were as detailed as the dragon on the ceiling and every morning when I woke up, it seemed as if they were in slightly different positions than when I fell asleep. To be honest, a good many of the furnishings in Hexe's private quarters seem to move about of their own accord whenever I look away. Being romantically involved with a warlock was taking a bit more adjusting to than I'd first imagined.

Speaking of which—I glanced over at Hexe's side of the bed. The sheets were rumpled, and his pillow still smelled of his unique personal scent—a masculine mixture of citrus, moss, and leather—but Hexe was already up and about his day. I sighed as I swung my feet onto the floor.

Waking up alone was something else I was having a little trouble adjusting to. It wasn't that Hexe had grown bored with my company in bed—far from it—it was just that his people don't need nearly as much sleep as humans do. I guess I can add that to the umpteen things I didn't know about Kymerans before moving to Golgotham.

I took a quick look at the ornate French mantel clock that sat on the nearby nightstand and muttered a few choice words under my breath. Then I hurried into the master bathroom and stepped into the claw-footed tub, pulling the curtain shut behind me. Water blasted out of the showerhead shaped like a medieval dolphin, delivering the necessary kick start for my day.

I was supposed to be meeting my best friend for lunch. After that, I was going to take a trip to my favorite junkyard in Red Hook to scrounge raw materials for a new set of metal sculptures to replace the ones destroyed by Boss Marz. Not that anyone was in a hurry to exhibit my work now that it had a reputation for marching out of the gallery under its own steam. It's a long story.

After a quick rinse, I grabbed a towel off the rack and headed back into the bedroom—only to discover a hairless winged house cat perched atop the footboard, gazing at me with blazing red eyes.

"So you finally decided to get out of bed, eh?" the familiar growled. "You numps sure like to lollygag. . . ."

I yelped in surprise and awkwardly tried to wrap the towel around myself. "*Scratch!* What are you doing in here?"

"If you *must* know," he said with a sniff, "this perfectly *delicious* sun spot is about to materialize on the floor for the next half hour, and I simply *must* get my sunbathing in."

"I don't care *why* you're in the room!" I snapped. "Just get out!"

"How dare you tell me to 'get out'!" Scratch replied crossly, furrowing his feline brow. "I *live* here! Long before you ever showed up, I might add."

"You heard me—*scat!*" I shouted, waving toward the door while trying to hold my towel closed.

"You did *not* just shoo me away!" the familiar gasped indignantly. "What next? Are you going to throw an old boot at my head?"

"What's all the noise about in here?"

I looked up to see Hexe standing in the doorway, dressed in a pair of corduroys and an old sweater, a cup of fresh-brewed coffee in one six-fingered hand.

"Don't look at me—*she's* the one doing the yelling," Scratch said, nodding his head in my direction.

"I just don't want you in the room while I'm getting dressed! Is that so hard to understand?"

"What's the big deal?" the familiar replied grumpily. "It's not like I *want* to look at your hairless ape-bits. Besides, I've seen Hexe naked nearly every day of his life."

"That's different," I said.

"How so?"

"It just *is*!"

Hexe stepped forward, motioning toward the door with his thumb. "You heard the lady, Scratch—get lost."

"The nerve of some people!" The familiar unfurled his batlike wings, and with a couple of brisk snaps, he sailed off the end of the bed, through the doorway, and into the hall.

Hexe closed the bedroom door and turned to face me, shaking his head in bemusement. "I understand you wanting your privacy, Tate. But you're going to have to get used to Scratch being around. He *is* my familiar."

"I understand that," I said as I tossed my towel aside. "But there's such a thing as being *overly* familiar."

Hexe sat down on the edge of the bed, watching me with his golden eyes as I hurried to get dressed. "To be honest, I have to agree with Scratch—what's the big deal about him seeing you naked? Do humans always keep their clothes on in front of the household pets?"

"Hexe, baby, where I'm from, the pets don't *talk*. And, more important, they don't *know* I'm naked."

"You've got a point," he conceded. "Come to think of it, I guess familiars *are* more like household servants than pets in your world."

"Exactly." I smiled in relief. "I'm glad you understand where I'm coming from. For me, being undressed in front of Scratch is like flashing the family butler. It just feels—inappropriate."

"Where are you going?" Hexe asked, reaching out to caress my naked hip. Every time he touched me, it was as if a mild electric current passed between us. I smiled, savoring the tingle.

"I'm meeting Vanessa for lunch."

"You don't have to hurry off right this minute, do you?" He smirked, snaking a muscular arm about my waist.

As Hexe began planting kisses on my bare midriff, I checked the time on the mantel clock. I did some extremely quick math in my head, and decided I could spare another fifteen minutes—maybe even twenty. If I was lucky, I might get there just before the margaritas ran out.

I met up with Vanessa Sullivan at Frida's, a Mexican restaurant in the East Village, the walls of which are covered with murals inspired by the artwork of its namesake. Vanessa was sitting in front of the self-portrait of the famed surrealist in her shape-shifter form, that of a deer-faced woman. My old college roomie had a basket of tortilla chips in front of her and a half-finished pitcher of margaritas at her elbow.

"About time you showed up!" She grinned, hoisting her drink in welcome. "I got tired of waiting."

"So I noticed." I chuckled as I sat down. "How's engaged life treating you, Nessie?"

"I'm drinking, aren't I?" she replied with a toss of her coppery head. "It's amazing how planning a wedding can drive otherwise sane people to absolute lunacy."

"Anyone in particular?" I asked as I helped myself to a margarita.

"After being a lapsed Catholic—no, make that *prolapsed*—my entire life, now my mother has decided I should have an old-school wedding—priest, cathedral, the whole shebang! And if *that* wasn't bad enough, my future mother-in-law is insisting on a rabbi."

"Oy." I grimaced. "So what are you going to do?"

"Adrian and I have decided that if our families don't get off our backs, we're going to chuck it all and have ourselves a nice, old-fashioned Druid marriage ceremony. That should shut both sides up. But enough about me—what's new with you? We haven't seen each other since your opening night at the gallery."

"It was also the closing night," I reminded her. "And now the gallery owner is suing me for breach of contract because I ordered my artwork to march out during the show."

"Please!" Vanessa groaned, rolling her eyes in disgust. "Derrick Templeton should get down and kiss your feet! The art scenesters are *still* talking about that show—when's the last time that gallery of his stirred up that kind of interest?"

"Yeah, it got everyone talking all right," I replied with a sigh. "Now they think my work's enchanted—no respectable art dealer will represent me."

"Screw respectability. I've found it to be highly overrated. All that matters, Tate, is that you're an amazing sculptor. Anyone with one eye in their head can see that. Just keep doing what you're doing, and the right people will find you."

"That's what I keep telling myself, Nessie," I said. "But I'm starting to wonder if I have what it takes to gut it out."

"Are you kidding me? You're the bravest woman I know! You'd have to be, to agree to be my maid of honor!"

"I never would have taken you as a flatterer," I said with a laugh.

To my surprise, Vanessa's demeanor suddenly became very serious. "Don't laugh. I am being one hundred percent irony-free. I don't know *anyone else* who would have gone to the lengths you did to help a friend in trouble."

"What else could I do?" I shrugged, humbled by the unexpected praise. "I couldn't stand by and let Boss Marz put that poor kid to death."

"What are they going to do with that creep, anyway?"

"Right now they've got him locked up in the Tombs,

awaiting trial on a number of charges. What's left of his gang is lying low for the time being, thank goodness."

"And how's your teenaged were-cat?"

"Lukas is doing great. He's got a job as a delivery boy for Dr. Mao's apothecary shop. Between work and his girlfriend, he doesn't hang around the boardinghouse that much. He's assimilating into Golgotham a lot faster than I am. Not that Hexe and I mind—we appreciate the privacy right now."

Vanessa arched an eyebrow. "So you finally made the move on your magic man, eh?"

"Yeah. It's been a couple of weeks since we took our relationship to the next level," I said, blushing slightly.

"Oooh, I like how you phrased that. It sounds a lot classier than 'since we started screwing like weasels.' " A look of alarm crossed her face. "Have you told Mrs. E?"

"Of *course* not!" I replied. "I may be eccentric, but I'm not crazy enough to tell my mother I'm romantically involved with a Kymeran."

"What about Hexe? Does he have family?"

"Yes, he has family," I replied evenly. Although I have to admit that if anyone besides Nessie had asked me that question, I probably would have been pissed. "He wasn't hatched from an egg! In fact, I've already met his mother."

"Really? What's she like? Does she rhyme with 'witch,' too?"

"No, thank goodness. She's actually very nice. I've only met her once, but I like her. Her brother's another story, though." I automatically frowned as I thought about Hexe's dreaded uncle. "He blames me for Golgotham becoming the new hipster hot spot, thanks to that photo-essay in the Sunday *Herald*."

"But those were Bartho's photographs—you had nothing to do with that!"

"It doesn't matter. As far as Uncle Esau is concerned, *all* humans are one and the same. However, I *am* responsible for Bartho deciding to move to Golgotham."

"Ah—so you *are* guilty!"

"Afraid so. Behold! I am Tate, Destroyer of Worlds," I said, lifting my margarita in a mock toast.

Chapter 2

A plate of enchiladas and two more margaritas later, I bid Vanessa adieu and hopped the F train to Brooklyn. I got off at the Carroll Street station, where I caught a cab into Red Hook. Once a warren of junkyards and derelict factories, inhabited by longshoremen and other blue-collar workers, the South Brooklyn seaside neighborhood was now showing signs of finally succumbing to the real estate developers. As the taxi wound through funky little side streets, I spotted a billboard advertising the IKEA warehouse located just off the Gowanus Expressway. Wine bars and condos wouldn't be far behind.

The cabbie dropped me off outside Keckhaver Salvage, two and a half acres of automotive scrap surrounded by chain-link fencing that offered an unparalleled view of the Statue of Liberty. I had been a regular customer for the last three years, and was on a first-name basis with the owner, Mike, who was standing outside the one-room hut just inside the front gate that served as his office.

He was a tall, wide-shouldered man in his late fifties, dressed in a pair of greasy overalls, with long gray hair that spilled down past his shoulders, and a braided salt-

and-pepper goatee with a ceramic bead swinging at the end of his chin. He smiled and lifted his hand in greeting as I entered his domain.

"Welcome back, Tate. Looking for something in particular?"

"Just scavenging for whatever strikes my fancy, Mike," I replied. "How's business?"

"Depends on how you look at it," the junkman grunted. "You see that construction over there?" He pointed to a couple of cranes off in the distance. "Some big-shot real estate developers are converting the old industrial piers into condos, stores, and a marina. They want to buy my property. I don't really want to sell—but I don't have a choice. The new property taxes have gone through the roof now that I'm gonna be next door to a fuckin' marina!

"The wife's thrilled—it's a lot of money. Me? I don't want to leave, but I can't afford to stay. This business has been in my family for three generations—" The phone in the office/shack started ringing, cutting off his train of thought. "I better get that—it's probably the real estate guys again. Anyways, you're welcome to browse the yard." He motioned to the wilderness of junked parts and rusted vehicles. "Better get what you can while the getting's good."

I spent the rest of the afternoon doing exactly as Mike had suggested, scrounging through the towering piles of scrap metal for buried treasure that would inspire my next creations. I ended up with the steering knuckles pulled off an old Ford Bronco, some differential covers, and a box of mixed gears.

I located Mike, who was elbow-deep in a '73 El Camino engine compartment, and pointed out the items I wanted. We then returned to his office to set up the delivery information. He frowned when I told him where I needed it shipped.

"That's the address for the Relay Station in Golgotham," he said.

"I've been living there for a couple months now," I explained.

Mike grunted and nodded his head and returned to his paperwork, but I could tell he was slightly perturbed by what I'd told him. As I fished out my cell to call for another taxi to return me to the subway stop, he motioned for me to hang up.

"Don't bother with that. You'll be waiting for fucking hours. I'll give you a ride back to the train. Besides, I got a junker to pick up in Carroll Gardens."

"Thanks, Mike."

"It's the least I can do for a steady customer," he replied with a shrug.

I climbed into the tow truck, the side panels of which read, in faded script, KECKHAVER & SON SALVAGE & TOWING. The "& SON" had been partially scratched out. It smelled strongly of WD-40 and diesel fuel, and a loose spring in the passenger seat kept goosing me in the ass as we jounced our way across the pothole-laden street. It was a far cry from my father's Maybach, but then again, I could not recall my father ever driving me anywhere without a chauffeur.

When we reached the subway stop, I thanked Mike once again for the ride and started to get out. Before I could exit the vehicle, the junkman gripped my elbow. His hand was large, the knuckles scraped and scarred from a lifetime spent under the hoods of vehicles, and yet it possessed an odd gentleness.

"Look, Tate—you seem like a nice kid. Hell, I got a daughter your age. I hope I ain't overstepping myself here, but you really ought to think about moving outta that place."

"I appreciate your concern, Mike." I smiled as I extricated myself from his grip. "But there's really nothing to worry about—Golgotham is a lot safer than most people think. It's certainly a lot less dangerous than walking around Red Hook after dark."

The mechanic gave a humorless laugh and shook his head. "Look, I've lived in this part of Brooklyn all my life—I can remember back when it was a *real* shit-hole, back in the nineties. I know how to handle myself, you know what I mean? But you couldn't *pay* me to set foot in Golgotham. The worst thing that can happen to you in Red Hook is you get yourself raped or murdered. In Golgotham you can end up damned."

With that the junkman drove off, leaving me to mull over his farewell as I waited for the train that would take me back home.

It was early evening by the time I reached City Hall Station, the closest subway stop to Golgotham. As I stepped out onto the platform, a throng of hipsters exited the car before mine, talking and texting. It was as if the entire Urban Outfitters catalog had come to life and decided to take a train downtown.

As I passed underneath the station's landmark stained-glass skylight, I noticed several of my fellow travelers clutching well-thumbed copies of *Manhattan Magazine*, the *Herald*'s Sunday supplement. I stifled a groan.

Two weeks ago *Manhattan* had published a photoessay by my friend, the up-and-coming "hot" new photographer "Bartho" Bartholomew, titled *Golgotham Nightlife*. The six strikingly composed black-and-white

photographs had shown, among other things, leprechauns playing darts at Blarney's Pub, centaurs hauling
carriages full of drunken revelers down cobblestone
streets, the regulars crowding the bar at the Two-Headed
Calf, a half-naked nymph standing in the doorway of a
Duivel Street bordello, and the glitterati enjoying themselves at the ultra-exclusive Golden Bowery. More important, Bartho's pictures had captured the citizens of
Golgotham with an authenticity reminiscent of Ouija,
the famed psychic photographer of 1940s New York.

Within twelve hours of the Sunday *Herald* hitting
the streets, Golgotham suddenly found itself besieged
by the young, bored, and semi-affluent. Unlike the majority of tourists who made their way to the neighborhood in search of magic or to score a new kind of kick
on Duivel Street, these visitors came to experience the
"real" Golgotham. The result was an unexpected and
unprecedented increase in the number of human faces
in the pubs, restaurants, and nightclubs that normally
catered to native clientele. While the money spent by
this recent spate of "looky-loos" was welcome, their intrusion into Golgotham's traditional social scene was
another matter.

As I emerged from under City Hall, the group ahead
of me cut across the plaza in the direction of Broadway,
making a beeline for the centaur-drawn hansoms and
satyr-pulled rickshaws lined up at the taxi stand, leaving
me standing at the curb. Since motorized vehicles aren't
allowed within Golgotham, I was now faced with a long
walk after a tiring day. Grumbling under my breath, I
shoved my hands deep into my coat pockets and set out
across Park Row in the direction of home.

I decided to head west and walk down Ferry Street,
skirting Witch Alley, the neighborhood's notorious open-
air magic bazaar. Although this took me a block or two

out of my way, it saved me from having to deal with the traffic jam created by the never-ending stream of tourists and bargain shoppers attracted by the various spell-slingers, potion-pushers, and charm-peddlers hawking their wares to those in search of quick luck or easy love.

"Need a ride?"

I looked over my shoulder and saw a familiar face smiling down at me. It was Wildfire, stablemate to Hexe's childhood friend and primary means of transportation, Kidron. The female centaur's long hair, currently worn in an elaborate French braid crowned by a wreath of interwoven sunflowers, was the same shade of sorrel as her lower body and tail. She was human from the withers up, and wore a leather bustier that also served as a harness to the Victorian-era hansom cab she was pulling. Save for the Bluetooth headset clipped to her right ear, she looked like she had just stepped off a Grecian urn.

"As a matter of fact, I do," I replied gratefully.

Wildfire pulled a harness line connected to her bustier, and the doors to the hansom cab flew open. I quickly jumped inside and made myself comfortable.

"It's very busy this evening," I commented as we trotted in the direction of the boardinghouse.

"Yes, we've been getting a steady stream of looky-loos since that article in the Sunday *Herald*," Wildfire said. "If things stay like this, we should be able to afford a down payment within the year."

"On a stable?"

"No, a ranch." The centaur explained, "We have our eye on a place in Wyoming. We've been working hard for several years now to save up enough money. Kidron and I plan on starting our own herd someday."

As she spoke, I realized, with a start, that Kidron and Wildfire weren't just roommates, but actually husband

and wife. I was both surprised and embarrassed that I had never made the connection before.

"The city is no place to drop a foal," the female centaur said. "Colts and fillies need space to roam and run free without worrying about being hit by a car. The ranch we're interested in is over three hundred acres, located thirty miles east of Laramie."

"It sounds nice," I replied. The idea of living out West didn't appeal to me in the least, but I also wasn't a horse from the waist down. "Where were you born, Wildfire?"

"I was foaled on a farm upstate, near West Winfield," she replied. "Kidron was stable-born here in the city. He's used to walking on pavement all day long, but I miss the feel of turf under my hooves, and the smell of fresh grass."

"Are you sure you want to move that far away? I mean, you could probably find a nice farm somewhere in Pennsylvania."

"Our ancestors came here on cattle boats from Greece in the 1850s, looking for a better life," Wildfire said with a toss of her mane. "Kidron and I are simply continuing in that tradition. We want our foals to look forward to something besides dragging coaches full of tourists around Golgotham when they grow up. All we want is the American Dream."

Wildfire dropped me off at the corner grocery a block from the house, where I made a last-minute purchase before hurrying home. Upon my arrival I found Hexe busy in the kitchen, brewing up something for one of his clients in the iron cauldron reserved for making potions.

"How was your day, honey?" Hexe asked as he stirred the bubbling concoction.

"Fairly productive," I replied, setting the grocery sack

on the kitchen table. "I would have been home sooner, but I stopped by Dumo's to pick up a little something. Where's Scratch?"

"What do *you* want?" The familiar sniffed, not bothering to get up from his resting place on the kitchen floor.

"I'm sorry I insulted you earlier today," I apologized. "I brought you a peace offering."

Scratch raised his head, ears perked and whiskers twitching. Suddenly I was the most interesting person he knew. "You brought me a present?"

"I hope this makes up for my being rude to you," I said, removing a bundle wrapped in butcher paper from the grocery bag.

Scratch was on his feet faster than I could blink, his bloodred eyes the size of saucers. "Yeah, well, that depends on what you brought me," he said, trying to sound nonchalant despite the drool dripping from his lips.

The moment I tossed the package onto the floor, the winged cat jumped on it, tearing the paper with his claws and fangs, revealing a nice juicy cow's heart. His mouth opened distressingly wide as he unhinged his jaw and swallowed the chunk of meat in a single gulp.

"You're forgiven," Scratch said as he licked his lips. "For *now*."

"What have I told you about spoiling him?" Hexe chided.

"Hey, *somebody's* got to!" Scratch grumbled. "All I ever get from *you* is that dry-ass Purina Familiar Chow."

"So—how is Nessie?" Hexe asked as he took the cauldron off the boil.

"A tad frazzled, but that's to be expected," I replied, pouring myself a glass of green tea from the fridge. "She and Adrian have set the date for their wedding."

"That's nice," Hexe said in a preoccupied tone of

voice. He was busily sorting through the various jars of dried herbs, roots, and worts scattered along the kitchen shelves, in search of whatever ingredient it was that needed to be added while the potion cooled.

"Did I mention I'm her maid of honor?"

Hexe turned around, holding a bottle containing a pickled cobra. "Does this mean I have to go, too?"

"We're a *couple* now," I reminded him. "That means if *I* suffer, *you* suffer, and vice versa. At least *you* don't have to wear the dress she picked out for the bridesmaids." I grimaced and shuddered.

Further discussion concerning Vanessa's wedding was derailed by the sound of someone hammering on the front door as if driving in a railroad spike. Hexe frowned and looked at me.

"Are you expecting a delivery?"

"Yeah, but not today," I replied. "It's probably one of your clients. Maybe someone got their nose turned into a balloon animal, or cursed with biohazard-quality halitosis?"

Hexe put a lid on the cauldron he was tending and hurried out of the kitchen. I tagged along after him, curious as to the reason for the frantic knocking. Hexe opened the front door, revealing our neighbor from across the street. Her name was Kama, and she was a witch-for-hire like Hexe, with a seafoam green bouffant and sequined harlequin glasses. She was on our front stoop, doing her best to keep the middle-aged human woman standing beside her from collapsing.

"Praise all the heavens! You're home!" the sorceress exclaimed in relief. "I normally would have called before coming over, but there's no time!"

"What's the matter?"

"My client's been afflicted with a Great Curse," she

explained. "I need help from a strong Right Hand if this poor woman is to survive."

Kama's client suddenly moaned in pain and clutched her abdomen, her sweaty face turning the color of oatmeal. She then vomited forth a handful of carpet tacks, which clattered across the hardwood floor of the foyer like the world's worst game of jacks.

"We don't have much time," Hexe said grimly. "Follow me."

Chapter 3

I hurried ahead of Hexe and Kama, opening the door to the study for them as they maneuvered the feverish, semiconscious woman through the house. The walls of Hexe's private office were covered with bookcases, and a stuffed crocodile hung from the ceiling like a cold-blooded piñata.

"Put her down over there," Hexe instructed, pointing to a red velvet fainting couch positioned under a taxidermied gorilla. "What's her name?"

"Madelyn Beaman."

"Madelyn, can you hear me?" Hexe asked in a loud, clear voice. The cursed woman groaned but otherwise did not respond. Hexe squeezed her hand until she opened her eyes and looked at him. "Did anyone give you something to eat or drink in the last two hours?"

Madelyn shook her head as if it took every ounce of energy to do so.

"She's one of my regulars," Kama explained as she knelt beside the suffering woman, gently combing the damp hair away from her brow. "She showed up on my doorstep ten minutes ago, complaining of severe nausea.

I barely had time to diagnose her as being afflicted when she began to spit up bobby pins. That's when I realized I was out of my depth."

"If what she said is true about not ingesting anything, it means that whoever's cursed her is using sympathetic magic," Hexe said.

"Is that bad?" I asked nervously. The last time I'd seen anyone look as sick as Madelyn was when we'd gone to say good-bye to Great-aunt Florence in the cancer ward.

"If the one who invoked this curse has hair or nail trimmings to work with, or some item of clothing that once belonged to her, it makes things . . . complicated, but not impossible to reverse," Hexe said carefully.

"Thank you for helping me, Serenity," Kama said gratefully. "If you hadn't been home, I don't know who I could have turned to."

"Glad to be of service," he replied, flashing Kama a reassuring smile. "I have to prepare for the widdershins ritual, and I need you to keep her warded until I'm done with that."

Kama nodded her understanding and began to recite an incantation in Kymeran, which resonated within the confines of the study like the chanting of Buddhist monks. As I watched in quiet awe, I could see what looked like a moonlit spider web shimmer into existence around the cursed woman.

"Come with me," Hexe said, taking me by the hand. "Kama needs to concentrate on her warding spell."

I followed Hexe back into the kitchen, where he began ransacking the cupboards and pantry. I sat down at the kitchen table, trying to stay out of his way as he searched for the ingredients needed for the widdershins ritual that would turn the curse away from its hapless victim.

"I don't quite understand what's going on. Why did

Kama bring her client to you?" I asked. "I thought you guys were highly competitive when it comes to your customers."

"Kama is a juggler—she practices both Right Hand and Left Hand disciplines equally," he explained. "Because of that, her Right Hand magic isn't strong enough to combat such a powerful Left Hand curse. It requires someone like me, who practices Right Hand magic exclusively, to turn an affliction of this magnitude widdershins. While Kama might be willing to inflict color blindness or stuttering on others for money, she doesn't deal in genuinely malicious curses. It's not in her nature. Nor is it in her nature to let another die, whether she profits from it or not."

"What's wrong with her patient?" I asked.

"This curse is known as allotriophagy, where foreign and foul objects are vomited forth from those who haven't consumed them. It can range from live creatures, such as snakes or toads, to pieces of iron, nails, pins, needles—or even worse. In order for it to work, a wizard must take the stomach from a pig or a goat and affix a piece of clothing or a lock of hair from the victim to it, and then gradually fill the stomach with increasingly dangerous items. Those items are then magically transported into the victim's belly.

"Hopefully I can lift the curse before Madelyn begins puking up razor blades and broken glass. Once it gets to that stage, there's nothing I can do. She'll hemorrhage to death from the damage done to her stomach and esophagus. It's an awful way to die."

"But who would want to do this to her?"

"No doubt someone who is extremely jealous of her," Hexe replied. "Perhaps an ex-lover, or her husband's mistress. Sadly, a good many people would rather pay a necromancer than alimony."

"So much for 'happily ever after,'" I said, grimacing in distaste.

"Allotriophagy is one of the nastiest Great Curses, which means I have my work cut out for me." He took a wad of white sage, bound with kite string, that was the size and shape of a cigar, and set one end on fire, waving it in the air in odd patterns. He then set the smoldering bundle of herbs aside and opened a bottle of distilled water, which he poured on his right hand; then he carefully dried his hand clean with a crisp white linen napkin.

"What are you doing?" I asked.

"Cleansing myself," he explained. "It helps focus my energy before the widdershins ritual."

"Is this going to be dangerous?" For the first time I felt a genuine spark of fear—not for myself, but for Hexe. While I had seen him practice magic before, none of it had been as serious as this.

"It *can* be," he conceded. "It all depends on the strength of the hands involved."

Suddenly there was a scream from the study, followed by a loud thump. We hurried back to find Kama picking herself up off the floor, a thin trickle of blood leaking from her nostrils.

"Are you all right?" Hexe asked. "What happened?"

"The curse is too strong," the sorceress explained as she got to her feet. "I shielded Madelyn the best I could, but it finally punched its way through."

The moment Kama spoke, Madelyn Beaman began to convulse and gag. Without thinking, I grabbed a nearby wastebasket and placed it beside the fainting couch, so the antique Oriental carpet wouldn't be ruined. To my horror, what flew from the cursed woman's mouth was a mixture of galvanized roofing nails—and blood.

"There's no more time," Hexe said, motioning for us to stand aside. "Tate—please turn off the light."

I nodded and switched off the Tiffany desk lamp made from an armadillo's shell. The room was immediately plunged into darkness, but after a second or two my eyes began to adjust to the gloom and I could see Hexe standing before the fainting couch.

Placing his left hand behind his back, he turned to face the East and raised his right hand. All six fingers were bent at angles no human digits could master as he began to chant in Kymeran. Even though I had no way of knowing what he was saying, I felt the hair on my arms start to rise.

As he touched the middle of his forehead with his right hand, a beam of brilliant white light suddenly shone down from above, as if some celestial stagehand was training a spotlight on him. The light was so bright I was forced to shield my eyes. After a few seconds the light took the form of a sphere, roughly six inches in diameter, hovering just above the crown of Hexe's head.

He then turned West and touched the middle of his abdomen, his chanting becoming deeper and more insistent. A second sphere of white light blossomed into existence in his solar plexus, as if he'd swallowed a ball of lightning.

Turning to the North point of the compass, Hexe angled his right hand so that he was pointing at his own feet. A shaft of light descended from the sphere hovering just above the crown of his head, fanning outward like the base of a pyramid.

A sulfurous wind began to blow out of the darkness, scattering the papers piled atop Hexe's desk and chasing them across the floor. I moved to retrieve them, but Kama grabbed my arm and shook her head. A second later Madelyn began to convulse, crying out in pain as her belly filled with yet more torment.

Turning to the South, Hexe touched his right hand to

his right shoulder, creating yet another sphere of light. As his chant grew in speed and volume, a beam of light shot forth from his right shoulder and ran down the length of his arm, until it came to rest in the palm of his hand. Hexe turned to face Madelyn and stretched his right arm out over her prone body, his glowing palm centered over her stomach.

The wind from nowhere increased in strength, knocking books off the shelves and making the stuffed crocodile suspended from the ceiling swing back and forth like an incense burner. Hexe was surrounded by light, gleaming in the darkened room like a giant living diamond. By now he was shouting as if trapped at the bottom of a well. His voice was so loud I had to cover my ears, yet I could still feel the words resonating against my sternum like a tuning fork.

A pillar of white light abruptly shot from Hexe's palm and into Madelyn's grotesquely distended belly, causing the cursed woman to sit bolt upright and scream at the top of her lungs. White light poured from her gaping mouth and eyes, as if she were a human jack-o'-lantern. Hexe didn't flinch or falter, but continued his litany as he channeled more and more light into her body.

Just as abruptly as it had begun, the stinking wind ceased its howling, and the cursed woman fell silent, dropping back onto the couch like a marionette whose strings had been cut. Hexe staggered as the celestial white light surrounding him winked out like a snuffed candle. I rushed to his side to help steady him.

"Are you okay?" I asked anxiously. Although I had seen him work spells before, I had never seen him drained to such an extent.

"I'm fine," he replied hoarsely, giving me a reassuring hug. "I just feel like I've run a twenty-mile race with a forty-pound pack strapped to my back. That's all." He lurched over to his desk and removed a metal lockbox from one of the drawers.

"I was able to turn the allotriophagy widdershins, but as long as the necromancer who inflicted the curse has an item that belongs to Madelyn in his possession, she remains in mortal danger. While that particular affliction will no longer work against her, there are still plenty of Great Curses to choose from," he explained as he removed a long gold chain, on the end of which hung a flat metal disk made of the same material, inscribed with Kymeran symbols. In the middle of the disk was set an extremely realistic glass eye. "Put this around her neck. It is one of the strongest gladeyes I've ever made. It should keep her protected as long as she wears it against her skin."

Kama took the amulet and slipped it around her client's neck. Madelyn groaned in pain as she began to regain consciousness, blood seeping from the corners of her mouth as a result of the damage done to her throat and stomach lining.

"Tate, could you be so kind as to bring me the bottle marked 'katholikon' from the kitchen?" Hexe asked. "It should be sitting in the ingredients rack above my workbench. I'd get it myself, but I'm still a tad woozy."

"Of course," I replied. I ducked back into the kitchen and scanned the wooden shelf above the antique workbench Hexe used to prepare his various healing potions and charms. I located the bottle between a jar of dried dung beetle and a vial of squid ink. It was the smallest container on the shelf, with a rubber eyedropper for a cap, like the medicine I had to use for the swimmer's ear I contracted while at sleepaway camp. I plucked it out of the rack and returned to the office. Hexe took the tiny amber bottle from me, handling it gingerly, as if it contained nitroglycerine.

"I'm afraid I'll have to give you a straight dose, Madelyn," he explained as he removed the dropper and placed a single drop of the katholikon on her tongue. "It's going to be unpleasant, but you have to swallow it."

"It burns like fire!" she wailed, clawing at her mouth. "You've poisoned me!"

"Hexe isn't trying to hurt you, Madelyn," Kama said soothingly. "Just swallow—it'll be over in a minute or two."

"What is that stuff?" I asked, eyeing the tiny bottle uneasily.

"What the ancient humans called 'panacea'—a near-universal cure-all. It can heal most internal injuries, provided you're conscious and capable of swallowing. But if you try to introduce it intravenously, it's like mainlining hydrochloric acid. All you need is the tiniest drop for it to do its work—unfortunately, it tastes like Ghost Pepper sauce mixed with gasoline. Normally I mix it with wild cherry syrup and honey to cut back on the taste, but we just don't have the time for such niceties right now. I had to give her an undiluted dose, but she should be fine in a few moments."

True to his word, the color instantly returned to Madelyn's face and her eyes grew clear. She looked around the room with a quizzical expression. "Where am I?" she asked. "This isn't your house, Kama."

"You're at my neighbor Hexe's," the sorceress explained. "He was kind enough to help me with your . . . condition."

"Why don't I fetch a something so she can clean up?" I suggested and hurried to the water closet located under the front staircase. As I was reaching for a washcloth, there came yet more pounding on the front door, followed by a man's voice.

"Madelyn!"

I answered the door to find myself staring at a middle-aged man dressed in clothes that were just a little too hip and a toupee that was styled just a little too young. Even if Hexe had never said anything about Madelyn's curse being inflicted by a jealous husband or a vindictive mistress, this guy would still have set off my hinky-meter.

"What do you want?" I asked suspiciously.

"My name's Charles Beaman and I demand to see my wife!" he replied gruffly. "I was told she was here—"

"By whom?" This question came from Hexe, who materialized behind me as if from thin air.

"Me," Kama replied. "Madelyn insisted I notify her husband."

"Very well." Hexe sighed and stepped aside. "Your wife is this way, Mr. Beaman."

As we filed back into Hexe's office, I saw that Madelyn had abandoned the fainting couch in favor of one of the chairs normally reserved for client consultations. She looked a thousand times better, despite the dried blood staining her face and clothes. The look of love and devotion she gave her husband as he entered the room made me want to punch him in the throat.

"Chuck! Thank heavens you're here!"

"Oh my God, Maddy!" he exclaimed in horror. "What have they done to you?"

"Besides save her life?" I retorted as I pushed past him to clean the gore from his wife's face.

"It's okay, Chuck." Madelyn smiled. "Kama and Hexe are my friends. I would have died if not for their help."

As Mr. Beaman bent down to hug his wife, Madelyn wrapped her arms about him, clinging to him like a drowning swimmer hugs a life preserver. I started to feel bad about wanting to karate-chop his larynx. After a long moment, Mr. Beaman pulled himself away and turned to address Hexe.

"Do you know who's responsible for afflicting my wife?"

"No, I'm afraid I don't. It could be any of a number of practitioners here in Golgotham." Although Hexe's face was otherwise unreadable, his golden eyes seemed to darken for a moment. "Great Curses are neither cheap nor simple to procure. Do you know of any reason why someone would pay thousands of dollars to curse your wife?"

"Of course not!" he replied with an overly loud laugh. "My Maddy's a wonderful woman! Not an enemy in the world!" He turned back to help his wife get to her feet. "Come along, Cupcake—let's go home."

"Not so fast, Mr. Beaman," Hexe said, moving to block the couple's path. "There is still the matter of my fee. . . ."

"Oh, of course!" Mr. Beaman said, reaching for his wallet. "How much is it? Five hundred? Six?"

"Ten thousand dollars."

"What?!" Mr. Beaman shouted, his toupee abruptly coming unseated. "Ten *thousand*—? Have you lost your Kymie mind? That's highway robbery!"

"As I said, your wife's affliction was not only deadly but expensive. The same holds true for its removal," Hexe replied evenly. "However, you're getting a priceless added value: Not only is Mrs. Beaman fully recovered from the mortal wounds inflicted by the allotriophagy, but she's also cured of any other ailment or disease she might have been suffering from."

"I don't care if you throw in a free set of steak knives and a glass cutter! I'm *not* paying you ten thousand dollars!" Mr. Beaman barked. Suddenly I was back to wanting to karate-chop him in the throat.

"Oh, for crying out loud, Chuck!" Madelyn groaned. "Pay the man his money! Lord knows he earned it!"

Mr. Beaman glared at his wife, his cheeks turning beet red. "You *know* I don't carry that kind of cash on me!"

Madelyn sighed and reached for her purse. "Will you take a personal check?"

"Of course, Mrs. Beaman."

Hexe waited patiently while Madelyn used her husband's back as a writing desk. As she handed the signed check to him, Hexe leaned forward and whispered in her ear, "Whatever you do, never, *ever* remove the glad-eye from around your neck for as long as you—or your husband—live."

Mrs. Beaman glanced at Mr. Beaman, who was busy trying to reattach his toupee, and I saw something flicker in the back of her eyes. Whether it was the birth of suspicion or the death of love was impossible to say.

As Hexe escorted his visitors from the house, he paused to take Madelyn's husband aside for a moment. "I would advise you not to try and put a stop-payment on the check your wife just gave me," he said in a quiet, firm voice. "You would *not* like the means by which I collect bad debts." He gestured in the direction of Scratch, who, having shed his "normal" appearance for that of his demon aspect, lay curled in the shadows at the foot of the stairs. Mr. Beaman's eyes bulged and his Adam's apple went up and down like a yo-yo as the dragon-winged saber-toothed tiger yawned and fixed him with a baleful stare. I was surprised his toupee didn't jump off his head and run out of the room.

Once the humans were safely away, Hexe turned to address Kama. "Let me guess—she's the one with the money?"

"Boatloads of it," the sorceress replied. "They've been married for nine years. It was a natural union, as far as I know—no come-hither or love potions involved. Madelyn is, at heart, a good woman, but an insecure one.

She was afraid he was going to leave her for another woman, so about six months ago she paid me to cast a Stay-With-Me spell over Chuck. I warned her that without an accompanying love potion, the spell wouldn't guarantee her husband's devotion. She said she didn't want to compel his love, just keep him from leaving her. I fear tonight we saw the upshot of that decision."

"People should be careful about what they wish for—they might just get it," Hexe said grimly. "If he couldn't leave her, he was going to make sure she left him—the hard way."

"He certainly wasn't happy about paying double—first to try and kill his wife, then to save her," Kama replied with a humorless laugh. "In any case, I can't thank you enough for your help, Hexe."

"Glad I could be of service," Hexe replied, holding up Madelyn's check for her to see. "We'll split the fee fifty-fifty, agreed?"

"Agreed, Serenity," Kama replied, bowing her head in ritual obeisance.

"Yes, well—what are neighbors for?" Hexe said, blushing to his purple roots. He always became uncomfortable when fellow Kymerans treated him like royalty. Once Kama had left, Hexe headed back into the kitchen, where he took the cauldron he'd been tending and up-ended it into the sink. "So much for *that* batch of Balm of Gilead," he muttered.

He had just saved a woman's life and pocketed a nice chunk of change in the bargain, but I could tell that something was bothering him—and it wasn't simply that he'd ruined a potion.

"Do you mind if I ask you a question?"

"Of course not," he grunted as he lugged the cauldron back over to the stove.

"Why did you tell Mr. Beaman you didn't know who was responsible for cursing Madelyn?"

"Because I can't tell who paid to have a curse inflicted," he replied, a little too sharply. "You *know* that."

"But you *can* read the signatures of other wizards and witches on the spells they cast. And you know damn well who inflicted that curse on Mrs. Beaman. I could see it in your eyes when her husband asked you about it. Why didn't you say anything?"

"Because," Hexe said, with a heartsick look on his face, "the necromancer who placed the curse on Madelyn was Uncle Esau."

Chapter 4

If there's one thing I've discovered about sorcery in the brief time I've lived in Golgotham, it's that after a hard day of inflicting and lifting curses, cooking up potions, and casting spells, all the average witch or warlock really wants is a hearty meal and a good drink. So Hexe and I headed out to his favorite local restaurant to celebrate his recent windfall.

However, just as we were leaving the house, Hexe's cell phone went off. "I better take this," he said, as he glanced at the caller ID. "What's up? Uh-huh. Nothing—going to grab some dinner at the Calf . . ." He turned to smile at me. "Yes, of course she's here. . . . No, why do you ask?" His smile abruptly disappeared. "That's rather short notice, don't you think? Hold on. Let me ask her." He clapped a hand over the mouthpiece, an exasperated look on his face. "My mother has just invited us over for dinner."

"Tonight?"

"It's up to you. We don't have to do it if you're uncomfortable with the time frame. . . ."

My initial surprise was quickly replaced by excitement. This was a Major Step. Although I'd met Hexe's mother on a couple of occasions, I hadn't spent any real time with her since we had started dating.

I took a quick physical assessment of myself, to see if I was presentable. While I wouldn't say I looked like something the cat dragged in, I was keenly aware that I was in dire need of a haircut. Still, the peacoat, turtle-neck sweater, and jeans I'd thrown on earlier could pass for dressy casual.

"Tell her I'd *love* to," I replied.

"Tate says it's okay with her," Hexe translated. "See you soon, Mom."

As he went to hail a cab, I started to get nervous. I told myself that it was only natural. After all, none of my previous boyfriends had mothers who were witches *and* queens.

Lady Syra lived on Beke Street, between Perdition and Shoemaker, which was only fitting, as it was named in honor of her ancestor, the founder of Golgotham. Her apartment building stood fifteen stories tall, towering over its humbler neighbors like a giant. With its multi-paned metal window casements, quatrefoil-pierced balconies, and crenellated parapets, it looked more like a neo-Gothic castle than a condo co-op.

"Now *that's* swanky," I said, pointing to the copper-sheathed observatory that crowned the penthouse.

"It was a gift from President Kennedy, after my mother warned him about Dallas in '63," Hexe said proudly. "Too bad he chose to ignore her concerning San Francisco in '68."

The ground floor of the apartment building boasted a limestone pointed-arch entryway with a massive oaken double door. As we approached, a handsome, broad-shouldered huldu, dressed in immaculate doorman's livery, stepped forward to greet us.

"Good evening, Serenity," the doorman said, his bull's tail swishing discreetly below the hem of his long coat.

"Hello, Knute," Hexe replied with a slight nod.

The lobby was as cavernous as a cathedral, lit not by electricity but by balls of blue-white witchfire that bobbed near the ceiling like helium balloons. As we headed to the elevator bank, the doors opened and a satyr tottered out of the car.

Up to this point, my only encounter with such a creature had been when one had tried to kidnap both me and Nessie while we were riding in a rickshaw. Although I knew I shouldn't judge an entire species by one bad apple, I automatically took half a step back.

Unlike the satyr who'd tried to carry me off, this one was nattily dressed in a tailored dinner jacket and matching waistcoat, with a lavender cravat tied about his neck. In one hand he carried a golden-headed cane engraved with the initials *GG*, which he used to steady himself. He sported a neatly trimmed goatee, and his carefully coiffed hair was styled to accommodate the curling goat horns that jutted from his temples.

Upon spotting Hexe, the satyr paused to screw a gold-rimmed monocle into his left eye. "Pan's beard!" he laughed. "How've you been doing, my boy?"

"I've been keeping myself busy, Giles," Hexe replied.

"So I see," the satyr replied archly, giving me an appreciative once-over. "Well, I must be off," he said, raising his cane in a farewell salute. "I mustn't keep a certain faun waiting. Tell your mother I said hello." With that he hurried across the foyer, his hooves clattering loudly against the marble-clad floor.

"Who was that?" I asked as we stepped into an elevator that now smelled of equal parts barnyard and high-end cologne.

"That was Giles Gruff, businessman and notorious bon vivant," Hexe explained. "He owns the rickshaw business in Golgotham, among other things. He is *extremely* conscious of how society views his people, and goes to great length to comport himself in as gentlemanly a fashion as possible. He can be a bit pretentious at times, but he's an okay sort. He's been our downstairs neighbor for as long as I can remember."

"I thought you grew up in the boardinghouse," I said.

"No, that was my mother's and Uncle Esau's childhood home," he explained. "I did spend a great deal of time there with my grandparents, Eben and Lyra, though. I remember playing hide-and-seek with my grandfather in the hedge maze when I was little."

Just then the elevator doors opened, revealing the foyer outside the penthouse. Having grown up surrounded by crystal chandeliers and antique furniture, I wasn't impressed with the lobby's decor so much as I was with the minotaur seated on a marble bench in front of the penthouse door.

The bull-headed man put aside the newspaper he'd been reading and snorted, causing the large metal ring hanging from the center of his nose to swing like a doorknocker. The horns jutting from his massive skull were the diameter of a man's wrist, the points capped by a pair of golden balls. His shoulders were as wide as an ox yoke, his body covered in rippling muscles that strained against the jogging suit he wore, and he had the biggest, softest, most beautiful brown eyes I'd ever seen.

"Greetings, Serenity," he mooed.

"Good evening, Elmer," Hexe replied with a smile.

It was then that I recognized the minotaur as one of the many half-beasts Boss Marz had held captive and forced to fight to the death for the amusement of gamblers. The last time I'd seen him, he was wearing a werewolf on the end of his horns.

"How do you like your new job?" Hexe asked.

"I like very much," Elmer said as he opened the penthouse door, speaking with a very thick Mediterranean accent. "Your mother . . . good woman."

"Yes, she is," Hexe agreed, as he escorted me across the threshold.

The first thing I noticed upon entering the apartment was a strange suit of armor set just inside the foyer, as if in challenge to unwanted visitors. The helm, breastplate, gauntlets, and greaves were elaborately detailed, much like those of a samurai warrior, and fashioned from a strange iridescent material that gleamed like the carapace of a scarab. In one gloved hand was a long metal pike similar to the hooks used to train elephants.

"What is this thing made of?" I asked, staring in fascination at the glittering armor. "I've never seen metal like this before."

"That's because it's dragon skin, Miss Eresby."

Lady Syra was standing next to her son, watching me with a little smile on her face. I had not seen or heard her arrive. She was dressed in a pair of black capri pants, ballet flats, and a cropped blouse with batwing sleeves. Her peacock blue hair was worn in an upswept style that accentuated her delicately arched brows and golden eyes. She still smelled, as I remembered, of roses and jasmine and wore what, at first glance, looked like an ivory necklace shaped like a serpent about her throat.

"May I touch it?" I asked, barely able to contain my excitement.

"Be my guest."

I could hardly keep my hands from trembling as I ran my fingers along the breastplate of the armor. It felt like a strange mixture of leather, horn, and fiberglass, and seemed both lightweight and extremely resilient. The last dragons had been put to death over a thousand years ago, and yet here was a relic fashioned from the remains of one. The realization that I now knew what a dragon's skin felt like was at the same time deeply exhilarating and tremendously sad.

"The ancient Kymerans made a number of items from the sheds of their dragons," Lady Syra explained as I inspected the armor. "This particular suit has been in the family since before the sinking of Kymera. It was worn by my ancestor Lord Bexe."

"The last Witch King," I said in wonderment.

"Or so the human history books would have it." She smiled wryly. "In any case, he was the last to rule over a true kingdom. The royal family still abides, as you well know. Tell me, Tate, what do you think of my new footman?"

"You mean Elmer? I thought he was your bodyguard!"

"Believe me, I have *all* the protection I might possibly need right here." Lady Syra laughed, placing a hand on the tiny albino snake twined about her throat, mouth-to-tail. "But as Witch Queen, I am honor-bound to help *all* of Golgotham's citizens, not just the Kymerans. It is a covenant that dates back to the Sufferance, and one the royal family takes very seriously. Elmer's such a dear boy—I would hate to see him fall back into the hands of those who would abuse his good nature. Plus, he is exceptionally handy when it comes to rearranging the furniture. Come, let's sit down. The foyer is no place to chat."

As I followed Lady Syra to the living room, we passed down a hallway whose walls were covered with framed photographs: Here was a picture of Lady Syra with Elvis; there was one of her having tea with Queen Elizabeth II; and over there was a photo of her at John Lennon's fiftieth birthday party, sitting at a table with Jimi Hendrix and Keith Moon. She had led quite the glamorous jet-setting life.

The living room was a large open area with a sunken conversation pit, and a signed Warhol serigraph of Lady Syra hung over the fireplace. Arranged on the mantelpiece was a collection of unusual bric-a-brac, from an African fetish doll bristling with nails to a fire opal the size of an ostrich egg set on a pedestal and sealed under a glass dome.

"Would you care for a smoke before dinner?" Lady Syra asked as we sat down, gesturing to the collection of hookahs arrayed on the coffee table. "I have a wide variety of *shisha* tobaccos—hazelnut, mocha ... perhaps some lemon mint?"

"No, thank you," I replied as she loaded the bowl of one of the water pipes with a sticky mixture that smelled of equal parts Turkish tobacco and cognac. "I don't smoke."

"Ah, yes! Cancer!" Lady Syra said, clucking her tongue in self-reproach. "How thoughtless of me! Would you care for a champagne cocktail instead?"

"That would be lovely."

Lady Syra clapped her hands and a Kymeran butler with a vermilion buzz cut stepped into the room, an empty silver serving tray balanced on his right hand.

"Yes, Your Highness?"

"Miss Eresby would like a champagne cocktail, Amos."

"Very good, ma'am."

The butler moved to where I was seated and leaned forward, extending the empty serving tray to me. I glanced at Hexe in confusion, but he did not act as if anything was at all unusual. When I looked back at Amos, I was startled to see a champagne flute full of bubbly on the silver platter.

"Thank you," I said as I took the proffered glass, trying not to look impressed. The last thing I wanted to do was come across as a nump in front of Lady Syra.

"So—why did you *really* invite us to dinner, Mother?" Hexe asked, folding his arms across his chest.

"What a question!" she replied, blowing twin streams of hookah smoke from her nostrils. "Is it so strange for me to want to share a meal with my only son and his new friend? Why, I've barely seen the two of you since that unpleasantness with Boss Marz."

"Dinner is ready, Your Majesty," Amos announced, even though, as far as I could tell, he had yet to leave the room.

"About time! I'm positively famished!" Lady Syra exclaimed. "Do bring your drink along with you, Miss Eresby."

"Please, Lady Syra—I'd rather you call me Tate."

"You're right." The Witch Queen smiled. "There's no need to be so formal. I will call you Tate and you shall call me Syra."

The dining room was off the living room, and easily the same size as the one in my parents' home. The table was long enough to accommodate up to twelve guests, outfitted with an Irish linen tablecloth, the finest cut crystal, and Tiffany flatware. In the middle was a centerpiece composed of deep-hued fruits arranged on a large platter around dark pillar candles. Overhead hung a French Renaissance Gothic chandelier decorated with gargoyle heads, with tiny balls of blue-white witchfire glowing inside their gaping maws.

As I made myself comfortable at the table, Amos the butler placed an empty plate in front of me. In the weeks

since arriving in Golgotham, I had acquired a taste for
certain Kymeran cuisine, such as rook pie and ostrich
steak. But there were some "delicacies" I simply could
not stomach. I hoped whatever Amos had in store for us
didn't involve bugs, snakes, or the boiled heads of barnyard animals. I tentatively sniffed the air, in hopes of
preparing myself for whatever culinary "treat" lay ahead,
but all I could smell was the butler's own unique scent of
black pepper and cinnamon.

"You've truly outdone yourself, Amos!" Lady Syra
exclaimed in delight.

I looked over at my hostess, confused as to why she
would be moved to compliment her butler so lavishly
for simply putting an empty plate in front of her. To my
surprise, I saw a heaping serving of crawfish étouffée,
even though Amos had yet to leave the room.

Baffled, I glanced down at my own plate and was rewarded by the sight of a sizzling, thick-cut medium-rare
New York strip and a loaded baked potato. I gasped in
surprise and looked back up at Amos. "Where did this
come from? How did you—? I mean, you haven't moved
an inch!"

"Amos is a wizard in the kitchen," Lady Syra explained, amused by my bewilderment. "He charms my
dishes, so that they manifest whatever it is you're hungry
for. It's a very rare skill, and I'm lucky to have him in my
service."

"Madame is too kind," Amos said, blushing slightly.
"If everything is to your satisfaction, I must finish charming the dessert cart."

Once the butler left the dining room, Hexe put down
his fork and turned to face Lady Syra. "I know when
something's up, Mom. You wouldn't have invited us for
a friendly little dinner on such short notice if you didn't
have an ulterior motive."

I was all too familiar with dinner table confrontations in my own family, and had long ago mastered the skill of keeping my head low and my eyes fixed on my plate. I started cutting into my steak, praying that the drama between mother and son would be relatively mild and over by the time Amos returned with that magic dessert cart of his.

Lady Syra heaved a deep sigh. "I had hoped we could forestall this conversation until after dinner. But the truth of the matter is, Hexe, I've been getting complaints about your behavior."

"What kind of complaints?" Hexe demanded sharply. "About what? From whom?"

"Some of the more conservative members of the Kymeran community have complained about you publicly flaunting your relationship with Tate. . . ."

I looked up, my dinner totally forgotten. Suddenly I was very much a part of what was going on.

"You call going out to dinner and walking hand in hand in public *flaunting*?" he snapped, wadding up his napkin and hurling it to the floor. "By the sunken spires, you make it sound like we've been having sex on our front doorstep!"

"I know it sounds outrageous," Lady Syra said, shifting about uncomfortably. "But you have to understand that this is *not* a good time for this sort of controversy. There is already significant anxiety concerning the increasing infiltration of numps—I mean, *humans*—into traditional Golgothamite venues. Some see you carrying on a romantic relationship with one of them as a conflict of interest regarding the gentrification issue."

"That's absolute spraint, and you know it. I'm not going to shun the woman I love simply to make a bunch of blue-haired bigots happy!"

"Do you *truly* love this woman?" Lady Syra's golden

eyes widened in surprise, as if it had never occurred to her that our relationship was anything other than physical.

Hexe paused and looked across the table at me. Suddenly the anger and irritation drained from his face, to be replaced by a gentle smile. For that brief moment, everything else disappeared, and we were the only ones that mattered in the room.

"Yes," he replied, reaching out to take my hand and giving it a reassuring squeeze.

I expected Lady Syra to smile and nod her head upon hearing her son confess his true feelings. After all, the whole world loves a lover, right? Instead, she began knotting and unknotting her cloth napkin. "Oh my." She sighed in exasperation. "That complicates things even further."

"What do you mean?" I asked.

"Dalliances are one thing, but a committed relationship is something else entirely!" she explained.

"So Hexe has a human girlfriend—what's the big deal?" I asked.

"The 'big deal,' as you put it, is that you're *not* a 'girlfriend.' There is no such thing when it comes to the Heir Apparent. There are only consorts and concubines," Lady Syra said pointedly. "Hexe, you know as well as I do that our private lives are not entirely our own. We have certain obligations to our people, no matter how difficult we find them to bear."

"Times have *changed*," he replied testily. "Just because you allowed Grandfather and Uncle Esau to ruin your happiness doesn't give you the right to destroy mine." Lady Syra flinched and quickly looked away. As soon as the words left his lips, Hexe's outrage disappeared, and he got up and put his arms around his mother. "I'm sorry I said that to you, of all people! It was a cruel and thoughtless thing to do."

"I understand your frustration, sweetheart," Lady Syra said with a sad smile as she caressed her son's cheek. "I know what it's like to face disapproval in the name of love. But you needn't fear, darling—I am not going to do as Papa did. I'm not going to forbid you from seeing Tate. However, I *am* concerned that the two of you don't fully understand the social and personal turmoil a mixed relationship such as yours creates. I don't want to see either of you hurt."

"I appreciate what you're trying to say, Lady—I mean, Syra," I replied. "And I realize it comes from genuine concern for our safety. I'm only now starting to comprehend the challenges Hexe and I are going to face as a couple; and I have to admit, it worries me at times. But, in the end, I believe that what we have is worth fighting for."

"You are both very courageous," Lady Syra said, dabbing at the corner of her eye with her napkin. "Far, far braver than I was at your age."

"It was different then, Mom," Hexe said gently.

"Not as much as you think." She sighed, patting his hand.

The quiet moment between mother and son was broken by raised voices on the other side of the dining room doors, followed by a loud rumbling sound, as if someone was hastily moving a large piece of furniture.

"Get out of my way, kitchen-witch!"

The doors to the dining room flew open to reveal Amos and Elmer arguing with Lady Syra's older brother, Esau. Great—as if things weren't already *I, Claudius* enough.

The minotaur took a tentative step forward, a pained

look on his face. "I am sorry, Lady Syra. I told man you were busy. But he threaten to turn me into ox."

"It's all right, Elmer," Lady Syra said, getting to her feet. "Please return to your station before you get caught in the chandelier again."

"Yes, ma'am," the minotaur replied, obviously grateful that he no longer had to be in Esau's company.

The necromancer strode into the dining room as if he were in his own home, shooing Amos away with an imperious wave of his hand. He was dressed in a black wool coat with caped shoulders, and he had shoulder-length hair of dark indigo laced with streaks of ice blue at the temples. While he had the same distinctive golden eyes as Lady Syra and Hexe, they lacked his sister's graciousness and his nephew's warmth.

"Syra! I need to speak to you *immediately*!" Esau announced, only to halt in midstep upon catching sight of Hexe. "Of course!" he sneered, his eyes narrowing. "I shouldn't be surprised to find you here, clutching your mother's skirts."

"What in the name of the Outer Dark are you doing here, Esau?" Lady Syra asked in exasperation.

Syra's brother ignored her question, and instead pointed a finger at Hexe. "How *dare* you lift my curse!"

"It is my duty as a healer and adherent to the Right Hand Path to serve a client to my fullest ability, no matter what the circumstance," Hexe replied stonily.

"Don't hand me that spraint about protecting clients!" Esau said with a nasty laugh. "The nump wasn't one of your regulars—she goes to that inept little juggler, Kama."

"It was Kama who asked for my assistance," Hexe explained. "I was honor-bound to help. Besides, I didn't realize the curse was your work until I removed it."

"Well, thanks to your meddling, my client is demanding a refund!" Esau said angrily. "In the thirty years I've been dealing in afflictions, I have *never* had to return money to a client! And I expect you to make good on what you've cost me!"

"Have you lost your mind?" Hexe snorted derisively. "You accuse me of hiding behind my mother, but you're the one who's constantly running to your sister to complain about me, instead of coming to my home and addressing your grievances to my face."

"You've made sure I'll never set foot in that house again," Esau snapped. "By renting out a room to a garden-variety nump, you've contaminated my childhood home and opened the door for others to follow!" Suddenly the necromancer did a double take in my direction. "What is *that* doing here?" he demanded, focusing a look of such venomous hatred upon me that my mouth went dry. I attempted to return his glare, but could not hold my gaze; it was like looking into the eyes of a king cobra readying to strike.

"Her name is Tate," Hexe said firmly, his hands curling into fists. "And she's here with me."

"I'd heard rumors that your son was dallying with a nump," Esau sneered. "Now I see it's true. I shouldn't be surprised that he's inherited his mother's poor taste in bed partners."

Lady Syra gasped as if her brother had slapped her. Hexe stepped forward, his eyes flashing like polished shields. "You'll apologize to my mother and my girlfriend right this minute!"

"Or you'll do what, exactly?" Esau scoffed. "You're not wizard enough to make me do anything, whelp!"

"Just try me and see, old man."

"That's enough, Esau!" Lady Syra snapped, struggling to recover control of the situation. "And the same goes for you, Hexe! This is neither the time nor the place for a duel."

If Esau heard his sister, he showed no sign of it. Instead, his black, hateful gaze was now riveted on Hexe. "It's time someone taught you a lesson about sticking your nose into Left-Handed business," he said, flipping his half-cape out of the way.

"I get enough of this foolishness already. I don't need it in my own house," Lady Syra shouted. "Esau, I command you to stand down!"

Suddenly an orb of fire shot from the necromancer's left hand. I recognized hellfire when I saw it, and I knew it burns whatever it touches to the bone. I automatically jumped to my feet, only to have Lady Syra snare my wrist, anchoring me to the spot as if I'd been grabbed by one of my own sculptures.

Hexe raised his right hand and with a flick of his wrist sent the fiery projectile back the way it had come, like a tennis player returning an opening serve. Esau lifted his own right hand in an attempt to deflect the returning volley, but the fireball's course remained unchanged and he was forced to jump out of the way as it zoomed past and struck the far end of the dining table, where it exploded like a paintball full of phosphorous. The flames spread rapidly, racing along the length of the tablecloth and jumping onto the adjoining chairs.

Lady Syra let go of my hand and stretched her arms above her head, tilting her head back as she began to recite an incantation in a language that was old when the first pyramids were raised. Water poured down from nowhere, soaking everyone and everything in the dining room. The charred dining table hissed like a snake as the hellfire was extinguished. The Witch Queen then closed her hands into fists and the downpour halted as if turned off at a faucet.

All of us were drenched, but Esau looked like he'd fallen into a carnival dunk tank, with his dark hair plastered to his skull and water dripping from his heavy woolen coat. It was the first time I'd ever seen the necromancer caught off balance, and I allowed myself a giggle. Esau glared daggers at me, but this time I held my ground, refusing to be intimidated by someone who looked like a half-drowned rat.

"How *dare* you—?!" the Witch Queen said in a voice as sharp and steely as a surgeon's scalpel. "You enter my home uninvited, threaten my servants, insult both me and my guest, attack my son, and then, to add injury to insult, set fire to my good tablecloth!"

"I'll admit that things got a *little* out of control," Esau said as he tried to wring the rainwater from his sodden overcoat. "But it's not my fault—your brat challenged me!"

"Yeah, you sure schooled me in the superiority of the Left Hand," Hexe snorted.

Esau opened his mouth to retort, only to fall silent under the Witch Queen's withering stare.

"I don't care *how* much business Hexe has cost you, Esau—not even a member of the royal family is permitted to raise a left hand against the Heir Apparent! By Kymeran law, what you just did qualifies as attempted regicide, with a penalty of death. For years I have tolerated your bullying and disrespect out of a misplaced sense of loyalty and, yes, guilt. But I can no longer ignore or excuse your behavior.

"What I am about to say, Esau, does not come easy to me, but you have left me no choice. You are my brother. When we were children, I loved you and looked up to you. But that was before you chose to walk the Left Hand Path. The lifestyle you embrace has turned the boy I once adored into a bitter, twisted stranger. I would give anything to have the brother I knew and loved restored to me, but I realize now that you are too far down the spiral to ever return." She took a deep breath and squared her shoulders, readying herself for what she had to say. "Esau: I now speak to you not as your sister but as the Witch Queen. As of this moment forward, you are banished from the royal presence. I never wish to see your face or hear your voice again. Should you cross my path, I will have no choice but to treat you as a hostile and engage you in ritual combat. Now leave me, and consider yourself lucky I do not banish you from Golgotham as well."

For the briefest moment there was a flicker of sorrow in Esau's golden eyes, like a cloud scudding across the face of the moon. Then the darkness returned, dimming what little light remained within him.

Lady Syra gestured to the door of the dining room, which swung open of its own accord, revealing a worried Amos standing on the threshold. Esau bowed stiffly to his sister, then turned on his heel and strode from the room without a backward glance.

Lady Syra watched him go, her hands clasped tightly before her. Save for the single tear running down her cheek, it was as if she was made of stone, neither breathing nor blinking until Hexe touched her shoulder. Only then did she start, as if waking from a dream.

"That was a very difficult and unpleasant thing for me to do. But it was inevitable," she said wearily. "I'm sorry you were subjected to such poor manners by a member of my family, Tate. Normally my dinner guests needn't fear dying in a house fire. I can see why my son is so taken with you—you possess a strong lick of courage. Not everyone would have kept their head under such circumstances. Now, if you don't mind—Amos and I need to address the damage done to my home. I trust you can find your way out."

Hexe nodded his understanding, and kissed his mother on the forehead. She smiled wanly and caressed his cheek before motioning for Amos to join her in the heavily sodden and badly charred dining room.

As we passed by the wall of photographs on our way out, my eye was caught by an old Kodachrome that showed a teenaged Lady Syra dressed in a miniskirt, standing with her arm about the shoulder of a handsome, slightly older Kymeran man with an indigo blue Beatles haircut, dressed in a paisley-print Nehru jacket. With a start, I realized the friendly, smiling face and kind, caring golden eyes belonged to Esau.

Chapter 5

Since we didn't have a chance to finish dinner, and were in dire need of a few stiff drinks after our ordeal, Hexe and I hailed a centaur and decided to go to the Two-Headed Calf. During the ride, Hexe didn't have much to say, and seemed lost in thought. From what I had gleaned from the conversation between him and his mother, there was considerably more family drama going on than I previously realized. Hexe had never mentioned his dad before, and I had assumed that Lady Syra was either a divorcée or a widow. Now it was becoming clear that things were far more complicated than just a messy divorce. Still, despite my curiosity, I refrained from asking any further questions concerning his father. I decided it would be best if he told me the story on his terms, instead of having it pried out of him piece by piece.

The Two-Headed Calf was situated a couple blocks down and over from the boardinghouse, and had been in business continuously since before the Revolutionary War. Above the entrance was suspended an old-fashioned wooden pub sign depicting its namesake: the left head goggle-eyed, tongue-lolling drunk, while the right head contentedly munched on a daisy. As Hexe opened the door for me, a cloud of cigarette smoke wafted out to greet us.

One of the more unpleasant aspects of Golgotham that I had been forced to get used to was the fact that damn near every Kymeran smokes like a clogged chimney, especially in public. Whether by sorcerous design or genetic fluke, they are not susceptible to cancer, so their attitude toward tobacco and other carcinogens is considerably different than that of human society. I counted myself lucky that Hexe didn't indulge in the habit, but I still had to deal with secondhand smoke whenever we went out on the town.

The Calf was jumping when we arrived, the bar elbow to elbow as a live band played in the back to a raucously appreciative audience—a good number of which appeared to be human.

"Who are they?" I asked, pointing to the musicians playing an earsplitting cross of punk and traditional Kymeran folk tunes on electrically amplified violin, hurdy-gurdy, and accordion.

"They're called Talisman," Hexe explained, speaking loudly enough to be heard over the music. "I went to grammar school with the lead singer, Polk. They're getting some interest from a major label. It's about time there was a *real* crossover Kymeran rock act. Bowie doesn't count."

A handful of college students sat in one of the booths, talking animatedly among themselves as they nursed tankards of barley wine and took pictures of their surroundings with their cell phones.

Lafo, the Calf's head bartender, chief cook, and bottle washer, left his place behind the horseshoe-shaped bar and came out to greet us. He was close to seven feet tall, and with his long, flowing, ketchup red beard and the elaborate tattoos swarming his forearms, he looked more like a pirate than a respected restaurateur. As he welcomed us, my hand was briefly engulfed by his.

"Good to see you two, as always," he said with a grin.

"Seems you've acquired a new clientele." Hexe nodded at the looky-loos and chuckled.

"There's a write-up somewhere online listing the Calf as 'The Weirdest Place to Get a Drink in New York City,' or some bullshit like that," Lafo explained with a shrug of his broad shoulders. "They've been pouring in like water all week. I appreciate the business, but by the sunken spires, what a load of whiny chuffers! They're always going on about the cigarette smoke and asking for nachos and light beer. Where do they think they are? Applebee's? Plus, now the regulars are pissed at me because I won't kick 'em out!"

As he spoke, the door to the Calf opened and another knot of young humans arrived, gaping at the bar's interior with a mixture of excitement and trepidation. As they entered, a couple of the regular patrons exited, roughly jostling the looky-loos on their way out.

"See what I mean?" Lafo grunted. "Some of my best customers have accused me of selling out. Ha! You'll know I've sold out the day you see cheeseburgers on the menu!"

"We were planning to stay for a drink and some dinner, but it looks like you're full up," Hexe said as he scanned the crowded room.

"I can fix that," Lafo assured him. The tavern owner walked over to a nearby table occupied by a couple of young college kids. "Hey, you!" he barked. "Go stand at the bar!"

"But we're sitting here!" the braver of the two protested.

"And I *own* where you're sitting. So you can either stand at the bar and finish your drinks, or you can show me some ID. Which is it gonna be, kiddos?" The students grumbled under their breath, but they still got up and took their drinks to the bar. "There ya go—best seats in the house!" Lafo said with a lavish flourish of his catcher's mitt–sized hand. "Make yourself comfortable. I'll send Chorea over to take your order."

"Oh—are she and Faro back from their honeymoon?" I asked.

"Well, *she's* back," Lafo replied. "I'm not too sure about Faro's whereabouts."

A few seconds later Chorea, one of the Calf's barmaids, appeared at our table, order pad in hand and a ballpoint pen tucked inside the wreath of ivy and grapevine that adorned her raven black hair. The looky-loos in the booth opposite from us snickered as they blatantly ogled the maenad's voluptuous body through her gossamer-sheer chiton. My cheeks burned with shame, not for Chorea but out of embarrassment for the behavior of my fellow humans.

"Congratulations on your marriage." Hexe smiled. "Faro is a lucky man."

"Not if I get my hands on him!" Chorea replied sharply. "Did you know that bastard ran off and left me on our honeymoon?"

"Oh, Chory, I'm so sorry," I gasped. "That's horrible!"

"He ditched me in Crete, two days after we were married." The maenad gave Hexe a suspicious look. "You wouldn't have happened to have seen him lurking about?"

"No, I haven't," Hexe replied. "But if I run into him, I'll make sure he knows you're looking for him."

"Fair enough," Chorea sighed, mollified by his response. "So—what'll it be? The usual?"

Within moments of our nodding yes, the barmaid had a pint of Old Hurdy-Gurdy and a glass of the house red sitting before us. As I lifted my glass to my lips, the person at the table next to us—a Kymeran man with long pumpkin-colored dreadlocks—lit up an elaborately carved meerschaum pipe, adding further aromatic billows to the already smoky room.

A young human woman wearing a beret and a disgusted look on her face leaned out of a nearby booth and tapped the orange-haired Kymeran on the shoulder. "Excuse me—sir? Sir?"

The dreadlocked Kymeran turned in his seat to scowl at her, but did not take the pipe out of his mouth. "What is it, nump?" he growled.

"Sir, do you mind *not* doing that?" the woman asked in a tone that made it clear she was making a demand, not asking a question.

"Doing *what*?" the Kymeran replied, continuing to puff on his pipe.

"Smoking!" she replied in a voice just short of a shout.

The entire room fell dead silent as every eye in the bar turned to stare at the defiant human. Asking a Kymeran to extinguish his cigarette or pipe on his home turf was right up there with burning a flag, in terms of cultural insult. The dreadlocked wizard took the meerschaum out of his mouth and studied it for a moment, then shook his head.

"I *do* mind, thank you very much."

The woman in the beret blinked, taken aback by the Kymeran's lackadaisical response. "Smoking isn't allowed in bars and restaurants in New York City," she said with overstated politeness. "What you're doing is against the law!"

"Who's gonna arrest me?" The warlock chuckled as

he blew a lungful of Borkum Riff in her face. "You and your nump pals there? This ain't Tribeca or the Village. You're in Golgotham now, girlie. You'd best remember that."

The woman and her companions hastily gathered up their coats and left the bar, muttering profanities under their breath. The moment the door closed behind them, the regulars gave a ragged cheer and a few came over to clap the pipe smoker on the back and buy him another round.

Hexe, however, did not seem to find the incident quite so amusing. "C'mon, Tate," he said. "Let's go upstairs to the dining room."

Suddenly there came a high-pitched, yet somehow masculine shriek from the back of the house. *"Put me down!"*

Chapter 6

I turned in the direction of the yell and saw a drunken college student dressed in an Islanders sweatshirt holding a wildly squirming leprechaun over his head as if he were the Stanley Cup, much to the amusement of his equally inebriated companions. Like all of his kind, the leprechaun sported bright red hair and bristling whiskers. However, instead of wearing the stereotypical breeches buckled at the knee and gartered hose, he was outfitted head to toe in scaled-down Versace.

"Don't let 'im go until he gives you his Lucky Charms!" one of the friends shouted. This particular witticism triggered a round of loud, braying laughter from the surrounding crowd. Since I had suffered my share of mischief at the hands of the local Wee Folk, I will confess to a certain schadenfreude at the fairy-fellow's predicament.

"That's racist!" the leprechaun yelped. "Let me go, ye bloody nump!"

"Don't do it, Jared!" one of the college student's friends advised. "If you capture one of 'em, they have to grant you three wishes!"

"What are ye, *five*?" the leprechaun snapped as he continued to try and free himself. "None of that shite from the fairy tales is true! Now put me down!"

"No way!" Jared said, shaking his head. "Not until you give me your pot of gold."

"Are ye daft as well as drunk?" the leprechaun growled. "I don't carry me gold around on me person. Besides, it's all tied up in commodities right now."

"And I say make with the gold, little dude!" Jared laughed, shaking his captive like a piggy bank, as if a cascade of bullion might pour from the leprechaun's tiny pockets.

Suddenly Lafo was standing in front of the college student, the sleeves of his shirt pushed up to reveal his muscular forearms. "I'll have no horseplay in my establishment!" he barked, his voice booming like surf against a rocky shore. "And don't you numps nowadays know enough not to antagonize the Wee Folk?"

"There's no reason to get all butthurt, bro'," Jared replied as he set the leprechaun down. "I wasn't gonna really *do* anything to the little fucker. Me and my friends were just having some fun, that's all." The college student turned to offer a conciliatory fist bump to the victim of his bullying. "We're cool, right, little dude?"

The leprechaun responded by pulling a short shillelagh from the sleeve of his jacket and pointing it at the college student. "So ye want me Lucky Charms, eh?" he asked, his high-pitched voice trembling with rage. "Well, by damn, you'll *need* them, boyo! *May you feast on hogwash and sleep in filth; may you root with your nose as the farmer till'th!*"

Jared doubled over as if punched in the gut by a phantom fist, and dropped to the floor. The college student's cries of confusion and pain quickly turned into porcine squeals as his hands and feet transformed themselves into trotters and his nose grew and broadened into a twitching pink snout. He frantically thrashed about as he tried to free himself from clothes that no longer fit his newly acquired physique, which came complete with a curlicue tail.

The sight of the transmogrified student's distress triggered a chorus of laughter from the Calf's regulars, who were every bit as amused by Jared's ordeal as the frat boys had been by the leprechaun's.

"Oh my God!" one of Jared's friends wailed. "What did you *do* to him? Turn him back, you little freak!"

"Never!" the leprechaun snarled defiantly. "And if you ask me, I have improved his appearance immensely."

"Damn it, Tullamore," Lafo snapped. "You know I don't allow spell-slinging in my joint! Last thing I need is the Paranormal Threat Unit breathin' fire down my neck."

A couple of frat boys lunged at the leprechaun, but Tullamore was ready for them. He nimbly sidestepped his bigger, clumsier opponents, moving so fast it was impossible to keep track of him. One moment he was thumbing his nose in front of his attackers, the next he was dancing a jig behind them.

The laughter from the Kymerans watching from the sidelines grew louder and nastier each time the disoriented college students tried to rush the toddler-sized Tullamore. Cackling with laughter, the leprechaun jumped onto a nearby table occupied by another group of humans and began frantically step-dancing like a pocket-sized Michael Flatley, sending their drinks flying in every direction.

One of the humans jumped to his feet, cursing loudly as he wiped thick, sticky barley wine off his suede coat. "You're paying for my dry cleaning, squirt!"

"You'll have to catch me first, nump!" Tullamore retorted as he flipped him the bird. The leprechaun jumped off the table and landed on the back of the transformed Jared, who squealed in fear and began running in and out between the close-packed tables and booths. Tullamore slapped the pig-boy's rump with the shillelagh like a jockey going for the winner's circle as he was chased by Jared's friends and the man in the ruined jacket.

While the regular patrons of the Two-Headed Calf might have been enjoying the chaos created by Tullamore's taunting of the humans, Lafo clearly had had all that he could stand. He yanked open the front door and gestured angrily toward the street.

"Take it outside, Tullamore!"

The leprechaun grabbed Jared by his porcine ears and dug his heels into the pig-boy's haunches, sending his steed squealing out of the bar and into the night, his pursuers chasing after him like an unruly pack of hounds. Most of the Calf's regulars poured out into the street as well, eager to have a good laugh at the numps' expense. To my surprise, Hexe got up to follow them. However, unlike his fellow Kymerans, he didn't seem the least bit amused.

"Where are you going?" I asked.

"Someone halfway sober has to keep an eye on this before it gets worse," he explained.

"Wait for me!" I shouted, grabbing my peacoat.

By the time we made it outside, there were at least sixty people, a third of them humans, gathered on the sidewalk in front of the Calf's bay windows, watching Jared's friends chase after Tullamore as he rode their buddy up and down the street like a racehorse. Thanks to curious passersby stopping to rubberneck and neighbors pouring out of their nearby homes and businesses to see what all the fuss was about, the crowd outside the

Calf grew to well over three hundred in the span of just a few short minutes.

The humans were shouting alternately at the leprechaun to turn their friend back into his true form and at Jared to stop running around, goddamn it. Meanwhile, the Kymeran onlookers continued to laugh and shout encouragement to Tullamore. One of the frat boys lunged at the leprechaun, but Tullamore tugged on Jared's ears as he would the reins of a horse, wheeling his mount about so he was headed in the general direction of Ferry Street, home to Golgotham's leprechaun community. Suddenly the man in the suede jacket moved to block his path.

"Ye'll have to do better than that, boyos, if ye want to catch me!" Tullamore shouted. In the twinkling of an eye, a pair of huge white wings, like those of a swan, unfolded from the pig-boy's shoulders. The leprechaun dug his shins into his mount's flanks and with a startled grunt Jared soared into the air with a single flap.

Jared's dumbfounded friends stood and stared as he sailed away over the rooftops, accompanied by gales of laughter from the assembled Kymerans. "Bring him back, you little bastard!" one of them shouted, shaking his fist at Tullamore's rapidly disappearing backside. "That's my roommate you're flying off with!"

Once he realized the leprechaun was not going to reverse his flight plan, Jared's roomie turned to face his companions. "What am I going to tell his mother?" he moaned.

A Kymeran with hair the color of lime sherbet stepped forward and clapped the distraught college student on the shoulder. I recognized the wizard as Oddo, one of Hexe's occasional clients, who came to the house whenever he needed a hangover cured, as he had a tendency to get drunk and sling spells in public—a definite no-no in Golgotham.

"Don't fret, lad," Oddo said, slurring his words only slightly. "Your pal will show up in a day or two. . . . Of course, he'll be a few dozen yards of sausage hanging in a butcher's window by then. . . ."

"Holy fuck!" the roomie gasped in horror.

Oddo guffawed and slapped his knee, pleased by the shocked look on the college student's face. "What did I tell ya? The nump fell for it, hook, line, and sinker!" he shouted to the Kymeran onlookers gathered on the sidewalk, who promptly added their belly laughs to the chorus.

"It's not fuckin' funny!" the roomie yelled, pushing Oddo aside.

The wizard staggered backward, more surprised than harmed by the attack. He pointed his right hand at his adversary, the six fingers bent at angles impossible for human digits to duplicate, and made a sharp upward motion, as if hailing a cab.

The college student shot six feet into the air like a marionette yanked offstage by the puppeteer, his arms and legs flailing wildly as he screeched at the top of his lungs: *"Stop it! Put me down!"*

"I will—but only after I make sure you and the other numps have learned your lesson about sticking your noses in places that don't want you," Oddo replied. He made a twirling gesture with his right hand and the levitating student began to spin like a top, going faster with each revolution.

"Please! Stop!" he wailed. *"I think I'm gonna—I'm gonna—"*

I assume the rest of his sentence was *puke*, because that's exactly what he did, in copious amounts under

high pressure. The cluster of humans directly underneath him nearly trampled one another in their attempt
to escape the unwelcome downpour, only to be shoved
back by Oddo's drinking companions, much to the delight of the assembled onlookers, who laughed even
louder than before.

In the confusion, one of the humans trying to escape
accidentally stumbled into Oddo, causing him to lose
control of the wildly spinning college student. The poor
bastard went flying like a rock from a slingshot, sailing
through the bay window of the Two-Headed Calf with a
mighty crash.

The crowd fell instantly silent as Kymeran and human alike stared, dumbstruck, at the smashed window.
The most shocked expression belonged to Oddo, who
seemed genuinely stunned by what had just transpired.
But before the green-haired magician could apologize
or find out if the victim of his prank was hurt or not, a
frightened voice cried out: *"The Kymies are trying to
kill us!"*

The underlying tension between the Calf's regulars
and the human interlopers finally burst forth, and within
seconds the humans were throwing tankards and barley
wine bottles at what they perceived to be the enemy.
Luckily, the majority of Kymerans weren't so drunk that
they automatically retaliated with sorcery; instead they
protected themselves with their right hands, flicking
aside the various missiles hurled in their direction before they could make contact.

Lost in the middle of the chaos, Oddo quickly found
himself surrounded by angry humans. An arm flailed out
and punched him in the face. Oddo put his right hand to
his mouth, his eyes widening in astonishment when it
came away bloody. Surrounded and outnumbered, he

dropped back, his eyes growing darker as he lifted his left hand.

Suddenly Hexe was no longer at my side, but pushing his way through the crowd. He grabbed Oddo by the left wrist, pulling the warlock's arm back and pinning it to the small of his back. *"Stop, Oddo!"* he shouted. *"It's bad enough as it is already, without you making things worse!"*

The drunken wizard struggled to free himself, only to stop upon recognizing Hexe. As the flicker of hellfire cradled in Oddo's palm winked out, a bottle came flying out of nowhere and struck Hexe in the head. A couple of Kymerans quickly darted forward and grabbed him and Oddo, dragging them into the protection of their circle.

I dove into the crowd and made my way toward Hexe, putting my formative years in the mosh pits to good use by throwing elbows and knees in every direction, and God help anyone or anything that got in my way. Suddenly a Kymeran with a turquoise mohawk stepped in front of me, deliberately blocking my path. He smelled dangerous, like gunpowder and a lit match.

"Keep to your own, nump!" he growled, raising his left hand in warning.

"Leave her alone, Skal!" Hexe barked, pushing his would-be protector aside. "She's with me!"

Skal lowered his hand and stepped away, but the loathing in his eyes as he looked at me did not disappear. I pushed past him and threw my arms around Hexe, only to gasp at the sight of blood running down the side of his face.

"Oh my God, baby—you're hurt!"

"Scalp wounds bleed like a bitch, but it's superficial," he reassured me, pointing to the laceration just above his left temple.

Suddenly the air was filled with the wailing of sirens, and a couple of old-fashioned paddy wagons drawn by centaurs outfitted in riot gear rounded the corner. The wagons had the letters *PTU* stenciled on their sides and flashing blue lights mounted on top.

Hexe muttered, "About damn time."

"You'll tell 'em I didn't *mean* to put the nump through the window, won'tcha, Serenity?" Oddo asked anxiously. "They'll believe it comin' from you."

"Of course I will, Oddo," Hexe said, doing his best to calm the worried sorcerer.

The doors of the paddy wagons flew open and members of Golgotham's peacekeeping force, the Paranormal Threat Unit, jumped out onto the streets. Composed of a mixture of Kymerans, "gifted" humans, and other paranormal races, they were outfitted in specially charmed and modified police gear designed to handle the dangers unique to the magic-using community they policed.

The leader of the PTU squad, a tall Kymeran woman carrying a bullhorn and dressed in full-body armor and riot helmet, stepped forward to address the unruly crowd. "Everybody calm down! My name is Lieutenant Vivi of the PTU and I want your hands where I can't see 'em!"

While the Kymerans did as they were told, placing their hands either behind their backs or in their pockets, the humans in the crowd exchanged confused looks, unsure as to what to do. Baffled by the instructions, one of the humans automatically raised his hands over his head.

"I *said* keep 'em where I can't see 'em!" Lieutenant Vivi snapped.

Pale green ectoplasm shot from her right hand, wrapping itself around the befuddled human like bandages around a mummy. Within a heartbeat the human was cocooned in the viscous substance from the neck down, rendering him completely immobile. The remaining humans started to shout obscenities and push and shove one another in a panicked attempt to escape, mistaking the restraint of an unruly suspect for another attack.

Lieutenant Vivi raised the bullhorn to tell the crowd they had nothing to fear, but her words were drowned out by the scream of sirens approaching from the other end of the block. The PTU officer frowned and turned to stare at the NYPD Emergency Services Unit truck lumbering its way up the cobblestone streets.

The look of relief disappeared from Hexe's face, to be replaced by one of alarm. The sight of New York City's finest in Golgotham was as jarring as spying a centaur trotting through Central Park.

"Bloody abdabs!" he gasped. "What are *they* doing here?"

As the PTU responders stared in disbelief, an armed ESU squad poured out of the truck, riot shields and tear gas guns at the ready. At their head was a tall, muscular man with a gray crew cut, dressed in a Kevlar vest. He, too, was carrying a bullhorn, which he used to address the crowd.

"NYPD! Everybody freeze! Put your hands up where I can see 'em!"

Now it was the Kymerans' turn to look bewildered. For a brief moment the groups of feuding humans and Kymerans were united in confusion as they alternately lifted and lowered their hands above their heads, uncertain which authority figure they were supposed to obey.

"I was wondering how tonight could possibly get worse," Hexe said with a groan of disgust. "Now I know."

The PTU commanding officer strode angrily over to the ESU leader. "Hey! Who do you think you are?"

"Lieutenant Daniel Trieux, New York Emergency Service Squad One, Lower Manhattan," he replied curtly. "And you are—?"

"Lieutenant Vivi, Paranormal Threat Unit. This ain't Lower Manhattan, Lieutenant—it's Golgotham. You're outside your jurisdiction. My team has things under control. I need you to stand down."

"Sorry, no can do, Lieutenant," Trieux replied sternly. "Nine-one-one received a call stating humans were under supernatural attack at this location. I'm under orders to extract all humans from the area and transport them to the Fifth Precinct."

"This is a PTU investigation, and the only place anyone's going is to the Tombs via PTU escort." Lieutenant Vivi scowled. "You can pick 'em up from there. Like I *said*, we have things under control here."

As Lieutenant Vivi argued with her NYPD counterpart as to who had the authority to haul the collective butts of the unruly crowd to jail, the Kymerans gathered outside the Two-Headed Calf began to mutter among themselves in their own language. Normally NYPD never ventured past the Gate of Skulls, leaving the peacekeeping in Golgotham to the Paranormal Threat Unit. Although I couldn't understand what they were saying, it wasn't hard to figure out that they were not pleased by the surprise arrival of New York's finest. The same was true for the locals thronging the streets, who eyed the ESU team the same way gazelles size up a lion at a watering hole.

"They're going to surrender me to the humans, aren't they?" Oddo moaned, mopping the sweat from his brow with a filthy handkerchief. "They're going to cut off my fingers because I attacked a nump." He held up his hands, flexing the extra ring fingers that allowed Kymerans to work their magic. "I'm not gonna let that happen," he said, his voice wavering on the verge of tears. "I'm not gonna to let them take my magic!" Before Hexe could convince him that his fears were unfounded, Oddo began pushing his way through the crowd, shouting at the top of his voice: *"The humans want my magic! They're gonna cut off my fingers!"*

The wizard's paranoia swept through the assembled Kymerans like wildfire. Within seconds what had been grumbling turned into full-fledged dissent.

"Go home, numps!" bellowed a Kymeran with a salmon pink afro. *"Nobody's taking our fingers!"*

"Golgotham is ours!" yelled Skal. *"Leave now, before it's too late!"*

"Everybody calm down!" Hexe shouted, trying to make himself heard over the sea of angry voices. "The police are just here to escort the humans out of Golgotham!" But it was no use; the mixture of alcohol, paranoia, and discontent had turned the unruly crowd into an angry mob.

"Gardy looooo!"

My hair stood on end at the sound of the traditional warning call of magic being unleashed. I turned and saw Skal draw back his left hand like a baseball pitcher winding up for a curveball and hurl a fistful of hellfire through the night air. A wild cheer rose up from the Golgothamites as the fireball landed atop the roof of the ESU truck, which proceeded to burn like it was made out of plywood.

I heard Lieutenant Trieux shout something through his bullhorn, followed by a series of dull *whumps*. Suddenly a dense reddish cloud rose up from the cobblestones like an evil fog. My nose began to burn and my eyes filled with tears. The surrounding crowd started coughing and hacking as the rapidly spreading fumes enveloped everyone in the vicinity—Kymeran and human alike.

Hexe grabbed my hand and dragged me through the wall of smoke. Although my vision was blurred, I saw Lieutenant Vivi point her right hand at her NYPD counterpart, encasing Lieutenant Trieux in his very own ectoplasmic cocoon. The last thing I saw, before a rolling, blood-tinged cloud obscured my view, was the ESU team turning their weapons away from the crowd and aiming them, instead, at the PTU forces.

"We've got to get back to the house before these fools start slinging blind," Hexe said as he led me through the chaos. All around us those caught up in the riot wailed and shrieked, urging one another to do battle, but the mob had no leaders or logic behind it, only blind animal fear.

Figures stumbled in and out of the low-hanging cloud of tear gas smoke, like lost souls trying to fight their way free from Hades. A crying Kymeran woman with coral pink hair staggered out of the fog, blood flowing down the back of her neck. Hexe motioned for her to join us, but she shook her head and went in the opposite direction upon realizing I was human. A satyr with a freshly broken right horn went clattering by, bleating in pain and fear, blood streaming from his broad nostrils. I glimpsed Skal, the Kymeran who had hurled the opening salvo, running through the haze, laughing maniacally, his left hand on fire.

Suddenly a policeman in full riot gear, his face obscured by a gas mask, materialized from out of the fog, blocking our path.

"Let go of the girl, Kymie." Although his voice was muffled, there was no mistaking the intent behind the semiautomatic pistol pointed at Hexe's chest.

I opened my mouth to yell at the cop and tell him that Hexe was trying to save me, not hurt me, but all I could do was cough and choke on the burning air. Hexe tightened his grip on my hand, but did not respond to the policeman's threat.

The cop took another step closer, raising the sight of his weapon to Hexe's forehead.

"I *said* let her go, Kymie."

Just then there was a huge *boom,* as if a giant had clapped his hands beside my head, momentarily robbing me of my hearing. The policeman turned to look at where the ESU truck had been a moment before. It took me a second to realize that the vehicle's gas tank must have exploded. As the policeman turned back to face us, Hexe quickly raised his right hand and the ESU squad member froze in place. We stepped around the living statue and continued running in the direction of Beekman Street, desperate to put the madness behind us.

Suddenly a blinding light stabbed down from above, accompanied by a thunderous roar and a wild wind, which tore apart the localized cloud of tear gas and the black smoke from the burning tires, dispersing it into the side streets and alleyways, as well as the nearby homes and businesses of countless innocent Golgothamites. I looked up to see an NYPD helicopter circling overhead like a mechanical vulture.

An armed police officer standing in the open bay of the copter pointed in our direction, and the spotlight swiveled to follow us. A second later the copter dropped so low I was afraid it might hit the roof of a nearby building. The backwash from its rotors was so strong it nearly snatched me out of Hexe's grip. He stopped to scowl at the machine hovering overhead and lifted his right hand before his face, as if shielding his eyes from the glare of the searchlight. A moment later, the light wandered away, the occupants of the helicopter apparently no longer interested in us. We managed to get back to the boardinghouse without running into any further trouble.

Once we'd made it inside, Hexe slammed the door behind us and then slid down onto the floor of the foyer in exhaustion, resting his back against the wall. As I knelt beside him and kissed him, he grabbed me and pulled me close. We sat there for a long moment, trembling like foxes that had just escaped the hounds, secure in the knowledge we were safe in our den.

Chapter 7

"**W**hy do I smell blood?"

I looked up to see Scratch's eyes glowing in the darkened front parlor. A second later the rest of the familiar became visible as he emerged from the shadows. He padded up to Hexe, only to freeze upon seeing the wound on his master's head.

"What happened?" Scratch growled. "Who did that to you? How do you want me to kill them?"

"I got hit in the head by a bottle," Hexe replied. "And you're not killing anyone. Besides, I don't know who threw it at me in the first place."

"You're no fun." The familiar sniffed. "You also stink of smoke—both of you. You haven't taken up arson as a sideline recently, have you?"

Scratch was right. Now that we were safely indoors, there was no mistaking the acrid odor. We smelled like we'd been standing in the middle of a bonfire. Something told me I would never get the stink out of my favorite peacoat. But then, my dry-cleaning bill was the least of my concerns.

"Are you all right?" I asked, alarmed to see how pale and drawn Hexe appeared.

"I'll be okay," he replied hoarsely. "I'm just—drained, that's all. I never got a chance to really eat anything, and this has been a very busy evening. Lifting a heavy curse, getting in a slinging contest with my uncle, putting that cop in stasis, then using my magic to make us invisible to the helicopter crew . . ."

"So *that's* why they stopped following us with the spotlight," I said. "You need that wound cleaned up. I'll go get a washcloth."

As I headed to the linen closet, I was surprised to meet my sixteen-year-old housemate, Lukas, on his way downstairs. He was dressed only in a pair of jeans, and judging by how high he raised his unibrow, the young were-cat was equally surprised to see me.

"Oh—! You're home early!" he exclaimed, nervously flipping his sandy blond hair out of his face. "I was just, uh, going to the kitchen to get some pizza from the fridge. . . ." He frowned and sniffed the air. "Have you been burning something?"

"Lukas—can you bring me back a soda?"

I looked up to see Meikei, the teenaged daughter of Lukas's employer, leaning over the second-floor balustrade, dressed in nothing but one of his T-shirts. Upon seeing me, the young were-tigress gasped in embarrassment and her exposed flesh briefly covered itself with dark stripes.

"We weren't doing anything, Tate!" Meikei blurted. "I promise!"

"Save it for your dad, Meikei." I sighed as I pushed past Lukas. "It doesn't matter to me what you two get up to on your own."

"I don't want you to think we were being disrespectful," Meikei continued anxiously. "It's just Lukas said you and Hexe were going to be out late tonight. . . ."

As I reached the second-floor landing, the sound of drunken, angry shouting echoed from the street, followed by breaking glass. Suddenly Meikei and Lukas no longer seemed quite so worried about explaining away their tryst.

"What's going on out there?" Lukas asked, trailing after me as I searched for a fresh washcloth and hand towel in the hallway linen closet. "I heard sirens a little while ago."

"A riot between humans and Kymerans broke out in front of the Calf," I explained. "The NYPD is in Golgotham."

"Oh, wow!" Lukas's jaw dropped open like a nutcracker's. "Are you *serious*?"

Meikei gasped once more, this time in fear. "Lukas, I need to go home *right now*! Father will be worried."

"You'll do no such thing!" I said sternly. "It's far too dangerous out there, Meikei. Call your father and tell him you're safe here and that Hexe and I insist you stay overnight. He'll understand. If he asks, tell him you're sleeping in *my* room. What he doesn't know won't hurt him. Believe me—I have a *lot* of experience telling fathers what they want to hear."

I left Lukas and Meikei to make their phone call and headed back downstairs to find Hexe in the kitchen. He was sitting at the table, the box from Strega Nona's Pizza Oven open by his elbow as he hungrily scarfed down a slice of andouille and artichoke. Scratch was perched on the corner of the sink, his hairless tail slapping against its enameled surface in agitation.

"C'mon—just let me out for a measly ten minutes!" the familiar wheedled. "That's all I'm asking. I'll have the streets clear in no time!"

"That's what I'm afraid of!" Hexe said around a mouthful of Cajun sausage. "There's not going to be any killing, slaying, slaughter, mutilation, or mayhem. There's enough chaos out there without you adding to it!"

"Stop tempting your master, Scratch," I chided as I soaked the washcloth in hot water.

"I *am* a demon, y'know," the familiar replied, hopping down onto the floor. "It's in my blood."

"More like an imp, if you ask me." Hexe snorted, only to flinch as I began to clean his wound.

"Is it really *that* bad out there?"

I looked up to see Lukas standing in the kitchen doorway, staring in disbelief at the blood matted in Hexe's hair. The young were-cougar was still barefoot, but had reclaimed his T-shirt.

"It's worse," Hexe grunted. He pointed at a hand mirror and a small ceramic container sitting on the shelf over his worktable. "Hand me those, will you?"

Lukas brought the items to the table, and Hexe opened the jar and daubed unguent on his wound, using the mirror to guide his hand. Meikei entered the kitchen, now dressed in her own clothes. She, too, seemed taken aback by the bloodstains on Hexe's shirt.

"I did what you said, and called my father and told him where I was," she said. "It's a lucky thing, too. He was about to go out on the streets and look for me."

"I thought it would be a good idea if Meikei stays here overnight," I explained to Hexe.

"You made the right decision," he replied as he watched his scalp heal in the mirror. "It's safer to stay put."

"Is your dad upset about you being here with me?" Lukas asked anxiously.

"He said he didn't care *where* I was, just as long as I was somewhere safe," Meikei replied. "But he *is* holding you responsible for my well-being."

Lukas squared his jaw and puffed up his chest as he

put his arm about Meikei's shoulders. "Don't worry—
I'm not going to let anything happen to you." Despite
his youth, there was little in the way of adolescent bra-
vado in his voice. After all, not many boys his age, were-
cat or otherwise, could claim to have survived Boss
Marz's fighting pit.

"You two are to remain in the house," Hexe instructed. "I don't even want you stepping out into the
garden before sunrise."

"Is everything going to be okay?" Meikei asked,
sounding more than a little scared. Although she was
trying to remain calm, I could see the worry in the young
were-tigress's eyes.

I saw Hexe take a deep breath in preparation of an
answer, and touched his shoulder. He glanced up at me
and then gave a small smile and a nod of understanding.
"I'm sure everything will be fine in the morning," he
lied.

While Lukas and Meikei ate what remained of the left-
over pizza in the kitchen, I went upstairs to my studio to
look out the window that faced the street, to see what was
going on. As I pulled back the heavy drapery, I saw a
tongue of flame flickering in the distance—no doubt the
guttering remains of the ESU truck—dyeing the night
sky an angry, hazy orange. The police helicopter continued to circle the neighborhood at a slightly higher alti-
tude than before, its cyclopean searchlight sweeping back
and forth across the maze of streets in search of unrulies.

For the first time since the riot broke out, I finally had
enough time and distance to process what had happened. The initial shock and fear I'd experienced on the
street were quickly giving way to outrage as I saw what
had befallen my adopted home and its citizens.

Lowering my gaze to the street below, I noticed broken glass glittering like discarded diamonds on the sidewalk in front of the herbalist shop on the corner. As I watched, a couple of figures emerged from the smashed storefront, their arms laden with stolen goods.

"Halt! PTU!"

The looters sprinted in the opposite direction of the angry shout, dropping a trail of bat's head root and kola nuts behind them. A moment later a bay centaur outfitted in riot gear came galloping past, a fellow PTU officer astride his back, holding on to his mane for dear life. The pair of peacekeepers quickly disappeared around the corner in pursuit of their quarry.

Hexe entered the room and stood behind me. "Tonight has changed everything in Golgotham," he said. "It's just a matter of figuring out how much." As he looked out the window, the sorrow in his voice took on a sharp, bitter edge. "I'm angry right now—not so much because I came close to getting my head blown off, but simply because all of this could have been easily avoided. What happened tonight was the result of ignorance, stupidity, and fear. As pissed off as I am by the police brutality, I'm even more disgusted by how my people kept egging the situation on until it blew up in everyone's face. There was no reason for things to get out of control the way they did. I'm just glad we managed to escape." He slid his arms about my waist and kissed the nape of my neck. "You *are* okay, aren't you?"

"I can't help thinking how close I came to losing you tonight," I replied, taking a deep breath to steady myself. "If that cop had pulled the trigger . . ."

"But he *didn't*," Hexe said, turning me around to face him. "I'm alive and okay, and so are you. That's the important thing. Besides, I wasn't going to let anything happen to you."

"I wasn't worried about me," I replied, reaching up to caress the faint scar that was all that was left of his earlier head wound. "How are you feeling?"

"I'm nearly recovered," he said. "Throw in a little tantric sex, and I'll be good as new."

"What do you say we take a nice, long, hot shower and wash tonight out of our hair?" I suggested, tugging at the bottom of his shirt.

"Sounds like a plan," he replied as he started to unbutton my pants.

As we left my studio, I glanced out the window one last time and was relieved to see that the far-off flames had been extinguished. "By the way, thanks for sparing the kids the gory details," I whispered.

"I didn't see any point in freaking them out any more than they were already," he said as he peeled off his bloodstained shirt. "Let them have one last night where the worst thing they have to worry about is Meikei's father finding out they're fooling around."

Chapter 8

Just after sunrise someone started banging on the front door. Hexe threw on a silk dressing robe embroidered with swarms of dragons and went downstairs to see who was calling so early in the morning. When he did not immediately return, I tossed on a pair of yoga pants and an old T-shirt and headed down myself. I found Bartho, the photographer responsible for the article that had made Golgotham popular with the city's youth, sitting at the kitchen table.

Bartho's right eye was the color of a ripe eggplant, the pupil swimming in a pool of ruptured capillaries, and his left wrist was swollen and badly bruised. "Sorry about getting you guys up at this hour," the photographer said sheepishly. "I would have come here sooner, but I was afraid to go outside while it was still dark."

"I understand why you stayed put," Hexe replied as he ground up a raw potato in his mortar and pestle. "Tate and I felt the same way, once we made it home."

"I saw you get hit with that bottle last night," Bartho said. "I'm glad you're both okay."

Hexe raised an eyebrow in surprise. "You were at the Calf?"

Bartho nodded, only to wince in pain. "I was in the back of the bar, taking pictures of the band. Talisman has hired me to be their official photographer. I still don't know what started the whole shit-storm. One minute I'm watching the band, the next thing I know there's this mass exodus. I went outside to see what was going on and started taking pictures of the crowd. Before I realized it, the NYPD and the PTU were throwing down on each other."

"Did the cops do that?" I asked, motioning to his wounds.

"Fuckin' A they did it," Bartho replied bitterly. "I was taking pictures, and one of the pigs smashed his truncheon right into my face—damn near drove the camera into my eye. I'm lucky I can still see out of it. If that wasn't bad enough, the asshole stole what was left of my camera! I guess he was trying to get rid of evidence. Luckily, I was able to palm the memory card before he got it away from me." He grinned as he reached into the pocket of his jeans with his good hand and pulled out a memory card the size of a postage stamp. "There are pictures of the NYPD opening fire on the crowd on this thing—which means this little baby is worth its weight in gold!" The smile quickly disappeared from his face, to be replaced by a somber sigh. "Maybe it can make up for all the shit that's gone down in Golgotham because of that stupid photo-essay of mine."

"There's no point in kicking yourself like that," I said, patting him on the shoulder. "There was no way you could have foreseen any of this. You were simply trying to show others the world as you see it. That's what artists *do*. You're not responsible for how people respond to your work."

"Tate's right," Hexe agreed as he smeared the contents of the mortar on a makeshift eye patch constructed from a piece of double-folded cloth. "What happened last night was a long time coming. It was bound to occur, whether you ever set foot in Golgotham or not." He gently placed the poultice over Bartho's eye and wrapped a couple lengths of sterile gauze around the photographer's head to hold it in place. "Keep that on for at least a half hour. It will reduce the swelling and get rid of the bruising. Now let me look at your wrist."

Bartho obediently held out his left hand for inspection, grimacing as Hexe gingerly bent the wrist back and forth while wiggling each of his fingers. "I got lost in the damn smoke from the gas canisters and tripped over a curb," he explained. "I automatically held out my hands to try and break my fall, but I'm afraid all I did was break my wrist."

"It's not broken," Hexe assured him. "It's just a bad sprain. You're lucky—I can handle soft-tissue damage and certain types of wounds. Anything involving bones or major organs, though, I leave up to the boneknitters and psychic surgeons at Golgotham General."

"Do you have a TV?" Bartho asked, looking about the room.

"Kinda," I replied. "I've got one in my room, but I still haven't unpacked it yet. . . ."

"I've got one in my office," Hexe said, and promptly disappeared from the kitchen. I frowned in confusion, as I had never seen anything resembling a television in there before. A few seconds later he returned carrying a two-tone green plastic case with a gold anodized handle and matching knobs on top, with ADMIRAL emblazoned on the faceplate.

"*That's* a television?" Bartho laughed.

"It was in 1956," Hexe grunted as he put the set down

on the kitchen table. "My grandmother Lyra used it to see into the future. And watch her soaps. Normally, the only channel that comes in clear is WICK, which isn't surprising, since it broadcasts out of Golgotham."

He plugged in the power cord and turned one of the knobs on top of the TV. There was a faint hum as the cathode-ray tube went from dark to light, and within a few seconds black-and-white images could be seen flickering across the ten-inch screen. The picture stabilized, revealing a two-person anchor team seated behind a news desk. The camera zoomed in on the female newsreader, who was pretty, young, and, except for the extra digits on her hands, no different than any other anchorwoman I'd ever seen reading a teleprompter.

"—a special WICK news report. I'm Eina—"

The camera switched to the older, dignified anchorman. "And I'm Reed—and if you're just tuning in, today's edition of *Good Morning Golgotham* has been canceled in order that we may air continuing coverage of the violence that has rocked our community."

The anchorman's face was replaced by shaky, handheld videocam footage of frightened and confused Golgothamites trying to escape the tear gas.

"A riot occurred in the heart of Golgotham last night. The Two-Headed Calf, a Golgotham landmark dating back to 1742, was ground zero for an angry confrontation between native Golgothamites and human tourists. The incident resulted in both the Paranormal Threat Unit and the New York Police Department being called to the scene—an event unprecedented in the history of Golgotham.

"While reports coming into the newsroom at this time are still sketchy, several eyewitnesses claim that the NYPD opened fire on innocent bystanders, forcing the PTU to retaliate. The chaos quickly spread throughout the surrounding area, resulting in looting as well as considerable property damage to local businesses and homes. The Two-Headed Calf was hit particularly hard...."

Suddenly Lafo's face filled the screen. He was standing outside his restaurant, and each and every one of its windows had been smashed. The Calf's famous sign swung crookedly from a busted hinge and looked in danger of crashing down come the next strong breeze. The restaurateur looked both angry and weary as he pointed to the devastation behind him.

"First I've got this human kid who doesn't know enough not to screw around with a leprechaun; then some idiot throws *another* idiot through the front window! The next thing I know, people are smashing up the furniture and stealing my liquor! It's going to take a few weeks before I can reopen the place...."

The image on the screen cut from Lafo shaking his head in disgust to footage of various Kymerans, leprechauns, and other nonhumans piling out of numerous cabs and rickshaws and hurrying into a large building identified as the Golgotham Business Owners Organization Headquarters. I recognized one of the figures as Giles Gruff, who arrived in the back of one of his own rickshaws.

"The GoBOO has called a special investigation into the events leading up to the riot, and whether or not sanctions will be levied against the City of New York."

A well-dressed Kymeran with a three-foot-long braided ponytail draped over his shoulder like a pet snake, identified by a superimposed graphic as Mayor Lash, spoke into a microphone held by a reporter.

"We intend to get to the bottom of this tragic event as soon as possible. Despite our trademarked slogan touting Golgotham as the Big Apple's strangest neighborhood, last night was a sharp reminder that, in reality, we are a city-state with its own sovereign laws and governance, existing within the boundaries of Manhattan Island. One thing I can say right now is that unprovoked attacks made upon our citizenry by anyone—including the City of New York—will not be tolerated!"

Hexe frowned and turned the dial on the TV. The picture rolled and shimmied, only to right itself after he gave the case a sharp rap on the side. The news anchor for WNBC sat in front of a green-screen projection of the smoldering ruins of the ESU truck, accompanied by a graphic that read GOLGOTHAM RIOTS! in a dripping horror-movie font.

". . . was officially founded in 1775, following the Treaty of Golgotham, which established a Kymeran homeland within the City of New York, as well as a series of protected preserves for shape-shifters and half-beasts throughout the continental United States, in exchange for Lord Beke's support during the Revolutionary War."

A graphic flashed onto the screen showing Thomas Jefferson and George Washington shaking hands with a Kymeran wearing a tricorn hat and a Freemason's apron. I recognized it as a copy of the engraving I'd seen hanging on the wall of the Two-Headed Calf.

"News 4 has just received information that Jared Wagner, the NYU student whose transmogrification and abduction appear to have triggered the street brawl that led to last night's unrest, has been located live, unharmed, and in human form. We take you now to our live reporter, Mitzi Bloomberg, on the scene in Golgotham. . . ."

The picture switched to show a young woman holding a microphone and standing across the street from what I recognized as Blarney's, the central watering hole for Golgotham's leprechaun community, located on Ferry Street. A hansom cab was standing at the curb, and several PTU officers were busy keeping a crowd of reporters and other onlookers at bay.

"Thank you, Chuck. I'm standing in front of Blarney's Pub, where we have been told Jared Wagner will be handed over to the Paranormal Threat Unit, Golgotham's law enforcement division, who will be escorting the NYU sophomore first to the nearby Tombs, where he will be turned over to NYPD officials and then returned to his parents, Mr. and Mrs. Carlton Wagner of Long Island. Sources tell me that Jared's return was negotiated by the head of the Wee Folk Anti-Defamation League, who will also be defending his fellow leprechaun, Neyland Tullamore, on charges of kidnapping and felony enchantment. Wait a minute! I think I see him!"

The reporter gestured toward the door of the pub, and the camera dutifully zoomed in to show Jared, barefoot and wrapped in a blanket, being escorted out of Blarney's by Lieutenant Vivi. The college student looked pale and extremely shaken, as well as unprepared to see a wall of reporters shouting at him at the top of their lungs. One particularly enterprising newshound managed to get close enough to shove a microphone in the boy's face.

"Jared! Oscar Hernandez for WNYX-TV! Can you tell us what your ordeal was like?"

"It was a nightmare," the young man replied, his voice wavering. "I kept trying to scream, but all I could do was squeal like a pig—"

Before Jared could say anything else, Lieutenant Vivi hustled him into the waiting cab. As the reporters surged forward, eager to get their pound of flesh one sound bite at a time, the PTU officer raised her right hand, palm outward, in a warding gesture. The journalists abruptly fell back; it was difficult to tell whether they were repulsed by a spell or simply cowed by the threat of magic.

"There is a time and a place for asking this boy questions," Lieutenant Vivi announced sternly. "It is not here and now. The Wagner family will be holding a press conference later today, after their son has been checked out by doctors."

"Lieutenant Vivi! Lauren DeAngelo from Eyewitness News. What do you have to say to the accusations that it was your overreaction to the NYPD police presence in Golgotham that triggered the riot?"

The PTU officer glared at the reporter and climbed in alongside Jared, but said nothing as the cab pulled away from the curb.

Hexe changed the channel yet again, landing on a live broadcast from the steps of the Tombs. I immediately recognized Tullamore, looking considerably more subdued and a tad hungover, standing next to a robustly built, clean-shaven leprechaun dressed in a scaled-down three-piece Armani suit.

"Who's that?" I asked

"Seamus O'Fae," Hexe replied. "He's the top dog at the WFADL, and an important member of the Business Owners Organization. He's also a criminal lawyer. The wonks in City Hall call him Little Big Man behind his back."

As the reporters drew closer, O'Fae stepped forward to greet the cameras with the practiced air of a courtroom attorney. Since both he and Tullamore were the size of toddlers, the reporters were forced to drop to their knees in order to conduct their interviews. Despite Seamus O'Fae's diminutive size, his voice was surprisingly deep. Little Big Man indeed.

"As chairman of the Wee Folk Anti-Defamation

League, I have arranged with Captain Horn for Mr. Tullamore to surrender himself, in good faith, to the Paranormal Threat Unit." He turned and gestured to the tall, solemn-looking Kymeran dressed in a police captain's uniform and standing off to one side. "I have also facilitated the return of Mr. Wagner—in his original state—to his family. Furthermore, I wish to take this moment to state that the WFADL is one hundred percent behind Mr. Tullamore's fight for justice—"

As Hexe flipped the dial again, an all-too-familiar voice suddenly came from the speakers: "Last night proves that numps have no place in Golgotham beyond those areas set aside for them—Golgotham is our home, not their playpen! Let them get drunk and make braying jackasses of themselves on Duivel Street, if that's what they want to do. But make sure that's as far into Golgotham as they can go!"

Hexe groaned and rolled his eyes in disgust at the sight of his uncle standing on the street outside the Go-BOO Headquarters. Esau had an armload of pamphlets, and was busily handing them out to passersby while he conducted his interview with the television reporter. Behind him were people carrying signs that read GOLGOTHAM IS OURS and SAY YES TO NO-HUMAN ZONES.

"The GoBOO is so intent on lining their pockets with money from tourism, they have endangered our security and cultural identity," Esau went on. "For centuries we've been encouraged to play down the fact that Golgotham is actually a sovereign territory, to the point that most numps think we're simply another part of New York City, like Coney Island or Chinatown. My great-grandfather didn't negotiate the creation of a Kymeran homeland just so a bunch of rowdy looky-loos could be amused by the 'local color.' That is why I have started the Kymeran Unification Party; to bring pressure on the

GoBOO to see to it that Golgotham's borders—both physical and cultural—are reinforced, recognized, and respected, by whatever means necessary."

"You're not advocating violence against New York City, are you?" the reporter asked.

"Of course not," Esau replied. "But should Golgotham become the target of human attacks, my people will not stand idly by. After all, no one wants to see a replay of the Sufferance."

"Race-baiting asshole," Hexe growled as he turned off the TV. "I knew we hadn't seen the last of him."

"Do you think anyone will take him seriously?" I frowned at the thought.

"Esau's separatist spraint is impractical as far as the average Golgothamite is concerned, but I'm afraid his message resonates with a certain demographic within the community," Hexe conceded. "I can see him starting some real trouble."

As Hexe saw Bartho to the front door, my cell phone began to ring. I glanced at the caller ID, but all the read-out said was: QPQ. I frowned and hit the TALK button. As I lifted it to my ear, a vaguely familiar voice on the other end asked, "Is this Tate?"

"Yes," I replied cautiously. "Who's this?"

"It's Quid, of Quid's Pro Quo."

"Hey, how's it going?" I smiled, my memory properly jogged. Quid was the favor broker who had procured a couple of Dodge transmissions for me, which I turned into sculpture for my ill-fated art show.

Quid ignored my attempt at small talk and went right to business. "You remember our deal, right?"

I nodded, even though there was no one with me to see it. "I owe you a favor, no questions asked."

"And no stories told. Do you still have your welding equipment?"

"Yes, of course."

"I'm sending a pony wagon over to your place within the hour. The drover's an ipotane named Gus—he'll do the heavy lifting getting the equipment in and out of where you're going. I'll be at your destination with the blueprints and raw materials for what you'll be constructing."

"Okay. I'll be ready."

As I hung up, I ran a mental checklist of what I might possibly need. Since I had no idea what I was expected to fabricate, I decided it would be wise to make sure I had both a welding and a cutting outfit with me. I returned to my studio and changed into the protective welder's jacket, leather pants, and steel-toed boots I normally wear whenever I work with metal. The jacket's made of fire-retardant brushed cotton with pigskin leather sleeves, and an upturned welder's collar that can be snapped shut to keep sparks from flying down my cleavage. It also makes me look badass and sexy. Or so I've been told.

I gathered my equipment, including my welding helmet and gloves, into my tool bag and headed back to the kitchen. Since I lacked the magical skills that had teleported them upstairs in the first place, I decided I would let the packer handle getting the acetylene and oxygen cylinders out of the house, as they weighed well over a hundred pounds apiece

Hexe was pouring himself a fresh cup of coffee as I reentered the kitchen. He arched a purple eyebrow in surprise upon seeing my attire. "Isn't it a bit early in the day to be starting work on your new statue?"

"I'm not fabricating my own stuff today," I replied. "I'm making a house call." Hexe's eyebrow rose even higher. "Quid called in his debt," I explained. "He needs me to do some welding—no questions asked. He's sending a wagon around to pick up both me and my gear. It should be here any minute now."

"How long will you be gone?"

"I have no idea," I replied. "But it's a safe bet it'll probably take all day." A thought suddenly came to me. "What if he wants me to burn open a safe or something?"

"Then that's what you do," Hexe replied. "Don't worry. According to Kymeran law, crimes committed in the repayment of a favor are perfectly legal. At least, as long as they're committed in Golgotham."

"I'll keep that in mind." I chuckled. "Are you *sure* you don't mind me going off like this, what with everything that's going on right now?"

"Go ahead and repay your favor." Hexe smiled as he kissed me on the cheek. "I'm certain Quid wouldn't do anything to put you in harm's way."

Chapter 9

It wasn't long before there was another knock at the door. I opened it to find an ipotane standing on the front step. Like most of his kind, he was stout and barrel-chested, with thick lips and a squat, pushed-in nose, and he walked about on a pair of horse's legs, the hooves of which were covered in padded booties to muffle their sound and impact on hardwood floors.

"The name's Gus, short for Augustus. Quid sent me. Where's the equipment ya need moved, lady?" he asked.

I directed the packer upstairs, and within fifteen minutes Gus managed to transport my welding equipment down two flights of stairs and into the back of a small wagon hitched to a bay centaur colt wearing a Peruvian wool hat. I knew from previous experience that it would have taken two strong men a half hour, and considerably more swearing, to accomplish the same task. Once everything was properly secured, I kissed Hexe good-bye and climbed up on the driver's seat alongside Gus.

"Put that crap away, Bayard!" Gus shouted as he kicked off the brake. "We got work to do!"

The centaur youth grumbled something under his

breath as he turned off his Nintendo DS and returned it to the fanny-pack cinched about his waist.

"Colts today got no work ethic," the Teamster sniffed in disgust as the wagon began to roll. "They'd rather play with those damn gadgets than try and get a union card."

"You're just jealous because you can't figure out how to use one," Bayard said, tossing his head in both adolescent and equine defiance.

As we rolled through the early morning in the direction of the East River, I got a good look at the aftereffects of the riot. The streets were strewn with garbage from upended litter baskets, as well as trampled odds and ends from looted stores. Everywhere I heard the sound of brooms and the crystalline tinkle of broken glass as storekeepers swept what was left of their shopwindows into the gutter for the street cleaners. As we passed by what was left of a bakery, the owner paused long enough in his cleanup to fix me with a hostile glare.

Eventually we arrived in Pickman's Slip, a section of Golgotham comprising ramshackle warehouses, flophouses, and gin joints that fronted the water and serviced the longshoremen who worked the large pier that stretched out into the East River. Bayard led us along a narrow cobblestone street that twisted and turned between Colonial-era houses before heading down a back alley barely wide enough to permit more than a glimpse of sky. The narrow, muddy passageway dead-ended at the back of an old building that, according to the faded signage, had once sold sailcloth. The sun was not yet strong enough to burn away the heavy mist from the river, and the overall atmosphere was dreary and gray, which did nothing to assuage the misgivings I was starting to experience.

Just as I was about to tell Gus to take me back home,

the door to the loading dock rolled open with a loud bang to reveal Quid, dressed in a canvas duster and knitted muffler, a blueprint tube tucked under one arm. The Kymeran favor broker was totally bald except for a pair of lime green eyebrows that resembled hairy caterpillars.

"Sorry about the short notice," he said by way of greeting, "but the client called me up out of the blue this morning, insisting that the work be started immediately. Since it requires a skilled metalworker, I instantly thought of you."

"Thanks, I guess," I muttered as I studied the blueprints he'd handed me. "What the hell is this thing?"

"'No questions asked' means exactly that," Quid chided, wagging a finger in reprimand. "It also means 'No stories told.' Come along, now—I'll show you where you'll be working."

I followed Quid up a flight of stairs to the second floor of the warehouse. The sconces that lined the walls were actually metal forearms holding torches lit with witchfire, which cast flickering shadows of things that were not there. The disembodied arms reminded me of the silvery clockwork limb that Boss Marz's goon, Nach, sported after he lost his flesh-and-blood one to Lukas. Not a good memory.

At the end of the corridor Gus opened a door to reveal a large room with high ceilings and windows that looked onto a blank wall. The only thing that was in the room besides my equipment was a workbench outfitted with a vise, a small anvil, and a stack of twenty-gauge copper sheeting.

"Gus will remain here and help you with the grunt work. Once you're finished, he and Bayard will take you and your equipment back home. I'll stop by in a couple of hours with some refreshments. Whatever you do,

don't go wandering. I can't vouchsafe your safety outside of this room. There's a water closet over there, in
case you need it." He pointed to the farthest corner of
the room. "It ain't pretty, but it works."

"Don't worry. You won't have to share it with me,"
Gus said with a laugh. "Personally, I don't see how you
can sit on one of those things. I go as nature intended—
standing up." He gestured to the manure catcher cinched
under the horse's tail growing from the base of his spine.

The only way for me to erase *that* visual was to get to
work, so I began setting up my tools and cutting the copper sheets to the dimensions required in the plans. According to the blueprints, the thing I was building was
comprised of three individual components, identified as
"the head," "the body," and "the feet."

While it was hard and dirty work, thanks to Gus taking care of the purely physical tasks, such as lifting the
cumbersome copper sheeting, it moved along far faster
than I would have thought possible. By the time Quid
returned with my lunch, I had finished with the cutting
and was ready to start piecing the individual sections together. After the chaos and confusion of the previous
night, it felt good to work with my hands and tackle a
problem that could be solved with nothing more than
the proper tools and the right amount of solder.

With nothing to distract me, I threw myself into the
work. When Quid returned, this time with dinner, I had
finished work on the three separate components and
was ready for the final assembly. Using a block and
tackle, Gus lifted the body and dropped it down onto
the legs as if hoisting a piñata for a child's birthday party.
The final third proved a little bit trickier, as it required
me to climb a ladder in order to join the head to the
body.

When I was finished, the thing I had labored all day

to build stood seven feet high and five feet wide, balanced on three sturdy legs, and had a long, tapered neck
and a turnip-shaped lower body, with a hatch big enough
for a grown man to wiggle through. With such uniquely
Kymeran flourishes as the dragon-headed flue atop the
neck and the tripod legs ending in lion's feet, it looked
more like the world's most ornate hillbilly still than a
piece of magical apparatus. But if that was what the client wanted, who was I to argue? Besides, it possessed a
goofy charm I found endearing. More important, my
debt to Quid was now discharged—until the next time I
required his unique services.

It was well after midnight by the time I packed up my
gear to return home. While trailing behind Gus as he
lugged my welding equipment downstairs, I noticed a
door across the hall standing slightly ajar. As I walked
by, I heard what sounded like clucking on the other side.
Despite Quid's earlier warning, I couldn't resist sneaking a peek.

I eased the door open enough to look around the
jamb, and saw a real estate developer's wet dream: a
huge industrial loft with exposed beams, aged brick walls,
and a large skylight. At first glance the room looked like
a larger version of Hexe's office, right down to the ubiq-
uitous stuffed crocodile hanging from the rafters.

The source of the clucking noise proved to be a
plump little black hen sitting in a nesting box inside a
cage atop a table just inside the door; she regarded me
with an inquisitive tilt of her head. I smiled and whispered to myself: "'Hickety-Pickety, my black hen, she
lays eggs for gentlemen. . . .'"

The smile slipped from my face as my gaze traveled
to the metal table positioned under the skylight. Atop it
lay a male cadaver, its flesh as pale as tallow, staring with

sightless eyes at the distant stars above. I quickly jerked my head out of the room and hurried after Gus, my heart beating like a hummingbird's wings.

By the time I got home, Hexe was asleep in bed, an open book resting on his chest. As I gently picked it up and placed it on the nightstand, I could see it was hand-bound in leather and printed in Kymeran. Beyond that, I had no way of telling if it was a grimoire of ancient lore or a bodice ripper.

I stripped out of my clothes and slipped into the shower to rid my skin of copper residue. As I crawled into bed, Hexe rolled over and gave me a sleepy smile, wrapping his arms around my waist.

"I missed you," he murmured as he nuzzled my neck.

"I missed you, too," I replied, snuggling in close to his warm, naked body. "How was your day?"

"Busy. I had a steady stream of clients after you left. Most of them were pretty banged up. I also had to fend off several different reporters wanting to interview me about the riot. You're lucky you missed it. How about you?"

"My debt is paid in full," I assured him. I was tempted to tell him about what I had seen in the loft, but my pact with Quid was "no questions asked and no stories told." If I wanted to be accepted by Kymeran society, I had to abide by its rules. Still, as I drifted off to sleep, safely wrapped in Hexe's arms, I could not help but wonder if the pact I'd made with Quid might not come back to bite me on the ass.

Chapter 10

The next morning began, yet again, with a loud and insistent knock on the front door. I rolled over and glowered at the clock on the nightstand. It was a quarter after too-fucking-early.

"Ugh. Is the whole world conspiring to drag my ass out of bed at the crack of dawn?" I groaned.

"I'll see who it is," Hexe said, as he slipped into his dragon-covered dressing robe. "Continue with your beauty sleep."

I didn't have to be told twice, and promptly dropped back into a doze, only to start awake a few minutes later at the sound of Hexe's voice telling me to get up.

"But what about my beauty sleep?" I yawned, knuckling my eyes.

"I'm afraid it'll have to wait." Hexe tossed a piece of parchment onto the nightstand. "We've been summoned by the GoBOO."

"What for?" I unfolded the parchment, which was written in elaborate Kymeran script, save for the word "GoBOO" stamped into the wax seal at the bottom.

"The Golgotham Business Owners Organization is

holding a special inquiry into the riot. They want to question us about it. We're to appear before them at ten this morning."

"Well, aren't *they* the early birds. But why do they want to talk to us? Do they think we're responsible?"

"No—but they *are* looking to place blame for what happened."

"Well, there's certainly plenty of it to go around," I grumbled as I put on my bathrobe and headed downstairs. "I must have coffee, and plenty of it, if I'm going to spend my afternoon being questioned by a bunch of—" I frowned in consternation. "What exactly *is* the GoBOO, anyway?"

"It's kind of a cross between a city council, the Chamber of Commerce and the United Nations," Hexe explained. "Each major ethnic group in Golgotham is represented by its most prominent member. They draw up and pass most of the laws in Golgotham."

"Your mother's the Witch Queen. Shouldn't she be the head honcho? I mean, your great-great-grandfather founded Golgotham, right?"

"Yes, he did, but the royal family surrendered the right to rule and hold power, as humans understand the word, with the Treaty of Arum. However, we have traditionally served as ambassadors to the heads of state in the human world. The royal family also serves as arbiter for disagreements between the various ethnic groups of Golgotham."

"So your mom's like Judge Judy?"

"We prefer the term 'justiciar,'" Hexe replied with an amused smile. "It all dates back to the Sufferance. When the leaders of the human world decided to exterminate the nonhumans, they first targeted the ones that didn't have magic, like the centaurs, satyrs, and ipotanes. Soon they were streaming into Arum as refugees. The reigning Witch King at the time, Lord Vexe, granted them protection if they swore fealty to the Throne of Arum and its heirs. Those who refused ended up paying for protection from what would evolve into Boss Marz's Malandanti. But the upshot of it all is that my bloodline is honor-bound to aid and represent all who live within Golgotham, not just the Kymerans."

"That's why Lady Syra gave Elmer a job," I said, the penny finally having dropped. "I really need that coffee. Politics makes my brain hurt."

A couple hours and cups of coffee later, I found myself riding alongside Hexe in Kidron's hansom, on our way to our meeting. I was still a little fuzzy around the edges from lack of sleep, but the cab ride in the cold morning air had succeeded in chasing out most of the cobwebs. I needed my wits about me if I wanted to sound like something other than a clueless looky-loo when it was my time to be questioned. Meanwhile, Hexe was doing his best to get me up to speed on Golgotham civics as well as its lawmakers and leaders.

"You have to understand," he explained, "that when Golgotham was first created, the only government the majority of its citizens had known was some form of tribal chieftainship. The concept of self-governance was even more alien to them than it was to their human counterparts. As for the Founding Fathers, recognizing a sovereign city-state within their borders was dicey enough, but to allow one that adhered to the feudal system was simply too much. Any sort of monarchy was forbidden on American soil, and thus the GoBOO was born. It was originally called the Grand Council, but in the 1950s it was 'modernized' into the Golgotham Business Owners Organization."

"I never really questioned Golgotham simply being another neighborhood in the city," I admitted. "It wasn't discussed much in our schoolbooks."

"I'm not surprised. Though Washington and Jefferson were broad-minded, forward-thinking individuals, the same could not be said for all of the Founding Fathers. It's been to our advantage not to call too much attention to Golgotham's unique status. But sometimes it's unavoidable."

The GoBOO Headquarters was located off Nassau Street, between Maiden Lane and Shoemaker Street, in a Belle Epoque building that looked more like an opera house than a seat of government. A gaggle of television and newspaper reporters stood gathered at the foot of the marble steps that led to the entrance, taking note of every individual coming and going. I inwardly groaned in anticipation of the phone call I was sure to receive from my mother once my face was bounced via satellite to every news agency in the country.

We were greeted just inside the door by a tall, angular Kymeran with heliotrope muttonchops and eyes so pale a blue they seemed almost white, who smelled faintly of chalk and old paper. He bowed stiffly at the waist, his right hand placed over his heart.

"Greetings, Serenity. I am Tuli, the Executive Coordinator for the GoBOO. I am to take you and Ms. Eresby to the council chamber."

As we followed our escort down the echoing marble-clad hallway into the bowels of the building, it seemed to me no different from any other city hall, save that its office workers and civil servants boasted outlandishly colored hair and were occasionally animals from the waist down.

Eventually we came to a set of heavy double doors, above which hung the seal of the Golgotham Business Owners Organization: an open six-fingered right hand with a cat's eye embedded in the palm, similar to the design on the amulet Hexe had given Madelyn to ward off evil.

Tuli opened one of the doors and ushered us inside a large chamber with a domed ceiling and a sloping floor that led past rows of pew-style benches to a long, horseshoe-shaped table set on a raised dais with a wide ramp on the left side. Behind the council table sat a smaller, even higher podium that overlooked the room like a judge's bench. On the wall above the highest seat, set in an alcove, was another, larger version of the Go-BOO seal, this one cast in twenty-four-karat gold.

I heard muttering voices, and looked up to see a gallery overhead, accessible via doors on the second floor. The GoBOO had banned television coverage inside the council chamber, but I recognized one of the spectators as a political reporter for the *Herald* who had written an article on my father's failed run for the senate back when I was in college. It looked like I was going to get into the papers again, no matter what.

"Please be seated," Tuli said, gesturing to the pews closest to the chamber floor. "The council will be arriving shortly."

As he spoke, a door beside the dais opened and a centaur, his lower quarters covered in a brocaded caparison and his hooves politely muffled, entered the chamber. Although his chest-length beard and shoulder-length locks were liberally laced with iron gray hair, what I could see of his equine self was still a deep chestnut.

"That's Chiron, owner of Chiron's Stables," Hexe whispered in my ear as the distinguished older centaur clip-clopped up the ramp to the council table. "He's the landlord for every centaur in Golgotham, as well as the owner of its largest blacksmith shop—every centaur in the city wears his horseshoes. He claims direct descent from the same Chiron who was mentor to Achilles and Jason."

"Is that true?"

"Beats me," he said with a shrug. "In any case, he represents the ipotanes as well as the centaurs."

The next figure to emerge was Giles Gruff, dressed in a velvet maroon waistcoat and a spotless Italian silk shirt. The satyr used his monogrammed cane to steady himself on his cloven hooves as he took his place at the table next to Chiron.

"You already know Giles. He speaks for the satyrs and the fauns."

After Giles came a very handsome blond man chewing a massive wad of gum. He was wearing a shirt open to the waist and a pair of pants so tight they not only informed the casual observer as to which side he was dressed, but whether or not he was happy to see them. As he turned to address Giles Gruff, I noticed a special vent cut into the seat of his pants to accommodate his bull's tail, which was the same color as the hair on his head.

"That's Bjorn Cowpen," Hexe pointed out. "He owns several 'gentlemen's clubs' on Duivel Street and represents Golgotham's huldrefolk. He's, um, quite the ladies' man, as you might guess."

"Who's she?" I asked, nodding at the woman sitting down on the other side of Cowpen. She was quite beautiful, dressed in a flowing seafoam green gown. As I watched her, she ran a delicate webbed hand through long hair the color and consistency of cooked spinach.

"That's Lorelei Jones. She owns a tiki place on a pier

overlooking the river, near Pickman's Slip. She speaks for the merfolk community."

"I thought mermaids were fish from the waist down," I said, waving a hand at my own lady bits.

"Only when they're in water," Hexe explained. "When they're on land, they have legs. But they have to be careful not to dry out. If they're out of water too long they start to mummify, just like a worm on a hot sidewalk. Not a pretty sight."

As Seamus O'Fae entered the chamber the cameras in the gallery began to click and whirr. The leprechaun did not look up at the reporters, but I could tell by the satisfied smile on his face that he knew they were there. He joined his fellow GoBOO members at the table, although he had to use a booster seat to see over its top.

"Seamus represents the brownie, pixie, troll, and dwarvish communities, as well as the leprechauns. Rumor has it he's bucking for Lash's job."

The final member of the GoBOO to enter the room was the mayor of Golgotham, who looked no different than he had on Hexe's ancient television, except now I could tell that the braided ponytail looped about his neck and shoulders like a living stole was periwinkle blue. Despite his eccentrically long hair, he wore an impeccably tailored, extremely conservative dark suit.

"Why's he dressed like a banker?" I whispered.

"Because he's the president of Midas National, the largest bank in Golgotham," Hexe replied. "He's been mayor since the 1970s, and is a big promoter of tourism. The riot has been a huge black eye for his policies."

I glanced over at the bench across the aisle and saw Captain Horn of the PTU, tricked out in his full-dress uniform. Seated next to him was a Kymeran woman, also in uniform, whose curly flame-colored hair cascaded past her shoulders. It wasn't until she turned to speak to Horn that I recognized Lieutenant Vivi. It was the first time I'd seen her minus a riot helmet.

Tuli, a clipboard under one arm, stepped into the well before the council table and announced in a voice that echoed throughout the chamber: "Hear ye, hear ye! The special inquest by the council of the Golgotham Business Owners Organization in regard to the 'Golgotham Riot' is now in session. The GoBOO has appointed the right honorable Skua as its querent in the matter."

"Bloody abdabs!" Hexe grimaced. "This might get ugly."

"Why?" I whispered.

"Skua's an expert projectionist, and no friend to humans, but that's not the ugly part—"

"Silence in the chamber!" Mayor Lash barked from his perch. "That includes you, Serenity."

"The council first calls Hexe for questioning."

Hexe sighed and squeezed my hand before getting up and taking his place in the witness box. The GoBOO's querent, Skua, was a slender Kymeran woman slightly younger than Lady Syra, dressed in a conservative pantsuit. Her short, asymmetrically cut powder blue hair and deep green eyes gave her an intense, hawklike appearance.

"Before we begin, I would like to thank you for appearing before the council on such short notice, Serenity," Skua said, slightly bowing her head in ritual acknowledgment

"It is my duty as a citizen of Golgotham," he replied matter-of-factly.

"Were you at the Two-Headed Calf the night before last, during the so-called riot?"

"Yes, I was."

"Are you willing and able to testify to what you experienced that night?"

"Yes, I am."

Skua motioned to Tuli, who stepped forward and handed her a scrying crystal the size of a large grapefruit, wrapped in a black velvet cloth. She cradled the crystal in her joined hands and held it out toward Hexe.

"Breathe, so that the truth shall be seen," she intoned solemnly.

Hexe leaned forward, closed his eyes, and exhaled onto the crystal, turning its surface cloudy. Instantly, images began to coalesce within the sphere, taking on life and movement. Skua turned to face the council table and raised her hands above her head, her eyes rolling back so that they showed only whites. The lights within the chamber dimmed, like those of a movie theater, as life-sized holographic projections of the images flickering about inside the scrying crystal blinked into existence in the air above her head.

I gasped in surprise to find a three-dimensional version of myself hovering six feet off the floor, drinking a tankard of barley wine. Not only was I replicated, but so was the entire interior of the Calf, right down to the smallest detail. Like the pasts I'd glimpsed in Hexe's own collection of scrying crystals, the image was in black and white and lacked sound. I searched the phantom crowd swirling about in midair for a sign of Hexe, before realizing I was seeing everything from his point of view.

The events unfolded before the council as they had happened in real life, while the GoBOO took notes and occasionally murmured to one another. When the college student, Jared, grabbed Tullamore the leprechaun, I noticed Seamus O'Fae scowl and his face grow beet red. However, when Tullamore turned his tormentor into a pig, causing Jared to run hither and yon in terror, each and every one of the GoBOO laughed. They laughed even harder when Tullamore hopped on the trans-

formed boy's back and rode him out onto the street. I
shifted about uncomfortably and glanced up at the gallery. None of the reporters seemed the least bit amused.
As we got to the part where Oddo levitated Jared's hapless roommate and accidentally sent him flying through
the front window of the bar, I saw the mayor frown.

"Querent Skua—please halt the testimony."

The images above Skua's head abruptly froze, as if
she'd hit the PAUSE button on a DVD player.

"Who is that juggler, Serenity?" Mayor Lash asked
sharply.

"I can answer that, Your Honor," Lieutenant Vivi
said, getting to her feet. "He's an unruly by the name of
Oddo. Tends to get munted and involved in pissing con-
tests. I've busted him on public magic more than once."

"I want him arrested and charged with sorcerous assault. Is that understood?"

"Your Honor," Hexe protested, "I can give you my
word that Oddo didn't mean to harm anyone. It was an
accident."

"Be that as it may," the mayor replied, "it does not
change the fact that a Kymeran used magic against a human of his own volition, not as a go-between. You know
the laws about that. And as for it being an accident, he'll
have his own chance to testify—provided his memory
isn't blurred. You may resume the testimony, Skua."

I wondered what Mayor Lash meant by "blurred,"
until we got to the part in Hexe's own playback where
he was struck in the head. Suddenly the images fell out
of focus, rendering faces fuzzy and indistinct, as if seen
through a fog, and remained that way all the way up to
the initial confrontation between the PTU and the
NYPD, when Skal threw the fireball. In fact, the only
way I could identify Skal at all was because I was there
when he cast the spell.

Suddenly, without warning, Skua dropped the scrying crystal onto the floor, where it shattered into a thousand tiny fragments. "Please forgive me, Your Honor," she said in chagrin. "I lost my grip."

"It's perfectly understandable during the course of such lengthy testimony," Mayor Lash replied. "You may start again with a fresh crystal, if you like."

"No, Your Honor. I believe we've seen enough from this witness," she replied quickly. "You may stand down, Hexe."

He exited the witness booth to a flurry of noise from the gallery as the reporters utilized the lull to hurry off and file their stories. When he resumed his seat beside me, I leaned over and asked why Skua hadn't asked him to identify the person who threw the fireball, but all he did was shake his head.

Tuli stepped forward again and read from his clipboard: "The council calls the human known as 'Tate' to testify."

As I started to stand up, Hexe leaned in close and whispered: "Just answer their questions. Don't volunteer any further information."

As Skua approached the witness box to question me, I caught the distinct odor of hemlock and wormwood. I had been living among Kymerans long enough to realize that the scents they exuded were subtle clues as to their personalities, and Skua's was telling me that she was far more dangerous than she seemed.

"Thank you for appearing before the council today, Ms. Eresby." Although her tone was pleasant, her smile did not extend to her eyes, which remained as cold and hard as emeralds. "Would you please state your full legal name for the record?"

"Timothea Alda Talmadge Eresby," I replied, trying not to grimace. I *really* hate my given name, especially when I have to say the whole ungainly megilla out loud. It's like being forced to unroll a particularly hideous rug foisted on you by your family.

"Are you a resident of Golgotham, Ms. Eresby?"

"Please, call me Tate." I said with a smile.

"Are you a resident of Golgotham, Ms. Eresby?" Skua repeated sharply. So much for trying to be friendly.

"Yes, I am. I reside at Fifty Golden Hill Street. I've lived there for the last three months, give or take a week."

"You are human, are you not?"

"Yes, I am."

"Do you possess what is commonly referred to as 'psychic powers,' such as clairvoyance, telepathy, psychokinesis, or the like?"

"No, I do not."

This bit of information was greeted with a murmur of surprise from not only the audience but some of the Go-BOO members as well. Humans with "gifts" living in Golgotham were one thing, but a garden-variety human dwelling among them was something else altogether. I wished I could look over my shoulder at Hexe, but I didn't dare do so.

"I *see* . . . ," Skua muttered, her gaze growing even harder and colder than before. "And what is your occupation?"

"I'm an artist. I work in metal."

"Ah." Skua nodded her head, as if I had confirmed a suspicion. "And were you present at the Two-Headed Calf the night of the riot?"

"Yes, I was."

"Do you recall the events that immediately followed what we have just viewed?"

"Vividly."

"A simple yes or no will do, Ms. Eresby."

"Yes, I do."

"Are you willing and able to testify to what you experienced?"

"I am."

"Very well." Skua motioned to Tuli, who stepped forward and handed her a slightly smaller scrying crystal. She turned back to face me, holding out the crystal as if offering me a bite of a very shiny apple.

"Breathe, so that we may see the truth."

I leaned forward and exhaled upon the crystal. Within seconds it was filled with a swirling mist upon which tiny black-and-white images flickered. As Skua raised the crystal over her head, the well of the council chamber was filled by a monochrome mob and a burning police truck.

The eerie part wasn't seeing my memories projected like a holographic laser show, but the fact that it was absolutely silent. Angry faces contorted as Kymerans and humans alike screamed, shouted, and cursed, but not a sound was made.

Suddenly a wall of phantom smoke filled the air as the NYPD team fired its tear gas canisters into the crowd. As the smoke spread, the memory began to blur and run, like a chalk drawing on a sidewalk caught in the rain. Before it dissolved completely, however, the council was able to see Lieutenant Vivi wrap Lieutenant Trieux in ectoplasm, followed by the NYPD team turning its weaponry on the PTU.

Captain Horn quickly got to his feet. "I think we have seen enough testimony to prove to the council that the PTU is not at fault in this matter. Lieutenant Vivi's actions were in the public good."

"I agree, Captain," Mayor Lash said. "You may end the testimony, Querent."

Skua lowered the crystal and as suddenly as it appeared, the rioting mob disappeared. I was relieved that my testimony had been cut short, as something told me the sight of the next Witch King being menaced by an armed policeman, no matter how blurry, would do little to ease tensions between the City of New York and Golgotham. I vacated the witness box and returned to my seat. Hexe smiled and patted my hand.

"You did great," he whispered.

"I'm just glad it's over."

"It is obvious from the testimony that the NYPD acted rashly," Chiron said. "They placed not only Golgothamites in danger, but their own kind as well. The blame for the riot lics squarely on their shoulders."

As the other members of the council nodded their heads and murmured in agreement, Hexe got to his feet. "I would like to say something, if I may, Your Honor."

"Of course, Serenity," Mayor Lash replied.

As Hexe prepared to speak, I looked past him and saw Skua sitting in a nearby pew, staring at him with open trepidation.

"While the NYPD's actions were indeed unwise, you cannot argue they were unprovoked. Believe me—the reporters who just poured out of the gallery won't leave *that* out of the articles they're filing. Lieutenant Trieux and his mcn had no business being here, but that doesn't change the fact that sorcery was used against them, in violation of the treaty. You cannot simply blame it all on the NYPD."

"Hexe is right," Giles Gruff said, adjusting his monocle. "The humans will not take our grievances seriously if we do nothing to address this. Tullamore changing a drunk into a pig is one thing, but hurling hellfire at New York City policemen is something else entirely. I shudder to think what would have happened if that fireball had struck one of their officers!"

"If you ask me, it's what they deserve for breaking the treaty and coming unannounced and uninvited into our territory," Seamus O'Fae growled. "I have it on good authority that one of the humans at the Calf is the son of a New York City alderman, who tweeted his old man when things started to heat up. The alderman called in a favor with Lieutenant Trieux's commander, who thought 'extricating' a bunch of young college students to keep 'em from being turned into toads and whatnot would make for a nice feather in his cap. I'd like to see ye muckrakers report *that* shite in yer papers!" he shouted, waving a tiny fist at the remaining journalists seated in the gallery.

"Calm down, Seamus," Lorelei Jones said, laying a webbed hand on the leprechaun's green-clad shoulder. "Getting angry hasn't solved anything yet."

"Serenity, do you know who is responsible for slinging that hellfire at the police?" Mayor Lash asked.

"I do not, Your Honor," Hexe lied. "As you could tell from my testimony, the blow to my head made it difficult for me to focus my attention."

"As much as I hate to admit it, the Malandanti actually served a useful purpose in our community," Bjorn Cowpen said with a sigh. "Doesn't matter if they're human or not, I don't like troublemakers in my club, and I certainly don't like it when they're wandering the streets. The Malandanti were a big factor in keeping the unrulies in line on Duivel Street. Now they're starting to get out of hand. I've had a noticeable uptick at my joints since Boss Marz and his croggies were hustled off to the Tombs."

"Come, now, Bjorn!" Giles Gruff said, clucking his tongue in disapproval. "You might as well praise the Nazis for keeping the trains on time, or the Witch Finders for giving free manicures."

"Thank you, Councilman Gruff, for making that point," Captain Horn said. "While I understand your fears, Councilman Cowpen, let's not go overboard by romanticizing a bunch of murderous thugs."

"Well, this seems as good a time as any to adjourn for lunch," Mayor Lash decreed with a rap of his gavel. "The witnesses are free to leave."

As the GoBOO council members and the other members of the audience filed out of the chamber, I could no longer restrain my curiosity. "Why did you lie to the council about Skal?" I whispered.

"The worst Oddo has to worry about for his part in the riot is a year or two in the Tombs with mittens on his hands. Tullamore will probably have to surrender his pot of gold to Jared and cobble shoes for the disadvantaged as community service. But what Skal did violates the treaty. The GoBOO could very well take his magic from him as a peace offering to the city."

"You mean—cut off his fingers?" The very idea made me shiver in disgust. "Do they still *do* that?"

"In special cases, where it's warranted, yes," Hexe said grimly. "They could take his entire left hand, if they wanted to. Skal is a bigoted fool, but he's just a kid. Something like that would destroy not only him but his mother as well."

"His mom?"

"Skua."

"So *that's* why she dropped the scrying crystal during your testimony."

Hexe shrugged. "Whether she did so by accident or design, who can say? It is highly likely she knew nothing of her son's involvement in the riot and only recognized him at the last moment, despite the blurriness of the image. But she *did* recognize him— that much I'm certain of. It would ruin her career, no question about it. I won't be party to that, if I can avoid it. Everyone deserves at least one chance—this is Skal's."

Without warning, I kissed Hexe on the cheek. He blushed and rubbed the side of his face. "What was that for?" he asked with a laugh.

"For being a sweet, wonderful guy, even to people who don't deserve it," I replied.

As we turned to go, a feminine voice called out from behind us. "Hexe! Ms. Eresby! A word, if I may."

It was the mermaid, Lorelei Jones, who had descended from the council table to join us. As she drew closer, I could see that her skin had the same texture as that of a dolphin and that she had gill slits on either side of her throat. I was afraid she might smell like a fish market, but was pleasantly surprised by the aroma of sea spray and kelp, with just a touch of driftwood, that accompanied her.

Hexe smiled broadly as he shook her webbed hand. "Lorelei! Good to see you again! You look as beautiful as ever."

"Flattery will get you everywhere!" she laughed with a voice like water bubbling from a deep spring. "I just wanted to tell you thank you for bringing some common sense to today's hearing. Between Seamus and Bjorn, there's precious little to be found right now."

"They're scared. That's all," Hexe replied. "Change rarely happens overnight in Golgotham."

"Why don't you bring your friend over to my place for dinner and drinks?" Lorelei suggested, smiling in my direction. "On the house, of course. But I warn you, I pour them strong! They don't say 'drinks like a fish' for nothing! Well, I'd best be going. Nice meeting you, Ms. Eresby."

"Please, call me Tate, Ms. Jones."

"Tate it is. And you can call me Lorelei. The 'Jones' is only because I needed a last name for the liquor license."

As we exited GoBOO Headquarters, the throng of TV reporters stationed outside the building surged up the stairs to greet us, shoving cameras in our faces.

"Hexe! Hector Lafcadio with WPIX! Is it true you're dating the heiress to the Eresby fortune?"

"No comment. Please, let us by—," Hexe said as he pushed the microphones aside. "I have nothing to say to the media."

"Hexe! Miranda Joyce with WCBS! Is it true that Kymerans attacked the New York Police Department?"

"No comment!"

"Miss Eresby! Sally Ann Klutter for *Entertainment Tonight*! Is it true you're living with a Kymeran? Is he your lover? Is it true what they say about Kymeran men?"

"What kind of question is *that*?" Hexe said heatedly. "And what business is it of yours, anyway?"

Before things could get out of hand, Lieutenant Vivi suddenly appeared, inserting herself between Hexe and the reporters.

"Step back!" she barked. "You heard him—they don't want to talk to the press! Now clear off before I run you all in for blocking the sidewalk and disturbing the peace!" The PTU officer glanced over her shoulder and gave us a crooked smile. "I'd make a break for the cab stand right now if I were you."

Hexe grabbed my hand and dashed to the nearest hansom. As we climbed into the cab, I looked across the street and saw Captain Horn standing there, gazing at Hexe with a contemplative look on his face. When he saw I had noticed him, his features became as unreadable as a slab of granite, and he quickly turned on his heel, disappearing into the crowd.

Chapter 11

When we returned home, we were promptly greeted by Scratch, who was seated expectantly in the foyer, his eyes glowing murder-red. "About time you two got back," the familiar yowled. "I'm positively *starving*."

"I'm so sure," Hexe scoffed. "When I opened the door, I thought Tullamore had turned another college student into a flying pig."

"Do *not* go there, if you want to come back in one piece," Scratch growled.

"Far be it from me to damage your fragile self-image by snarking about your girlish figure." Hexe laughed as he removed his coat. "Anything happen while we were out?"

"A delivery person from the Bestiary dropped off a package addressed to Tate. Lukas accepted delivery and put it in your office before he left for work."

I frowned. "I didn't order anything from anyplace called that. What is it?"

"How would *I* know?" Scratch replied with a shrug of

his wings. "I'm not the one who signed for it—no thumbs, remember?"

"I suggest we go see for ourselves," said Hexe.

There was a small plastic travel crate, the kind used for transporting animals on airlines, sitting next to the desk. A sticker glued across the side read LIVE ANIMAL. As we entered the office, the crate began to rattle and I heard a piteous little yelp.

"Somebody, somewhere definitely made a mistake," I said. "I didn't buy a dog."

"There's no mistake," Hexe said, his smile breaking into a grin. "*I* bought him!"

"You bought a *what*?!" Scratch exclaimed, his eyes bugging out in alarm.

"Thought about what you said the other day, and decided you might appreciate having a real pet—one that doesn't talk back."

"Owning a dog is a big commitment," I protested. "You have to walk them, groom them, make sure they get their shots. . . . I don't know if I'm ready to handle something like that right now."

"I just wanted you to feel at home," he explained. "Just take a look at him, then decide if you don't want him."

I knelt down and unlatched the travel crate. Without warning the wire door swung open and a Boston terrier puppy came bounding out into the room. My first impression was that he was black and white and made mostly of head and belly. The puppy celebrated his freedom by running in figure eights between Hexe's feet and my own, ears and tongue flapping like flags. As I've said before, I'm a sucker when it comes to animals, and the minute I looked into those big brown eyes, I was instantly and irreversibly smitten.

"He's *adorable*!" I squealed, scooping my new dog up in my arms.

The puppy responded by licking every square inch of my face as fast as he could, while wriggling so hard I was afraid he would pop out of my hands like a wet bar of soap.

"I can still take him back if you want me to," Hexe offered.

"Don't you *dare*!" I gasped, cradling the puppy in the crook of my arm.

"So—do you like him?"

"Like him? I *love* him! Thank you, baby—he's wonderful—and so are you!" I gave Hexe a big fat kiss, only to have the puppy join in. I laughed and put the dog back on the floor so I could properly express my appreciation.

Scratch warily eyed the newest member of the household as the puppy continued exploring his environment, sniffing the corners, the carpet, and other furnishings in the room. "*That's* a dog?" the familiar grumbled. "It looks like a cross between a monkey, a bat, a goldfish, and a potbellied pig. Are you *sure* they didn't slip you an unfledged gargoyle instead?"

"He's a Boston terrier," Hexe explained.

"Where's his snout? He looks like he chased a parked car," Scratch grunted.

The puppy came to a halt and did a double take, as if he'd just seen Scratch for the first time. As the winged cat turned his back in disgust, the puppy gave the familiar's hairless butt a tentative sniff.

"*Hey!*" Scratch snarled, spinning back around. "*Watch where you're sticking that thing, buddy!*"

Instead of yelping in fright, the puppy dropped down into play stance, his chin and forepaws resting on the floor, his hindquarters wriggling in the air.

"Isn't that cute?" I cooed. "He wants to play with you."

"Gag me with a grapefruit spoon." Scratch groaned. The familiar glowered reproachfully at Hexe. "How could you do this to me after all these years?"

As Scratch turned to leave the room, the puppy bounded after him, landing with all four feet on the end of his hairless tail. The familiar whipped about a second time and hissed like a bag of angry cobras, spreading his batlike wings in warning. *"Bang off, chuffer!"*

The puppy took a couple of steps back, as if surprised by Scratch's response, then nimbly jumped forward and licked him on the face, and then just as quickly jumped back and began to dance around the familiar, yapping for him to come play.

"I don't think he's scared of you, Scratch," Hexe observed.

"He will be after I bite off an ear!"

I snatched the puppy up and held him in my arms. "Don't you *dare* hurt Beanie!"

Scratch rolled his eyes. "Is *that* what you're calling him?"

"You've got a better name for him?" I challenged.

"Yeah—'Snack'!"

"Scratch! Stop threatening to eat Beanie!" Hexe admonished.

"*She's* the one who named it after food!"

"Don't argue with me!" Hexe said sternly. "You are forbidden to kill, eat, maim, or otherwise hurt Beanie. Do you understand?"

Scratch sighed, his wings drooping in resignation at his master's command. "I gotcha. No eating the stupid dog. What about burglars, salesmen, and door-to-door missionaries?"

"Those are still permitted."

"Praise the pits for small favors," Scratch grumbled, as he flapped away in disgust. "Please excuse me while I go piss in your sock drawer. . . ."

The rest of the afternoon was spent "puppy-proofing" the house, which consisted of putting down newspapers and constructing makeshift barricades to ensure that the newly christened Beanie didn't wander anywhere he wasn't supposed to. The last thing we needed was for him to end up on the third floor, which had a bad habit of disappearing into alternate dimensions, if Hexe's great-uncle was anything to go by.

I used my iPhone to look up information on the proper care and feeding of a new dog, and was immediately overwhelmed by the list of dos and don'ts from various experts. While the store where Hexe bought Beanie had included a bag of dry dog food, along with the travel crate, as part of the purchase price, it was becoming increasingly clear that taking care of a puppy was going to require more than some wee-wee pads and a chew toy.

Although the PTU had rescinded its previous curfew, we decided it was still a little too soon to be wandering the streets after dark, and chose to order in for dinner. I put a call in to Strega Nona's Pizza Oven for two pies—a small Trojan Horse for myself (pepperoni, feta, spinach, portabellas, garlic, and sun-dried tomatoes) and the Six-Fingered Discount for Hexe (hot dogs, maple syrup, artichokes, flash-fried crickets, and pickles). I love that man to death, but I learned the hard way never to go half and half on the toppings with him.

Just after I finished ordering, my phone rang. The "Psycho Theme" ringtone alerted me to who was calling without my having to look at the caller ID.

"So—we don't hear from you for weeks, and *this* is

how we find out you're shacking up with some Kymie lothario!"

"Hello to you too, Mother," I said with a sigh. "Hexe isn't a 'lothario,' whatever that is, and what do you mean by 'this'?"

"The *television*!" I could hear the faint rattle of ice cubes in her Old Fashioned in the background. "It was one of those horrid entertainment gossip shows—not that I watch them, of course. Muffie Potter Aston rang me to say she'd seen you in the company of some purple-headed wizard. I was positively *mortified*!"

"Hexe and I testified before the GoBOO—I mean, the Golgotham Business Owners Organization—today," I explained.

"Why on earth would their Chamber of Commerce want to talk to you?"

"They wanted to question us about the riot, Mom."

My mother's bafflement quickly switched to alarm. "Wait—what would you know about a riot?"

"Hexe and I were there when it broke out. We were practically in the middle of it."

"Merciful God—are you all right, Timmy?"

As much as I dislike my given name, it is nothing compared to how much I loathe my childhood nickname. But since my mother sounded genuinely upset, I chose to ignore her use of it. "I got exposed to some tear gas, but not too bad. Hexe was hit on the head with a bottle—"

"Timothy—did you hear that?" my mother called out to my father, not bothering to muffle the mouthpiece. "Timmy was caught in that riot!"

There was the sound of footsteps crossing the hardwood floor of the grand salon, followed by one of the numerous extensions in my parents' penthouse being picked up. "Princess? Are you okay?"

"I'm fine, Dad. Honest. I was just telling Mom I'm okay...."

My father heaved a weary sigh, which indicated that he was getting ready to lay down the law. "Sweetheart, I know you want to find yourself, and we've been tolerant of that ... but between what happened at the gallery and now this riot thing, your mother and I think it's time you came home. Golgotham is just too dangerous."

"Dad, I appreciate that you and Mom are worried about me, but I'm perfectly safe," I lied. Like I told Mei-kei, I have a great deal of experience in telling fathers what they want to hear. "I have friends here, and I know my way around. Nothing bad is going to happen to me. I promise."

"Yes, well ... about your 'friends'—your mother is *extremely* alarmed about this Hexe fellow. She believes he has some kind of control over you."

"Mom's just being paranoid. And racist. You know how she is."

"I'm afraid so," my father admitted.

Suddenly my mother was back on the line—she must have gone off to freshen up her Old Fashioned. "Would it have *killed* you to pick up the phone and tell us what was going on? We had no *idea* you were involved in that horrible riot downtown!"

"Mom, Dad—maybe if you actually came down here and checked out the neighborhood, maybe met a couple of my friends, it might ease your mind," I suggested. "Right now isn't the greatest time, but maybe after things cool off and get back to normal ...?"

"Me—? Go downtown? To *Golgotham*?" my mother gasped. I could see her clutching her pearls at the very suggestion. "Have you lost your mind?!?"

"Now, Millie," my father countered, "Timmy does have a point—"

"Sure! Take *her* side!" my mother replied huffily. "Like you *always* do!"

My father heaved another sigh, even wearier than the one before. "Princess, we'll have to call you back and discuss this another time. Your mother and I need to talk."

"Of course, Dad. I understand."

"Love you, Timmy. Stay safe."

"I will, Dad. Same to you."

I'd known that suggesting that my parents visit Golgotham would set my mother off like a blasting cap, but it was the only way I could get them off the phone. I felt a twinge of guilt for setting my father up the way I did, but I told myself it had to be done in the name of peace, particularly my own.

My father may not understand or appreciate my desire to be a sculptor, but he has never denied me. My mother, on the other hand, has been a living boat anchor for as long as I can remember—doing her best to keep me from realizing any ambition outside of becoming a Lady Who Lunches. She always gets overridden by my father, but that doesn't keep her from making catty remarks every time we talk. I wished our relationship wasn't so acrimonious, but sometimes things just are the way they are. Water's wet, fire is hot, and my mom's a be-yotch.

I looked down at Beanie, who had worn himself out playing and, in true puppy fashion, fallen asleep right where he was. One second he was wrestling with a knotted-up tube sock, the next he was sprawled on his side, snoring through his little pushed-in nose, which was almost flush with his onion-shaped head. He was as limp as a rag doll, as relaxed as only small children and puppies can get, as I picked him up and cradled him in the crook of my arm. Somehow he managed to yawn and stretch without opening his eyes or interrupting his snores. I glanced up to see Hexe standing in the doorway, one shoulder propped against the jamb, a little half smile on his face.

"So—does it feel like home now?" he asked.

"*Better* than home," I replied with a smile.

Chapter 12

For the next few days I was kept busy taking Beanie to get his shots, and shopping for squeak toys, collars, and dog sweaters. And since animals with only one head and/or no ability to speak were comparatively rare where I lived, this meant trips outside of Golgotham. It also meant that by the end of the day I was usually too pooped to go out. Which wasn't that big a deal, since after our experience with first the riot and then the media, Hexe and I had decided it was probably a good idea to stay home and live off takeout for a few days, rather than risk going out after dark. Besides, it gave us time to bond with Beanie and help him get accustomed to our day-to-day routine. Still, after four days, as much as I adore Strega Nona's pizza and stromboli, when Hexe suggested we go to Lorelei's for dinner, I jumped at the chance.

Hexe's childhood friend Kidron picked us up in his hansom cab at seven. I had made sure to take the puppy out into the backyard before crating him for the evening. While Scratch had promised not to harm Beanie, I decided it might not be a good idea for the pup to push his luck while I was gone.

Lorelei's was situated near Pickman's Slip, at the foot of Ferry Street, on the end of a long pier that jutted into the East River. The building was huge, and looked like a fanciful cross between a Maori meetinghouse and a Hawaiian war canoe, with an inverse curved roof that measured sixty feet at its highest point. Flanking the front door were two massive, twenty-foot-high *maoi*—the famous stone faces of Easter Island—with volcano-like flames burning from the tops of their heads.

As Kidron pulled up to let us out, a young merman with webbed hands, green seaweedlike hair, and gill-slits along his throat, and dressed in a colorful Hawaiian shirt, hurried forward to help me down from the cab.

"Welcome to Lorelei's." The merman smiled. He pushed against the edge of the octagonal-shaped front door, which turned on a center pivot to allow entrance to the building. "Have a wonderful evening."

The first thing I noticed upon crossing the threshold, besides the mouthwatering smell of ribs slow-cooking in wood-fired ovens, was that instead of the usual tables and booths found in most restaurants, there were individual thatched huts. Some were big enough for two, while others were large enough to accommodate up to twenty or more people, giving the illusion of a tropical native village under a single roof.

Just inside the front door was a triple-tiered fountain filled with dry ice, which sent mist boiling across the carpeted floor, while the sound of jungle drums throbbed from hidden speakers. A beautiful mermaid hostess, dressed in a boldly printed sarong, stepped forward to greet us. She wore a lei of flowers around her neck that partially obscured her gill-slits, and held an iPad in her webbed hands. Her long dark green hair was piled high atop her head and kept in place by an ornately carved mother-of-pearl comb.

"Welcome to Lorelei's," she said with a smile. "Do you have a reservation?"

"I'm a friend of the owner," Hexe explained. "She said she'd put us on the list. The name's Hexe."

"Ah, yes!" The hostess nodded as she consulted her iPad. "Right this way, Serenity!"

As we were led into the restaurant, no matter where I looked I found something to amaze or amuse the eye. Grimacing war masks hung on the walls alongside shel-lacked sea turtles, and every doorway had Maori motifs painted along its edges. The entire left wall was covered in richly decorated vintage tapa cloths, made from the bark found in the South Sea Islands, and dominated by an imposing forty-foot-high tiki-god head with a roaring fire built inside its gaping mouth. The opposing wall, however, was made entirely of shatterproof Plexiglas, and housed the largest saltwater habitat I had ever seen outside of a public aquarium. I spotted a multitude of tropical fish, including adult sea turtles and manta ray, as well as several merfolk swimming inside it.

I stopped to stare in fascination as a mermaid, her hair floating about her head like a bed of kelp, glided past. With her clamshell-and-seaweed bra and dolphin lower body, she looked like an escapee from a children's picture book. As I watched, she disappeared inside a larger version of the "Neptune's Castle" found in more modest aquariums, leaving a trail of bubbles in her wake.

Our hostess showed us to an intimate grass hut for two, illuminated by multicolored glass float lights sus-pended in handwoven nets and a puffer-fish lamp that dangled from the rafters like a prickly piñata.

We carefully studied the menus, which were shaped like Easter Island heads and big enough to use as sema-phore signals. I ordered the Polynesian Spare Ribs with Molokai Sauce, while Hexe picked the Island Flaming

Chicken, which came skewered on a sword and was set on fire at the table. As for drinks, I opted for the Zombie, which left me feeling comfortably numb by the time we finished our entrées, and Hexe ordered a cocktail that arrived in a cup of dry ice that quickly engulfed the tabletop in a cloud of crawling mist.

"What's that one called again?" I asked as I turned on my cell phone camera.

"A Smoking Eruption."

"I'd see a doctor about that if I were you," I said with a giggle.

"Is Lorelei here tonight?" Hexe asked the waitress as she cleared away our dishes.

"She's tending bar in the Fishbowl," she replied, pointing to the back of the restaurant.

"C'mon," Hexe said, levering himself out of his chair. "Let's go say hello and thank her for dinner."

To reach the restaurant's lounge, we had to walk over a bamboo bridge that spanned an artificial stream fed by an equally artificial waterfall. On the other side was a Plexiglas tank that stood four feet deep, twenty feet long, and twelve feet wide, with a wooden bar top built along its rim. Inside the tank were several different species of tropical fish, and in the middle, set on its own private island complete with palm tree, was a shelf full of liquor and an array of tiki drinkware. Standing—or, rather, floating—behind the bar was none other than the restaurant's namesake and owner, dressed from the waist up in a twist-front bikini top that displayed her upper body to its best effect. She bobbed in place behind the bar as she vigorously shook a cocktail mixer without displacing the water or spilling a drop of alcohol into the "fishbowl."

"I was wondering when you'd finally claim your free dinner." Lorelei grinned as we stepped up to the bar.

"It's been a busy week," Hexe explained.

"For some more than others," the mermaid replied with a sigh.

"You seem to have a good crowd tonight," Hexe observed.

"The riot scared off my regulars, as well as the tourists. This is the first night people seem to feel comfortable going out after dark, praise Poseidon."

"I think people are getting over their shell shock," Hexe replied. "I tended to several locals who were injured in the riot the very next morning, but I haven't had a client knock on my door since then until today. I think the worst has finally blown over."

"I certainly hope so."

While Lorelei and Hexe discussed the effect of the riot on Golgotham's economy, I allowed my attention to wander as I continued to ogle the exotic war masks, ceremonial spears, and stuffed trophy fish decorating the lounge. As my eye traveled down the bar, I spotted a familiar head of electric blue hair seated on the very last stool, drinking from a large ceramic bowl shaped like a Hawaiian war-canoe.

"Look who's here," I said, nudging Hexe in the ribs.

His eyes widened in surprise upon espying the lonely drinker. "Faro!" he called out. "Is that you?"

The owner, and sole employee, of Faro's Moving turned on his barstool to greet us, a chagrined look on his face. "Yeah, it's me."

"I'd ask how married life is treating you," Hexe said acerbically, "but Chorea told us you ditched her during the honeymoon."

Faro cringed, a worried look on his face. "You talked to Chory? By the Outer Dark, whatever you do, don't tell her you've seen me! I'm trying to get our marriage annulled, and I'm laying low until it's all over and she finally cools off. I'm even steering clear of my office in the Rookery. I don't want her to know where I am."

"Annulment?" Hexe raised a purple eyebrow in surprise. "Granted, you two had a whirlwind marriage, but Chorea's still a hell of a gal."

"You're telling me!" Faro snorted. "I spent most of our so-called 'honeymoon' running for my life through the hills of Arkadia! We went to Greece so she could show me some of her old haunts, right? She starts drinking and dancing, and the next thing I know she's coming after me with blood in her eyes! I ended up having to teleport myself back to Golgotham. I didn't have my GPS on me, so I'm lucky I didn't end up at the bottom of a river or stuck in a wall."

"Well, she *is* a maenad, Faro," Hexe pointed out. "You knew that when you met her. Look at it this way—at least she really cares about you; maenads tend to kill the ones they love when they are in a Dionysian frenzy, like Agave tearing her son, King Pentheus, limb from limb."

"*Now* you tell me!" Faro groaned.

"Hey, it's not *my* fault you opted out of Classical Studies in favor of Applied Teleportation in high school," Hexe replied. "Chory's a wonderful woman, when she's sober. Maybe if you get her into AA, you can save your marriage. You know the makeup sex is gonna be *killer*."

"That's what I'm afraid of," Faro replied glumly.

Having tipped our waitress, we wished Faro well with his domestic problems, thanked Lorelei for her hospitality, and made our way out the door. Kidron was waiting patiently for us when we exited the restaurant.

"Where to next?" the centaur asked as we climbed back into the cab.

"It's such a lovely night," I said, squeezing Hexe's hand. "Why don't we take our time going home?"

"You heard the lady," Hexe told the driver. "Take the scenic route."

"I had a wonderful time tonight," I said, resting my head on Hexe's shoulder as Kidron slowly made his way through the winding, narrow streets. Although traffic was lighter than normal, I was relieved to see activity at the various pubs and restaurants along the way. It seemed that Hexe was right, and that the citizens of Golgotham were finally returning to their normal routines.

"So did I," he replied. "Lorelei's is no Two-Headed Calf, mind you, but it does have its strong points."

Kidron came to an abrupt halt. "Do you smell that?" he asked, his wide nostrils flaring in agitation. "It's blood. *Kymeran* blood."

Suddenly three figures darted out of a nearby side street and ran right in front of the centaur, causing him to rear up onto his hind legs and nearly overturn the cab. Hexe threw his arms around me to make sure I didn't tumble out onto the cobblestone street.

The trio were dressed all in black, two of them in ski masks, and they carried aluminum baseball bats. A second later a red-haired Kymeran woman, her face swollen and bloody, staggered from the direction they had come from, only to drop to her knees upon reaching the curb.

"Call nine-one-one!" Hexe said to Kidron as he jumped out of the hansom. "Tell them we'll need an ambulance."

"Way ahead of you," the cabbie replied, tapping his Bluetooth headset.

I hopped out of the cab and hurried after Hexe, who was kneeling beside the woman. As I got closer, I realized that what I had mistaken for red hair was actually mustard yellow, dyed carnelian by the blood flowing from her scalp. Her right eye was already swollen shut, and her lower lip was split open.

"Go help Jarl," she croaked, pointing behind her to a man with apricot-colored hair who lay sprawled in a rapidly widening pool of blood.

"Stay here with her," Hexe told me as he dashed to help the second victim.

"Don't worry," I said as I helped the bleeding woman back onto her feet. "My friend is a healer. Here, let me help you." I fished a handkerchief from my purse and handed it to her so she could stanch the blood flowing from her split lip.

"Thank you," she murmured gratefully, only to freeze upon seeing my hand. My stomach cinched itself into a knot as she recoiled, a look of fear in her eyes.

"It's okay, I'm not going to hurt you," I assured her. "I saw the men who mugged you—I know they were humans, but I have nothing to do with them."

"They weren't muggers," she replied. "They didn't want our money. They jumped us as we were coming back from dinner. They started hitting us with bats before Jarl or I realized what was happening. There wasn't time to raise a hand to defend ourselves. It was horrible— they kept beating my husband even after he went down. The one without the ski mask said they were the sons of Adam, and that they were going to make us 'dirty Kymies' pay."

As the woman related her story, a crowd began to gather around us, curious to discover what had happened. There was not a single human face to be seen.

"Did you hear that?" an older Kymeran man with mold green muttonchops loudly announced. "They were witch-bashed by a bunch of numps!"

An annoyed buzz rippled through the assembled onlookers, as if someone had just kicked a hornets' nest.

"What's this nump bitch doing here?" asked a teen-aged Kymeran girl in an Arcade Fire T-shirt.

"Get your stubby hands off her, nump!" another hostile voice shouted.

Suddenly Hexe was between me and the rapidly contracting ring of onlookers. "Leave her alone!" he barked. "She didn't have anything to do with this!"

Most of the assembled Kymerans backed away upon recognizing Hexe, but the warlock with the moldy muttonchops held his ground. "Why are you taking up for some nump bint, Serenity? What's she to you?"

"She's his concubine!" the teenager chimed in, holding up her Android phone. "It says so right here on TMZ!"

"So that's it, eh?" the moldy warlock sneered. "Kymeran women aren't *good* enough for you now, Serenity?"

"Everyone calm down!" Kidron shouted as he pushed his way through the crowd, forcing the onlookers to part or risk being trampled. "The PTU are on their way. They'll handle this."

"In seven hells, they will!" The warlock spat as he returned to the pub from which he'd come. "They'll roll over for City Hall, just like they always do, and you know it. No nump will ever be brought to justice for what they do in *or* out of Golgotham!"

Within seconds of the would-be mob's clearing the streets, a centaur with a snowy lower body, the mark of an ambulance bearer, rounded the corner, harnessed to a whitewashed coach marked GOLGOTHAM GENERAL closely followed by a PTU response wagon.

A couple of Kymerans dressed in scrubs jumped out of the back of the ambulance, carrying a stretcher between them. Hexe hurried to greet them. "He's got multiple skull fractures. You're going to need to stabilize him before he's moved."

The boneknitter nodded his understanding and knelt down beside Jarl, gently placing his hands to either side of the wounded man's head. He muttered an incantation in Kymeran and a pale white glow, similar to St. Elmo's Fire, flickered into being around Jarl's skull. A few seconds later he was carefully lifted onto the stretcher. As they carried him past me, I was shocked to see his face was little more than a mass of pulped meat, shattered bone, and twisted cartilage. It was a good thing the psychic surgeons at Golgotham General were capable of magic, because he was definitely going to need a miracle to survive his wounds.

As Jarl was strapped down in the back of the ambulance, I helped his wife climb in beside him. She seated herself on the passenger bench inside the coach, then turned to look at me.

"You've been very kind," she said. "I'm sorry the others treated you like that. And I'm sorry *I* treated you like that, too. I should have said something. . . ."

"They weren't in the mood to listen, even if you had," I said with a rueful smile. "And for what it's worth—I'm sorry, too."

She nodded her head, and then turned her attention back to her husband. The last I saw of Jarl and his wife before the ambulance pulled away, she was tightly squeezing his hand, as if to tether his life to hers.

"Looks like you two can't stay away from trouble."

I turned to see Captain Horn regarding Hexe and myself with a bemused look on his face. Normally a PTU officer of his rank wouldn't show up to a routine mugging, but these were not normal times.

"Did you see what happened?" he asked, fishing a digital voice recorder from his breast pocket.

"No," Hexe replied. "But we saw *who* did it."

"There were three of them, dressed in black. They ran

that way," I said, pointing in the direction of Pickman's Slip. "They were definitely human. Well, at least the one without a ski mask was."

"Do you think you could describe what he looked like?"

"I think so."

"Good. I'll send around a picturemaker first thing in the morning. Until then, I would recommend that Ms. Eresby go home and stay there," Horn said grimly. "News like this travels fast in Golgotham, and there will be those looking to make any human they happen upon pay for what transpired tonight."

"We understand, Captain," Hexe said as he escorted me back to the waiting Kidron. "Thank you for your concern."

"This is all so awful," I groaned as I climbed back into the hansom. "The evening started off so wonderful, only to turn into something ugly."

"Yes," Hexe agreed with a sigh as he took his place beside me. "So much for all of this blowing over."

Chapter 13

I woke up early the next morning, chased from my slumber by troublesome dreams where I pursued three shadowy figures down a narrow alleyway, while Golgotham burned around me. Unable to return to sleep, I threw on my clothes and went downstairs. I started a fresh pot of coffee and went to see if the *Golgotham Gazette* was waiting for me on the front step. It was.

COUPLE VICTIMS OF VICIOUS WITCH-BASHING, the headline screamed above the fold. I guessed I could forget relaxing with a nice cup of coffee while working on the Word Jumble.

As I shuffled back into the kitchen, Hexe came padding downstairs, dressed only in last night's jeans, carrying Beanie under one arm like a football. "Somebody needs to go potty," he said around a yawn.

"Here, I'll take him," I said.

"It's a deal." Hexe handed over the wriggling bundle of dog.

One of the nicest things about Hexe's boardinghouse was that it had not only a backyard—a rarity in itself, no matter where you live in Manhattan—but also a garden.

Secreted away behind a high stone wall, it was far larger than it looked from the outside, much like the house itself, thanks to what Hexe referred to as "architectural origami." It was here that he grew many of the herbs necessary in his practice, and even kept a huge living-hedge-maze. As I stood on the back porch and waited for Beanie to finish sniffing every blade of grass in his immediate vicinity, I took a moment to enjoy the peaceful solitude the garden provided. It was hard to believe that on the other side of its ivy-covered walls people were trying to kill one another over something as silly as an extra ring finger.

Once Beanie was finished, I picked him up and returned to the kitchen, where I found Hexe reading the *Gazette*. A cup of coffee sat waiting for me on the table. As I sipped my morning brew, Beanie scampered across the faded linoleum, making a beeline for his food and water bowls. I chuckled as I watched him eat. His head was so big compared to the rest of his body that his rear end tilted up in the air, lifting his hind feet off the floor. I heard a decidedly feline growl of disgust and looked up to find Scratch perched atop the fridge.

"Morning, sunshine," I said by way of greeting. "What are you doing up there?"

"It's the only place I can get any peace when that honyock's awake," Scratch explained. "The idiot never looks up. It's as good as being invisible—even better, since I don't have to waste energy on a cloaking spell."

"That's because dogs *can't* look up," Hexe replied from behind his paper.

"Sucks to be them, then. What's this about a witch-bashing?" Scratch asked, gesturing to the headline with one of his wings.

"You can read?"

"No need to sound so *surprised*, nump," the familiar

retorted. "Of *course* I can read! In fact, I can read every language known to mankind, plus a few you bloodthirsty bastards don't know about."

"Pull your claws in, Scratch," Hexe warned, putting aside the newspaper. "Just because Tate is human doesn't mean she's responsible for what happened last night."

"I won't say I'm sorry, because that's not how I roll," Scratch said. "But I *will* say I'm not *unsorry*. How's that?"

"A double negative is close enough to an apology for me," I replied with a shrug. "And about last night—what I don't understand is how three humans, armed just with baseball bats, could get the drop on a pair of Kymerans. I mean, all Jarl and his wife had to do was point a hand at them—left or right—and wiggle some fingers, and they'd have been toast."

"It's not as simple as that," Hexe explained as he refreshed his cup of coffee. "While all Kymerans have *some* kind of magic, we're not all dab hands at spellslinging. Just like some humans have a natural aptitude for music, and others are born accountants—we all have our individual strengths and weaknesses. According to the paper, Jarl is an alchemist who distills katholikon and elixir vitae. His wife is a lapidary—her talent lies in the ability to transform pieces of quartz into scrying crystals. I'm certain neither of them was a quick draw, especially if they were ambushed. "

"So you're saying the douche bags that attacked them were lucky. If they had picked a Kymeran like you or Oddo . . ."

"Or, heavens forbid, Uncle Esau." Hexe grimaced. "If that had been the case, the results would have been far different." Suddenly there came a knock on the front door. "I'll go put on some proper clothes," Hexe said as

I went to answer the knock, Beanie trailing at my heels. "If it's a client, tell them I'll be there shortly."

I opened the door to find a petite Kymeran woman who smelled faintly of menthol and pencil shavings standing on the front stoop. She had kumquat-colored hair worn in a loose bun and she carried an artist's sketch case tucked under one arm. Around her neck was a lanyard attached to a laminated identity card.

"I'm Gale," she said with a smile. "I'm the picture-maker for the PTU. I hope I'm not interrupting your breakfast."

"Please come in," I said, stepping aside. "Captain Horn mentioned you'd be stopping by."

As Gale crossed the threshold, Beanie darted forward and loudly sniffed her shoes, his eyes bugging even farther from their sockets. "How—cute," she said diplomatically. "Is that a baby gargoyle?"

I led Gale into the front parlor, and motioned for her to take a seat on the purple velour sofa. She sat down and opened her sketch case, placing a tablet of blank paper and several pencils on the table in front of her.

"We were just having coffee—would you like a cup?" I offered.

"No, thank you, Ms. Eresby. I find it interferes with my work—it makes my hands jittery."

"So what do I have to do?" I asked, taking a seat opposite her. "Do I give you a description? Do I look through a mug book?"

"It's quite simple," she replied as she picked up a pencil with her left hand, leaned forward, and pressed the fifth finger—the Kymeran extra "magic" digit—of her right hand against my brow, where the "third eye" is located. "All you have to do is take a deep breath, clear your mind, and picture the face of the man you saw running away from the crime scene."

I closed my eyes, and within seconds the images from the night before began to unspool within my mind. As I tried to focus on the face of the witch-basher, I heard Gale's pencil scribbling across the sketch pad.

I opened my eyes to see Gale, her own eyes shut fast, frantically drawing with her left hand as if it possessed a life and purpose all its own. I glanced down at the picture, expecting it to be nothing more than a mass of unconnected squiggles, but was surprised to see an incredibly detailed portrait of a young Caucasian male in his mid- to late twenties, with medium-length hair. I looked over my shoulder and saw Hexe, now fully dressed, standing in the doorway, watching the picturemaker do her job.

A few moments later the pencil fell from Gale's fingers and her hand dropped into her lap as if dead. The picturemaker emerged from her trance and stared at what she had drawn with blurry eyes.

"Are you sure this is the human you saw?" she asked, tapping the sketch.

I nodded. "That's him."

"Very good. I won't bother you any further, Ms. Eresby," Gale said, gathering up the tools of her trade and returning them to the sketch case. "The Paranormal Threat Unit thanks you for your cooperation and good citizenship."

"We're always happy to be of service," Hexe assured her.

Once the picturemaker was gone, I returned to the kitchen and poured myself another cup of coffee. I had the nagging feeling that something was amiss, but I was at a loss to identify exactly what. As I stood at the sink, trying to puzzle out what was bugging me, Hexe wrapped his arms about my waist.

"What's wrong?" he asked as he nuzzled the nape of my neck.

"What makes you think something's bothering me?"

"Your brow's furrowed," he replied, reaching up to smooth the fold from between my eyebrows. "Whenever I see lines on that pretty forehead of yours, I know something's on your mind. So what is it?"

As Hexe gently massaged my knitted brow, I suddenly realized what it was that was bothering me. "It's about the witch-basher's portrait," I said. "I've got the weirdest feeling that I've seen that guy's face before."

"Of course you have," Hexe replied with a laugh. "You saw him last night."

"No, that's not it," I said with a shake of my head. "There's something *familiar* about him that I just can't place. I'm pretty sure I've run into him before, but I can't remember what the circumstances were. I'm fairly certain he's not a friend of a friend, but I can't completely rule it out, either. I just wish I could remember *where* I saw this douchenozzle before it drives me nuts. . . ."

"Perhaps you ran into him at the Calf?" Hexe suggested helpfully. "There were dozens of humans there the night of the riot."

"That's probably it," I agreed as I turned around to kiss him. Still, although it seemed the logical answer, deep down I knew it wasn't the right one. No doubt it would come to me when I least expected it, and someplace really annoying, like in the middle of a shower, while working on my new art project, or just before falling asleep.

The next day Hexe and I went shopping for such staples as Perry's Peanut Butter Fudge ice cream (for me), canned haggis (for him), and fresh-ground Colombian coffee (for both of us). While on the way to Dumo's

Grocery, I saw copies of Gale's sketch plastered on every pole, news box, and storefront, each of them with the heading: WANTED FOR WITCH-BASHING!

On our way back home, our little red shopping cart filled with canned goods and toilet paper, I heard a strange, mournful call, accompanied by the steady thud of a drumbeat. An odd and somber procession was slowly making its way down Horsecart Street, coming from the direction of Chiron's Stables, the high-rise that housed Golgotham's centaur population.

For the first time since I moved to Golgotham, the myriad cabs, carts, and wagons that normally filled its narrow cobblestone streets seemed to disappear, leaving the roadway clear of traffic. The passersby on the sidewalks fell silent and stopped whatever they were doing upon hearing the lonely wail.

"What's going on?" I whispered.

"It's a centaur funeral," Hexe replied.

As he spoke, I saw an ipotane dressed in a swallowtail formal coat marching down the center of the street. He wore a top hat, similar to those of Victorian undertakers, complete with a black bombazine bow, the ends of which hung behind him like a second tail. The haunting sound I'd heard came from the bukkehorn held to his bearded lips.

Following him was a second ipotane, in identical somber dress, lugging a drum muffled in black crepe, which hung from a strap about his thick neck and on which he kept the beat for the mourners' funeral march.

Directly behind the drummer was a huge black hearse drawn by two Clydesdale-sized centaurs, who wore the same type of hats and coats as the ipotanes, the splits in their swallowtail coats carefully arranged across their broad, equine backs. The Victorian-era hearse was the size of a circus wagon, with glass sides and elaborate gilt and silver scrollwork along its posts and wheels. The casket it was carrying was big enough for a baby grand piano, and covered in flowered wreaths shaped like horseshoes.

Behind the hearse followed the mourners, who numbered a dozen centaurs and several ipotanes. Both male and female centaurs wore black ostrich feather headdresses and decorated funeral drapes of black bombazine that covered their haunches. The centaur males wore dark Shadbelly riding coats on their upper bodies, while the centaurides were dressed in black jackets cropped at the waist, with puffy leg-of-mutton sleeves, and had funeral veils affixed to their plumed headdresses. Some of the bereaved wept into black-edged handkerchiefs, while others used mourning fans made of black ostrich feathers with tortoiseshell handles to hide their grief.

"Where are they going?" I asked in a hushed voice.

"They're headed to Pickman's Slip," Hexe explained. "There the ferryman will take them on a funeral barge to an island in the East River known as Necropolis. That's where Golgotham buries its dead."

The group of mourners at the rear of the procession was composed entirely of ipotanes dressed in black togas, wearing garlands woven from dead, dried flowers. I was surprised to see Gus among their number. Big fat tears rolled down the drover's bearded cheeks as he mopped his eyes with a bandana. As he walked past, I reached out and gently touched his arm. Startled from his grief, he stopped to stare at me in confusion.

"Gus, it's me—Tate," I said. "What happened? Who died?"

"It's Bayard," the ipotane answered tearfully, once he recognized who I was. "He died a couple days ago."

"You're kidding!" I gasped. The idea of death coming

for someone so young was so dreadfully wrong I could barely absorb it. "What happened?"

"They say he OD'd on ketamine," Gus replied, the sorrow in his voice giving way to anger. "But I don't believe a word of it. I may have given the colt a hard time now and then, but he was a good lad! He wouldn't get mixed up in that kind of thing."

"I'm so sorry for your loss, Gus," I said sadly. "Please give my sympathy to Bayard's stable."

The ipotane nodded his head and loudly blew his nose into his bandana. "Thank you kindly, Miss Tate. I'll pass along your condolences. You excuse me—I need to catch up with the others." With that, Gus rejoined the funeral cortege as it wended its somber way down to the river and to poor Bayard's final rest.

"Are you all right?" Hexe asked gently as I brushed a tear from my eye.

"I'm okay," I replied. "It's just sad, that's all. He was so young. . . ."

"How did you know him?"

"He and Gus were the other members of that little work team Quid put together last week," I explained. "But I can't say any more. You know the rules: 'No questions asked—'"

"'No stories told,'" Hexe said, nodding his head in understanding. However, as we continued on our way home, he kept sneaking concerned looks at me whenever he thought I wasn't paying attention.

Later that same evening, as I was happily pounding away at my latest sculpture, my cell phone started to ring. I glanced at the caller ID and saw that it was Nessie, no doubt calling to regale me with an account of her latest misadventure in wedding preparations.

"Hey there, Bridezilla," I said by way of greeting. "Ready to elope yet?"

"Do you have access to the Internet?" Her voice sounded so serious that the smile instantly disappeared from my lips.

"Of course," I replied. "I'm in Golgotham, not Outer Mongolia."

"I'm sending you a link. There's something on YouTube. . . . I don't know if it's real or not, but you and Hexe need to see it before it gets taken down."

"Nessie, what's going on? You're starting to freak me out."

"I can't really describe it," she said in a strained, sad voice. "Once you watch it, you'll understand why."

I hung up and took my laptop downstairs. I found Hexe in his office reading a large, leather-bound book with iron hasps. The pages were yellowed with age and covered with hand-lettered Kymeran script. Before he closed it, I glimpsed an illustration of an eye in the middle of a pyramid surrounded by arcane symbols.

"I just got off the phone with Nessie," I said as I placed the laptop on his desk. "She sounded really weird."

"And this is news how?"

"No, I'm serious. She sounded *really* upset. She said there was something online we need to see."

I powered up the laptop and pulled up my Mozilla Thunderbird. Sure enough, there was an e-mail from Nessie with the subject heading VIDEO LINK: URGENT! I clicked on the link, and seconds later found myself staring at a YouTube page with the heading SONS OF ADAM MANIFESTO. Inside the video box was a dimly lit room, the walls of which were draped with black plastic sheeting held in place with duct tape. Since the windows were covered as well, it was impossible to tell if it was the middle of the night or high noon. Hanging directly in front of the camera was a makeshift flag fashioned from a white bedsheet and a can of red spray paint that read SOA.

What really got my attention, however, was that the man standing in the foreground was the same person I had seen running from the witch-bashing. Now that I had a chance to take a good look at him, I could see things I had not noticed before, such as his eyes being a pale, almost translucent gray, like those of a newborn baby. I was also surprised at how young he seemed to be—his face was amazingly smooth, without character lines or wrinkles. Behind him stood his two compatriots from the night before—or at least I assumed they were the same ones—their arms folded across their chests, their faces unreadable behind their black ski masks. All three men were of the same general height and build, with barely a centimeter's difference between them, as if they had all been stamped out with the same cookie cutter.

The man in the foreground cleared his throat, and when he spoke it was with an angry, forceful voice. "Greetings. I am Cain, and these are my brothers, Abel and Seth. We are the Sons of Adam. Perhaps you are already familiar with our work? We are the ones who used the Kymie couple in Golgotham for batting practice.

"For too long filthy, demon-ridden Kymie scum have been allowed to dwell in the midst of our great city, tempting God-fearing men and women with their unholy magic and nameless sins. They, and their inhuman cohorts—the centaurs, leprechauns, and other soulless abominations—lie nestled against New York City's bosom like some vile, venomous snake, waiting for the moment to strike! The time has come to sweep these monstrosities from our streets and chase them from our city! The Big Apple belongs to Mankind, not to the Kymies!

"We, the Sons of Adam, formally declare war against the evil witches, warlocks, and monsters that plague Mankind. My brothers and I shall not rest until Golgotham is no more, and its streets reclaimed by their rightful owners: the people of New York City! And to prove our dedication to our cause, we will show you *exactly* what the Kymies and their friends can look forward to from here on in."

My blood turned cold as Cain stepped aside, revealing what had, up until that moment, been hidden from the camera. A man lay on the floor, hands tied behind his back and a pillowcase over his head. Cain motioned to one of his younger "brothers," who stepped forward and yanked the makeshift hood free. I covered my mouth in horror and turned to look at Hexe. His face had gone as white as paste.

"Bloody abdabs—that's Quid!"

The favor broker's face was bruised and badly swollen from the beating he had suffered at the hands of his kidnappers, but there was no mistaking his woolly, lime green eyebrows. He lay there, his mouth sealed with duct tape, his cat-slit pupils expanded to the size of saucers, as sweat rolled down his naked scalp and dripped into his face. The terror in his eyes was that of a man who has seen his death, and knows it to be brutal.

The trio picked up their aluminum bats and arranged themselves around the prostrate Quid. I struggled to swallow the greasy knot rising in my throat as they raised their weapons. In the end, I could not bring myself to watch the beating, but I could hear the sickening thuds as the bats made repeated contact with flesh and bone, as well as the sound of Quid's muffled screams.

"Enough!" Hexe shouted, slamming the laptop shut so hard it cracked the screen.

We stood there for a long moment, staring at one another, unable to believe the unspeakable evil we had just witnessed. Then Hexe grabbed me and pulled me into his arms, holding me as tightly as if we were standing in the middle of a whirlwind.

We spent the rest of the night grieving our friend and comforting one another the best way we knew how, while praying to whatever gods might listen that our love would protect us from the madness beyond the safety of our bed.

Chapter 14

They found Quid's body just before dawn, dumped at the yawning maw of the Gate of Skulls, the official entrance to Golgotham, like some horrible sacrifice. No one saw who did it. Or at least no one was willing to admit to seeing.

As for the video posted on YouTube, it was promptly yanked once the site realized its content, but not before the link spread throughout the Internet like ink in a glass of water. Judging from the appalling comments left on the page before the video was taken down, there were a good number of viewers out there who either shared the SOA's opinion of Kymerans or simply thought beating one to death was funny. I could only hope the latter posters thought it was faked, and not a real snuff film—but I was probably being optimistic.

Unfortunately, it was proving almost impossible to trace the video back to its original source. According to news reports, whoever this Cain bastard was, he was smart enough to use daisy-chained anonymizer proxies in order to upload his little manifesto. Captain Horn held a press conference and told the cameras that the

PTU was meeting with the NYPD as well as the FBI to deal with what he called "the terrorist situation." The FBI was providing facial and voice recognition software so law enforcement could try to identify the man called Cain and, hopefully, locate him before anyone else was hurt.

As we watched the head of the PTU field questions from reporters on Hexe's ancient portable television, I found myself with a few queries of my own.

"I wonder why the other two don't show their faces?"

"They're probably afraid of getting busted for first-degree murder," Hexe replied.

"And this Cain guy isn't?"

"He's the leader," he said with a shrug. "He's a narcissist, just like every other crackpot leader in the history of the world. He wants people to pay attention to *him*. What's the good of being the boss, and getting all this press, if nobody knows what you look like?"

"You've got a point," I conceded. I checked the clock over the stove and cursed under my breath. "I better get going, or I'm going to be late."

"Do you really have to go?" Hexe frowned. "Can't you reschedule for another time?"

"I wish I could," I explained. "But this bridal salon is by appointment only, and if Vanessa cancels, it might be weeks, even months, before they can fit her in again."

"Very well." Hexe reached inside the pocket of his coat and fished out an amulet on a long gold chain. I recognized it as a gladeye charm like the one he'd given Madelyn, save that this one was shaped like a pyramid. "Take this with you," he said, placing the amulet around my neck. "It's to protect you when I'm not around. It will turn aside even the strongest curses and keep you safe from harm—at least of the supernatural variety."

"That's very sweet of you, darling," I said, tilting the

amulet between my thumb and forefinger, so I could look into the artificial eye embedded in its center.

"You have to wear it against your skin, if it's to work," he reminded me.

"Do you really think I'll need it?" I asked.

"Better safe than sorry," he replied as he lifted the gladeye by its chain and dropped it down my cleavage. "These are strange times, even for Golgotham."

I wanted to tell Hexe that he was being overprotective, but from the moment I left the house I was happy to have the gladeye on my person. The mood on the street was positively leprous. As I headed toward City Hall Station, more than one Golgothamite spat on the sidewalk as I passed by. For the first time since relocating to Golgotham, I was genuinely relieved to see the traffic snarling Broadway, which was the demarcation line between it and the rest of Manhattan.

Suddenly a leprechaun dressed in a green track suit stepped into the middle of the sidewalk, blocking my path. "Here ye go, lassie," he said, shoving a xeroxed flyer into my hand. "Big rally tonight. Spread the news and bring some friends." Upon noticing that I had only five fingers, he scowled and moved to snatch the paper back. "On second thought, ne'er ye mind! No numps allowed!" However, I was too fast—and tall—for him, and I held the flyer beyond the leprechaun's reach. The red-haired fairy made a rude noise, and a ruder gesture, before continuing on his way.

I frowned at the flyer, which was written in both English and Kymeran and depicted a pentacle, in the center of which was a six-fingered left hand. The caption read GOLGOTHAM IS OURS: KYMERAN UNIFICATION PARTY RALLY AT MIDNIGHT: HODGSON HALL.

I decided to duck inside the Emerald Spa, a corner newsstand that claimed to carry every magazine published in every known language, plus genuine egg creams and souvenir snow globes of the Gate of Skulls, to get the morning edition of the *Golgotham Gazette*. As I headed toward the register, a Kymeran woman with moss green hair plaited into a long single braid and coiled atop her head like a rope beehive blocked my path.

"I told you to stay away from our men, nump," she snarled. "I guess you don't listen too good."

With a start, I recognized the woman as Dori, one of Hexe's old girlfriends. The reason I hadn't noticed her before was that her scent had changed. The first time I'd met her, she smelled of bergamot and white orchids. Now she reeked of ash and black pepper. I could tell she had just come from her stall at the Fly Market, because she was still dressed in her patchwork skirt, the distaff version of the traditional "coat of many colors" that Kymerans wore to indicate they had magic to sell.

"You've got a lot of nerve, traipsing around Golgotham like you have a right to be here. Do you think you're safe, simply because Hexe has you in his bed? Is that it? You think that gives you impunity to walk among us, eh? Well, let me tell you, nump, you may think you're something special, but you're nothing more than a dalliance for him; a pretty way to pass the time between the sheets—that's all. Believe me, I know," she said, flashing a nasty smile. "He was all sweet on me, too—calling me 'darling' and 'dearest.' He couldn't keep his hands off me."

Dori grabbed her own far-from-insubstantial breasts and began squeezing them to illustrate her point, lewdly grinding her hips against an imaginary lover. I tried to sidestep around her, but she continued to block my path.

Every customer at the newsstand was watching us, most of them with amused smirks.

"Oh, it was good between us. *Damn* good! Until I had enough of barely covering the rent and decided to make a living with both hands, instead of the one. He didn't like *that*, oh no! He's only with you because you can't challenge him the way *I* did. But one day he'll wake up and realize that a nump like you can *never* give him what a Kymeran woman can. And when that morning comes, his Serene Highness will kick you out of bed so fast it'll make your head swim. Do yourself a favor and get the hell out of Golgotham before it's too late. You don't belong here—and you certainly don't belong with *him*!"

Like the sailorman says, I'd taken all I could stand, and I couldn't stand no more. I was sick of people telling me where I did and didn't belong, where I should and shouldn't live, and who I could and couldn't love. If it wasn't my parents, it was Hexe's family members—but I'd be damned if I would take it from some green-haired skank in a Deadhead skirt.

"It seems to me, if he wanted what a Kymeran woman has, he'd still be with one," I said acidly as I pushed her aside. I threw my money onto the checkout stand without bothering about the change and headed out the door. I did not look back, even though Dori was still screaming after me.

"You think he'll make you his consort? Dream on, bitch! When the time comes, he's going to want someone who can guarantee him a blue-haired, golden-eyed heir! And he won't pick some chuffin' nump!"

I was tired of being embarrassed and worrying about offending those around me, especially since I was going to be hated and distrusted no matter what I did or didn't do. So I shot her the Kymeran equivalent of the bird—

using my ring finger instead of the middle one—and
kept on walking.

I was halfway down the block when I felt something
hit me in the chest. It wasn't hard enough to knock the
wind out of me, but just sharp enough to make me wince.
A second later there was a sudden heat against my skin,
and I realized it was the amulet Hexe had given me.

I stepped into a nearby doorway and fished the gladeye out from its hiding place between my breasts. The
pyramid-shaped amulet was unusually warm, without
actually being hot to the touch, and I could see that the
artificial eye at its center was now cloudy. I didn't need
Hexe to tell me that it had just diverted a curse with my
name on it.

Chapter 15

"So—what do you think?" Nessie asked as she exited the dressing room in a gorgeous flowing, off-the-shoulder bridal gown that made her look like a goddess.

"Hmm—what?" I blinked and gave my head a tiny shake to clear my thoughts. "Oh. Yes. It's very—white."

"I think it looks positively *lovely* on you," the personal assistant said, somehow managing to smile while shooting me a Medusa look.

The bridal salon—excuse me, *atelier*—that Vanessa had chosen for her wedding gown was one of those Lexington Avenue boutiques where the bride-to-be and her party get the run of the whole store—excuse me, *workshop*—complete with personal sales assistant, champagne, and hors d'oeuvres. Normally something like this was far outside Nessie's budget—hand-thrown urns for cremated pets don't pay *that* well—but her father had offered to foot the bill, possibly out of lingering Catholic guilt for ditching the first Mrs. Sullivan for a sleeker, younger model during Nessie's sophomore year in high school.

The personal assistant was right, though. I *deserved*

that Medusa look. Nessie and I had been looking forward to this afternoon for weeks, and now that it had arrived, I was ruining it by staring off into space and being so distant I might as well be on Mars.

"Could you excuse us for a few minutes?" Nessie asked politely.

The personal assistant, an older woman with frosted hair and horn-rim glasses with a tailor's tape draped around her neck like a feather boa, removed the half-empty bottle of champagne from the ice bucket. "I'll bring something a little fresher," she said with a sigh, and disappeared from the room.

Vanessa sat down on the chaise lounge beside me and took my hand and gave it a squeeze. "God, I'm *so* sorry I dragged you to this place. But it was either today or three months from now."

"It's okay, Nessie," I replied. "I needed to get out of Golgotham anyway. Things are extremely . . . *tense* down there."

"I can just imagine. That video was . . ." She closed her eyes and shuddered. "Did they identify the victim?"

I nodded my head sadly. "His name was Quid. He was a friend of ours."

"Oh, Tate—I'm *so* sorry," she gasped. "I didn't realize! I would have canceled this whole thing if I'd had any idea."

"I know you would've." I smiled. "That's why I didn't say anything earlier. This is really important to you, and I didn't want to ruin it."

Nessie threw her arms around me and gave me a quick hug. "You are *the* best friend I've ever had. And you know I love you like a sister, so don't take what I'm about to say the wrong way—but do you really think it's a good idea for you to go back there?"

"Golgotham's my home, Nessie. Even now, I'm *still*

happier there than I ever was on the Upper East Side. I know you're worried about me, but so far the only ones getting hurt are Kymerans."

"Yeah—*so far.* Aren't you afraid of a backlash?"

"Yes, to tell you the truth, I am," I admitted. "But I can't live my life being afraid, Nessie. Besides, Hexe has my back."

"I'm relieved to hear it. Still, if it gets too hairy down there, you're more than welcome to stay with me until things settle down. It'll be great. We can sit up all night and eat ice cream and make fun of crappy movies, just like we did in college."

"What about Adrian? Doesn't he have something to say about me crashing on his couch?"

"Him? He can go stay with his brother." She laughed. "Besides, he's not supposed to see the bride before the wedding, anyway."

"That sounds very tempting, but I'm going to take a rain check. I'm afraid Scratch will do something like stuff Beanie up the chimney or roll him up in a window shade if I'm gone too long."

"You and that dog," Nessie said ruefully. "Every time I check your Facebook page, all I see are photos of Beanie sleeping, Beanie eating, Beanie asleep in his food! You're going to make a hell of a mom someday."

"Bite your tongue!" I laughed. "I'm nowhere near ready for something like that! If there are two things that don't go together, it's acetylene torches and diapers. I've got my hands full enough as it is with just a gassy Boston terrier and a talking hairless cat. Now, about this gown . . .''

After trying on several more wedding dresses, and emptying another bottle of champagne, Vanessa finally decided on a strapless Junko Yoshioka with a mermaid skirt, a satin ribbon waist-belt, and a lace shrug. The sales assistant seemed impressed by the final choice—and relieved to be free of us.

As Nessie climbed into her cab to return home, I promised I would stay safe and out of trouble. Once we went our separate ways, I headed down to the East Village to do a little shopping of my own before going back home.

It was dusk by the time I emerged from the subway. Normally I make my way home down Perdition Street, through the Gate of Skulls, but I couldn't bring myself to walk over the spot where Quid's body had been found, so I headed down Morder Lane instead.

The first couple of blocks the traffic on the street was fairly heavy, and there were plenty of human faces to be seen, thanks to nearby Witch Alley, but once I put the open-air magic bazaar behind me, those numbers dwindled fast. As I passed the shuttered Two-Headed Calf, I saw the scorched cobblestones that marked where the NYPD's response vehicle had exploded.

Upon arriving home, I opened the door to find Hexe putting on his coat.

"There you are!" he said. "I was just getting ready to leave. How was your afternoon with Nessie?"

"It was okay," I replied. "Where are you going?"

"I got a call from one of my clients; I need to make an emergency house call. You didn't run into any trouble getting to and from the subway, did you?"

"Not really," I replied. I decided not to launch into a retelling of my run-in with Dori. Maybe, after some time had passed, it would mellow into one of those "look back and laugh" incidents, but for the time being it was still too new and unpleasant for me to relish reliving it.

"That's good. Still, I'm glad you got back home be-

fore it got too late. I don't think it would be a good idea
for you to be out on the streets tonight."

"Because of the rally?" I asked, showing him the flyer
the leprechaun had handed me.

Hexe nodded, a disgusted look on his face. "I'm afraid
my uncle's using this Sons of Adam atrocity to push his
anti-human agenda."

"Are you going to check it out?" I asked. I'd been
seriously considering crashing the rally ever since I saw
the flyer, and had even gone so far as to stop by Trash
and Vaudeville on St. Marks Place to score electric-
green temporary hair dye for camouflage. I figured if I
wore tinted shades and kept my hands stuffed in my
pockets, I'd be able to pass as Kymeran long enough to
get an earful of whatever Esau was spouting.

He shook his head, a sour look on his face. "Some in
the audience might read my being there as an endorse-
ment. I'm not going anywhere near it—and the same
goes for you. I don't want you to leave the house, except
to take Beanie to the garden. Understand me?"

"I don't like it, but I understand," I said grudgingly.
Although part of me resented being told to stay home, I
knew it was simply because he was concerned for my
safety.

"Good. I've got to run," he said, giving me a quick peck
on the cheek as he headed out the door. "Don't bother
waiting up for me—odds are I'm going to be late."

Beanie came scampering up to tell me hello, and I
could tell by the excited way he was dancing around that
he needed to go outside. As I ushered the puppy into the
backyard, I told myself that I hadn't really just lied to
my boyfriend, because I never actually said I *wouldn't*
go to the rally, just that I *understood* why he didn't want
me to leave the house. And as much as I wanted to be a

good girlfriend, I was determined that I was *not* going to be run out of my new home without a fight. And if that meant sneaking into an anti-human rally disguised as a Kymeran to see what I was up against, then that was what I had to do, boyfriend or not.

I took the amulet Hexe had given me out from under my clothes in order to reexamine it. The eye was no longer cloudy; in fact, it seemed to wink at me in the light from the rising moon, as if it knew what I was scheming.

Chapter 16

Hodgson Hall was located on Shoemaker Street, between Vandercliffe and Pearl Streets. It was a large, neoclassical-style building with a redbrick exterior trimmed with granite. A large banner that read GOL-GOTHAM IS OURS hung from the rooftop, obscuring a good portion of the Ionic columns and arches that decorated the facade.

I watched from my vantage point across the street as a steady stream of Golgothamites headed up its wide stone steps. The entrance was manned by individuals wearing large buttons on their lapels bearing the Kymeran Unification Party logo: a six-fingered left hand inside a pentacle.

I stepped out of the doorway and cast a furtive look at myself in a nearby shopwindow. I was wearing a leather jacket I'd picked up in a vintage clothing shop, instead of my usual peacoat, and the temporary hair dye had turned my hair from brunette into an irradiated chartreuse. Anywhere else in the city I would have stood out like King Kong's sore thumb, but in Golgotham I might as well have been a mousy blonde. I fished out a pair of tinted aviator glasses, so no one would notice that my eyes lacked the characteristic cat-slit pupil, and my disguise was complete.

I shoved my hands into the pockets of my jacket and lowered my head as I joined the others filing through the door, hoping my camouflage was good enough to pass casual muster. I heaved a tiny sigh of relief as the KUP members standing guard at the door didn't give me a second glance.

Once inside, I found myself in a huge lobby area, with open square staircases on either side. I went up the flight of stairs to my right, which led to the main floor. Here I found yet another lobby area, this one with a concession stand that ran the length of the back wall and huge doors that opened onto the concert hall.

The main floor sloped toward a raised proscenium stage that stood six feet off the ground and allowed even those standing at the back of the room a decent view. There was no individual seating, so the audience was forced to stand and face the stage. I looked up toward the paneled ceiling high overhead and saw a large balcony four rows deep wrapped around the second floor, with a third, smaller balcony box occupying the wall directly opposite the stage. Although the doors had opened only a few minutes earlier, the main floor was crowded, and both upper tiers were already filling up.

Banners with slogans such as SAY NO TO NUMPS and TAKE BACK GOLGOTHAM hung from the rafters, and traditional Kymeran folk music played from unseen speakers.

I looked around to try and get a feel for the crowd. While the majority of attendees were Kymerans, there were a fair number of leprechauns, satyrs, and ipotanes, even a few centaurs, milling about on the main floor. By my estimation, there were close to three thousand Golgothamites attending the rally, and, as far as I knew, I was the only human.

What really worried me, however, was the smell of the crowd. During my time in Golgotham, I had come to understand that the personal scents of Kymerans provided biochemical signifiers to their basic personalities. To put it bluntly, nice people smelled nice, and bad people didn't. Normally, the odor generated from a large gathering of Kymerans was a heady mix of fragrances, as exotic as the spices wafting from an Indian restaurant. But the predominant aroma inside Hodgson Hall was astringent, a combination of birch tar and quinine, which suggested I was surrounded by a lot of bitter witches and warlocks.

I was so busy studying the crowd that I failed to look where I was going, and accidentally jostled a middle-aged Kymeran with a puce mullet, causing him to slosh the barley wine he'd bought at the concession stand. He growled something in Kymeran that I couldn't understand, but from the tone of voice I assumed it was "Watch where you're going." I nodded and grunted something I hoped sounded conciliatory, then quickly got out of the way.

The music faded, the houselights dimmed, and the colored spots high in the rigging swiveled to focus on the stage as the heavy curtains parted, revealing a huge backdrop bearing the symbol of the Kymeran Unification Party. A ragged cheer rose from the audience, accompanied by the stomping of feet and hooves and the clapping of hands.

A young Kymeran dressed in a black turtleneck sweater and a dark gray jacket stepped out onto the stage. It took me a second to recognize him as Skal, the unruly who had thrown the fireball at the police, as he had traded his bicycle-spoke mohawk for a crew cut. No doubt his mother, Skua, had suggested the radical change in appearance in case anyone else was summoned before the GoBOO to give witness to what happened the night of the riot.

Skal walked out to the middle of the stage and held up his left hand. At first I thought he was merely acknowledging the applause, or making a request for silence, but then I realized that the audience members had lifted their left hands in return.

"As deputy chairman of the Kymeran Unification Party, I am honored to welcome you to this, our first public outreach program, and to introduce you to our party chairman and founder, Esau!"

The applause and stomping resumed even louder than before, as a dense, swirling bank of fog abruptly rolled out from the wings and onto the stage, accompanied by a distant rumble. Flashes of multicolored lights rippled through the thick mist as a sourceless wind began to swirl it around like a potter spinning a handful of clay.

The rumbling grew louder and louder, as if an army of kettledrums was on the march, and then a figure coalesced within the heart of the whirlwind. Suddenly there was an eye-searing flash of lightning, accompanied by a deafening peal of thunder, and the dark veil dispersed, revealing Esau at its heart, his left hand raised high above his head.

And the crowd went fucking nuts.

I heard a loud, high-pitched shriek, like that of a bird of prey, and looked up to see a monstrous vulturelike creature, easily twice the size of an Andean condor, with the long, toothy bill and reptilian head of a pterodactyl balanced on the uppermost balcony. The winged horror dropped from its perch and spread its wings, swooping down to the stage. The monster-bird then fluttered its fifteen-foot-wide wings and, in the blink of an eye, transformed itself into Esau's pet raven, Edgar. The familiar landed on his master's shoulder and cawed loudly. As much as I despised the man, I had to admit he knew how to play an audience.

Esau smiled and stroked the bird's jet-black feathers as he soaked up the adoration from the crowd. Once he'd had his fill, he lowered his left hand to his side and the din died down enough for him to speak. Although he didn't have a microphone, his voice still managed to fill the auditorium.

"Two hundred and forty years ago, my great-grandfather, Lord Beke, offered his services as a wizard to the founders of the United States in order to create a safe harbor for not only those of his blood but all who swore fealty to the Throne of Arum. And for generations we have been left to our own devices, to live as we see fit. But now all that is changing, and it is up to us, fellow Golgothamites, to decide whether our way of life survives or is lost under the never-ending flood of humanity.

"From the very beginning Golgotham's economy has been based upon providing certain services, both physical and metaphysical, to the surrounding human population. The operative word in that sentence, my friends, is 'surrounding.' Traditionally, numps have been welcome in our world, provided they stick to those areas set aside for them, such as Witch Alley, the Rookery, the Fly Market, and, of course, Duivel Street.

"But recently numps have been infiltrating deeper and deeper into Golgotham, venturing into bars and restaurants they never would have dared set foot in a few years ago, emboldened by the GoBOO's ceaseless and unwise flogging of tourism. Some have even gone so far as to make Golgotham their home! Now, I'm not talking about oracles, mediums, and dowsers—these outcasts from human society have always hidden under Golgotham's skirts. No, I mean garden-variety, cud-chewing, credit-card-carrying *numps*. This recent development is not just a slippery slope, but one lined with razor blades—and we're sliding down it as I speak!

"Some may think I am overreacting, but mark my words: As soon as your lease expires, don't be surprised when your landlords raise the rent fifty to one hundred percent more than you are already paying! Why would they do such a thing, you ask? Because while you, my brethren, might not be able to afford such an increase, the numps eager to move in to experience our 'quaint' atmosphere certainly can! And they most certainly *will*! After all, they do it to their own kind time and time again—what makes you think they'll have any problems doing it to *us*? Numps are greedy, selfish beasts, all eye and belly. Whatever they see, they want. And right now, my brothers and sisters, they have their sights set on Golgotham!"

This brought a loud chorus of hisses from the audience, and it wasn't until I saw the spectators nodding their heads in agreement that I realized they weren't booing Esau, but voicing their contempt for humans.

I pulled my shoulders in even further and shoved my hands deeper into my coat pockets, as the participants on either side of me began rhythmically stomping their feet and pumping their left fists in the air.

"It is time that the citizenry of Golgotham—Kymeran and otherwise—stood together against the rapacious humans and their bought-and-paid-for puppets in the GoBOO! Our home lacks infinite capacity for settle-

ment, and if we do not act now, we will soon find ourselves squeezed out by human interlopers!

"There is not a species or a race that calls Golgotham
home that does not know the depths to which Mankind
will stoop—am I right? Who among us does not have an
ancestor who suffered on the rack, or served as fuel for
their *autos-da-fé*?"

The audience murmured in agreement, and I saw au-
thentic grief and loss flicker across the faces of those
around me, as well as hatred. Although the Unholy
War—or the Sufferance, as the Kymerans called it—had
ended nine hundred years ago, the horrors born of that
dark time were far from forgotten. Esau knew he had
his listeners under his thrall, and he was eager to push
the advantage. His voice grew even deeper and took on
a conspiratorial urgency, as if he shared special knowledge that only the chosen were privy to, forcing his audience to lean forward to hear him.

"My friends, Golgotham is under attack from nump
culture! The numps are waging a second Unholy War
upon us, and most of you don't even realize it. The last
time they were bold—they took up swords and siege
machines against us. But now they must be stealthy and
devious, for fear of angering their god, who forbade continued genocide in his name. So now they must work in
far more subtle fashion to rob us of our magic.

"This time it's nothing so crude as snipping off a finger. No, they're *much* too clever for something like that!
Instead, they lure us into dependency upon their dam-
nable technology. What better way to steal our sorcery
than to make us as soft and fat and lazy as they are?
Why astral-project when you can just pick up the phone
or text someone? Why use a scrying device to divine the
past when you can Google? Why teleport when you can

ride in a car? Why levitate when you can fly in a plane? Why waste the energy to do *anything* magical when you can use the humans' wondrous technology to achieve the same ends?

"Because we are magical creatures, and technology makes us weak—*that's* why!"

As I looked around the crowd to try and gauge reactions to the speech, I spotted a teenaged Kymeran with raspberry-colored hair rolling his eyes. Apparently Esau's message about the corrupting influence of technology didn't resonate with the younger members of the audience.

"We have already surrendered our dragons and our kingdom to Mankind. Our magic is all we have left. And it is what they fear and crave the most. Once our magic becomes too weak to be of any use to them, the numps will rise up and wipe us from the face of the earth. We will become nothing more than stories they tell their children to frighten them into good behavior, or lull them to sleep, like dinosaurs and cowboys. I don't know about you, but I do *not* want to live in a world where the only place I can find a centaur or a mermaid is in a picture book!"

That brought the spectators sitting in the balconies to their feet, and for several seconds their applause and cheers made it impossible for Esau to speak. So he simply stood and silently luxuriated in their approval as he waited for the clamor to subside.

"Who can we look to in order to stem this tide?" he asked, once they had finally fallen quiet. "The Go-BOO?"

"*No!*" came the reply, shouted by button-wearing KUP members scattered throughout the audience.

"The PTU?"

"*No!*" These shouts were even louder and more vehement, which suggested a good number of the KUP's recruits were unrulies with lengthy arrest records.

"Don't. Make. Me. *Laugh!*" Esau spat, his face contorting in disgust. "They are puppets of the nump mayor and his cronies, and happy to sell out their constituents for a handful of gold from City Hall! The reason I founded the Kymeran Unification Party was to defend the rights of the average Golgothamite against the interests of the encroaching humans and to give voice to those who resent their steadily increasing intrusion into our world! The time has finally come to speak out against the numps usurping our eateries, shops, bars, and homes before they annex Golgotham entirely! If the GoBOO refuses to address the question of nump incursions into Golgotham, then they will find themselves facing a crisis of unimaginable proportions—a crisis of their own making!

"Although the majority of numps are content with slowly weakening us with flashy bits of technology, there are still some who seek to wage war against us as their ancestors once did. I speak, of course, of the so-called Sons of Adam. When I saw the footage of our poor brother Quid, beaten to death by those grunting knuckle-draggers, anger and outrage bubbled in my soul. From that loathing and horror was born a resolve to capture and punish these ape-born savages.

"Starting tonight, I will be sending special citizens' patrols, composed of KUP members, out into the streets of Golgotham in order to watch for—and take into custody, if possible—the nump known as Cain and the other members of the SOA. When they are caught, I swear, by the blood of my ancestors, that I will do *all* that is in my power to see they are brought to justice by *Golgotham* standards! The crimes they committed were against Golgothamites, and it should be *our* laws, not those of New York City, that ultimately decide their fate!

"I have only one more question to put to you tonight: Who among you are willing to join me in keeping our streets and people safe from the Sons of Adam? Who among you will add your hand to ours?" Esau asked, lifting his left hand over his head as he looked out into the audience.

To my surprise, every attendee on the main floor raised his or her left hand, except me. I nervously looked around and saw Puce Mullet staring in my direction, a confused scowl on his face. He took a couple of steps toward me, sniffing the air like a hound trying to catch a rabbit's scent. Before leaving the house I had practically bathed in my favorite perfume in order to pass the smell test as a Kymeran; but after nearly an hour spent in a crowded auditorium, I was starting to sweat.

I decided that I had seen enough, and started to slowly inch my way out of the crowd, but Puce Mullet continued to advance toward me. As I turned my back on him, he said something to me in Kymeran. I had no idea what he'd said, except that it was a question of some sort, so I shrugged my shoulders as if to say "Beats me," while keeping my hands hidden in my pockets.

Within half a heartbeat, Puce Mullet closed the distance between us. As I tried to pull away, he grabbed my left wrist and growled in English: "I *said*: 'Why won't you raise your hand?'"

Before I could react, he yanked it free of its hiding place.

"Nump!" he yelled at the top of his lungs, upon seeing my five fingers. "There's a nump in the audience!"

Every face turned in my direction. Whether Kymeran, leprechaun, or centaur, they all had the same angry, outraged gleam in their eyes.

"She's a spy!" a leprechaun wearing a green bowler hat shouted. *"Grab her!"*

"I got her!" Puce Mullet twisted my left arm behind my back hard enough to make me yelp.

A huldu with a KUP button affixed to the lapel of his jacket pushed his face into mine. "Who sent you? Who are you spying for? The PTU? GoBOO?"

"I'm not a spy!" I shouted over the jumble of raised, angry voices.

"Not a spy, are you?" snarled the huldu, tugging on my hair. "Then why did you dye this green, eh?"

"I—I—!"

"Answer me, nump!" he bellowed, striking me across the face with his tail hard enough that I tasted blood.

Suddenly I was jerked free of Puce Mullet's grip and pulled up into the air, as if a giant hand had closed about the nape of my neck and lifted me aloft like a newborn kitten. I screamed as I shot upward, my arms and legs kicking frantically, struggling to free myself as I bobbed twenty feet in the air.

Although I was no longer being attacked by the crowd below, I was now totally exposed to the angry occupants of the balconies, who lost no time hurling the first thing they could lay their hands on in my direction.

"Nump go home!" shrieked a Kymeran woman with fluorescent orange hair as she hurled a soft drink cup at me.

I raised my arms to shield my face as the drink hit me in the chest, exploding in a spray of crushed ice and sticky syrup. A second later a box of popcorn struck a glancing blow to my head, followed by several more beverages. I was thankful that at least Hodgson Hall's concession stand didn't sell drinks in bottles and cans.

Suddenly I was flying sideways through the air, the

far wall of the auditorium rushing up to greet me. I screamed and put my hands over my eyes, only to be pulled back at the last possible second. I peered through my fingers and saw Esau on the stage below, moving his hands like a puppeteer controlling a marionette. As I was twirled about in midair like a child's piñata, my shrieks of terror were drowned out by the jeers from the audience.

As I shot past the upper balcony, the laughter abruptly died away and I saw a look of surprise cross the faces of the rally-goers. My trajectory came to a sudden halt, leaving me suspended near the rafters. Peering down between my feet, I saw the crowd below part itself as a familiar figure strode down the open path to the stage. Even though I could see only the top of his head, I would have known that purple hair anywhere.

"Let the woman go, Esau!" Hexe shouted.

"If you insist, nephew," the necromancer replied with a sardonic laugh.

Suddenly the invisible hand holding me aloft was gone, and I plummeted like a stone dropped down a well. Halfway to the floor, I felt a second, far gentler unseen hand reach out to slow my descent. I floated over the heads of my tormentors as Hexe made a beckoning gesture with his right hand, summoning me to his side. When my feet once again made contact with the floor my legs were shaking so badly I had to throw my arms around his neck to keep from collapsing.

"I should have known leaving you at home wouldn't keep you out of trouble," he said wryly.

"You sin against your own people, Serenity," Esau sneered. "Golgotham faces the greatest threat to its existence ever, and what do you do? Cozy up to the enemy!"

"Tate has as much right to be here as anyone else," Hexe replied, triggering a barrage of hoots and jeers from Esau's supporters. "You want to protect Golgotham—am I right? Tate calls Golgotham her home. That makes her a Golgothamite."

"That's impossible," Esau replied sharply. "She's human."

"There is nothing in the charter our ancestor drew up that declares Golgotham a human-free zone," Hexe countered. "Lord Beke declared it a homeland for 'all those gifted with powers and skills beyond those of the common Man.' That would include not only human psychics and the like, but also artists such as Tate."

"I can't believe we share blood!" Esau spat in disgust. "Are you so besotted with this woman, you've forgotten what the numps did to us?"

"No, I *haven't* forgotten," Hexe replied, doing his best to make himself heard over the derision of the crowd. "But I *have* forgiven. The people responsible for the Sufferance are long dead, and the humans of today are not the same as the ones back then. What good does harboring resentment and hatred over ancient injustices ever do? The centaurs trampled the humans' crops and stole their livestock; the satyrs raped their women and plundered their vineyards; the sirens lured their ships onto the rocks; our dragons burned their villages to the ground! The humans hated and feared us because of the horrors our ancestors visited upon them, and they struck back by burning us at the stake, cutting off our fingers, and drowning us in ducking ponds. This pointless tit-for-tat—it's like a serpent eating its tail. What can it possibly lead to, except anger and war? Is that what you truly *want* for Golgotham?"

The audience fell silent, waiting for Esau's reply as

the necromancer scowled at his nephew. But before he could answer, the doors to the auditorium flew open with a loud crash, and Paranormal Threat Unit officers came swarming in, right hands raised and ready to sling.

"PTU!" Lieutenant Vivi shouted. *"This is a raid! Everybody keep their hands behind their back!"*

Pandemonium broke out as those members of the audience with outstanding warrants—which was damn near everyone—tried to make a break for the nearest exit. Hexe and I were instantly forgotten as the crowd ran frantically about like rats hunted by a pack of terriers. I followed Hexe to a door hidden off to one side of the stage that opened onto an adjacent alley. As we stumbled out of the building, I sucked in the relatively fresh, clean air, relieved to be finally free of the rally.

We headed toward the mouth of the alley, only to halt at the sight of PTU officers indiscriminately throwing people into the phalanx of paddy wagons that filled Shoemaker Street. Not wanting to join the ranks of angry KUP supporters in the back of the wagons, we turned and headed in the opposite direction, only to have our way blocked by escapees from the raid, who were still pouring into the alley. To my dismay, Puce Mullet was among them.

"It's her!" he exclaimed angrily, pointing at me. "The nump spy!"

Hexe motioned with his right hand, and Puce Mullet turned as silent as a statue, his mouth frozen in mid-shout. But it was too late; the others had already seen me.

Suddenly an albino centauride, her upper human body as ghostly pale as her milk white equine lower half, pushed her way through the crowd, forcing the unruly mob to retreat or risk being crushed by the ivory phaeton carriage behind her. Her snowy mane was so long it nearly touched the ground, and her eyes flashed red as rubies in the dim light of the alley. She wore a white enameled breastplate over a silver chain mail long-sleeved tunic, and carried a mace, also enameled white, in her right hand. Hexe quickly boosted me into the rear of the carriage and then jumped in after me.

"I warned you it would end badly," Lady Syra said from the driver's seat.

"Someone from the family had to stand up and denounce what he's trying to do," Hexe replied. "It might not change Esau's mind, but it could make a difference with some of his followers."

"We'll argue about which of us was less right or more wrong later on, when we don't have your uncle's croggies howling for your girlfriend's blood." Lady Syra turned to the centauride. "Get us out of here, Illuminata!"

The female centaur obeyed by swinging her shining white mace in a wide arc, opening enough room for her to gallop through the angry throng, the royal phaeton jouncing along behind her. As we neared the far end of the alley, there came the sound of wings beating through the air, and a shadow fell across Illuminata's snowy flanks.

The centauride gave an equine scream of pain as the familiar Edgar, in demonic form, swooped down and dug his talons below the hem of her chain-mail tunic, where her human torso met with her horse's withers.

Lady Syra shouted something in Kymeran and a bolt of white energy leaped from her right hand, striking the familiar. There was an angry shriek and the smell of singed feathers, and the devil-bird abandoned his attack, flying off with a single flap of his monstrous wings. Illuminata continued to make good her escape, despite

the crimson rivulets running down her milk white forelegs.

As we finally exited onto the open street, I turned to
look behind us and saw Esau standing on the roof of
Hodgson Hall, his arms folded across his chest, his familiar perched on his left shoulder.

Chapter 17

Once we were safely away, Illuminata dropped down from a gallop to a trot. Lady Syra turned to look at me with obvious displeasure.

"I'm very disappointed in you, Hexe. You should have known better than to bring a human to such a gathering."

"It's not his fault," I explained. "It was my idea to sneak in there. He didn't even know I was in the building."

"It doesn't matter *whose* idea it was or wasn't—it was still a stupid one!" she exclaimed in exasperation. "You could have been seriously hurt! What were you thinking?"

"I was thinking that all my life I've been looking for the place I belong, and I've finally found it in Golgotham. If Esau and his croggies are going to try and force the humans out, I want to know what I'm up against."

"You didn't need to go so far as to infiltrate an anti-nump rally!" Hexe said tersely. "I would have told you what happened when I got home."

"How was I to know that?" I countered defensively. "You said you weren't going to the damned thing!"

"I was afraid if I said anything about it to you, you'd insist on accompanying me!"

"Damn straight, I would have!" I shot back. "You know I don't believe in quietly knitting by the fireside."

"Now, now, children," Lady Syra said, holding up her hands for quiet. "This is neither the time nor the place for your first lovers' quarrel." She turned to look at me for a long moment and then shook her head. "I don't know whether to condemn you for your stupidity or commend you for your bravery, my dear. Either way, that hair color definitely does *not* suit you."

Lady Syra dropped us off at the boardinghouse, stopping only long enough for Hexe to run inside and fetch a healing salve for the lacerations on Illuminata's back.

"Thank you for what you did back there," he said as he handed the ointment to the centauride. "It could have gotten really ugly."

"I only did as my lady commanded," she replied humbly. "It is my honor to serve her, as, Chiron willing, one day it will be my honor to serve you."

"Stop trying to butter up the next boss," Lady Syra chided. "You're not going to be rid of me anytime soon."

"By the way, Mother, before you leave, do you mind telling me how you not only knew I might need help making a speedy getaway, but also that Illuminata should break out her ceremonial armor?"

"A contact in the PTU informed me of the raid on Hodgson Hall," Lady Syra replied, appearing flustered by her son's question. "I deemed it wise for my driver to dress for the occasion. Now, if you'll excuse us, I must return home and tend to Illuminata's wounds."

Scratch was waiting for us inside the door, as always, his hairless tail upraised like a living question mark. He gave a wary growl as he sniffed the air. "I smell brimstone and feathers."

"That would be Edgar," Hexe replied as he hung up his jacket. "We had a little run-in with him earlier."

"That overglorified feather duster?" Scratch grumbled. "What was he doing? Pecking at his reflection in a mirror?"

"He attacked the royal carriage."

The familiar's eyes widened in surprise. "So ol' Esau is finally taking off the gloves."

"It would appear so," Hexe said with a sigh.

"This could get very interesting." Scratch grinned, licking his lips. "It's been generations since the last palace coup."

"That's because there's no palace anymore, just a condo," Hexe pointed out.

I headed upstairs to take Beanie out of his crate. The moment I walked into Hexe's bedroom, he began scratching at the door of his kennel.

"Mommy's home, sweetie! Are you glad to see Mommy?"

Beanie replied with an excited little yap that was his way of saying *Yes, I'm glad you're home. Let me out now!*

As I opened the crate, I heard a knock on the front door. I scooped up the puppy and looked over the balustrade at Hexe, who was standing at the foot of the stairs.

"I'll see to that," he said firmly. "You stay up there— just in case it's one of your 'admirers' from the rally."

I leaned against the newel post on the landing, listening to Hexe as he opened the front door while Beanie licked my face.

"Please forgive me for calling at this hour, Serenity. . . ."

I exhaled in relief as I heard Captain Horn's voice,

and promptly hurried downstairs to see why the head of the PTU was stopping by in the middle of the night.

Horn was in the front parlor, awkwardly perched on the purple velour sofa, with Hexe seated in the chair opposite him. As I entered the room, Captain Horn got to his feet and removed his hat, revealing close-cropped maroon hair.

"Hello, Ms. Eresby. Please forgive the lateness—" He stopped in midsentence and smiled as he saw Beanie tucked under my arm. "Well, hello, li'l fellow!" Beanie wiggled in delight as Horn scratched him behind the ears; then he nibbled on the PTU officer's fingers.

"Beanie! Stop that!" I scolded.

"I don't mind at all, Ms. Eresby," Horn chuckled as he resumed his seat, wiping the puppy slobber off with a handkerchief. "I had a gargoyle when I was a lad, too."

"So, Captain, what brings you to my home at this hour?" Hexe asked pointedly.

"Come, now, you know perfectly well why I'm here," Horn replied with a good-natured smile. "I saw you and your lady friend take the side door out of Hodgson Hall with my own eyes."

"You know we were at the rally, then."

"Yes. And I know *why* you were at the rally," Horn said. "It was brave of you to call out your uncle the way you did. There aren't many in Golgotham willing to stand up to Esau right now."

"How do you know about that?" Hexe asked in surprise.

"There were a couple of undercovers in the audience, keeping tabs on things," Horn explained. "I had Lieutenant Vivi and the rest of the PTU waiting down the block, in case trouble broke out. We swung into action when we got word Esau was using a human as a living

yo-yo. I had no idea it was Ms. Eresby, at the time—
though I really shouldn't be surprised. She does have a
knack for finding herself in the thick of things, if I remember correctly."

"You're my mother's contact at the PTU," Hexe said,
realization suddenly dawning in his golden eyes.

Horn nodded his head. "Lady Syra is a very old, very
dear friend of mine. And as a loyal Kymeran, I would do
almost anything for both her and the royal family. Including turning a blind eye to the fact that you have
been harboring an unlicensed shape-shifter in your
boardinghouse for several months."

"You know about Lukas?" I gulped.

"Of course I do." Horn chuckled. "There is very little
that goes on in Golgotham that does not reach my ear at
one point or another. As for Lady Syra, when I discovered that you were actively confronting your uncle at
the rally, I contacted her immediately. I am glad you and
Ms. Eresby were able to get out of that madhouse in one
piece." The PTU chief leaned forward, his voice becoming serious. "Your uncle is stirring a very toxic cauldron,
Hexe. The people of Golgotham are scared and anxious.
And when people are scared, they can be manipulated
into doing things they normally would never counte-
nance. Esau understands that, and he is exploiting the
riot and this Sons of Adam business to force his way
onto the Council and gain a platform on which to run for
mayor."

"I agree with your assessment of my uncle's agenda,
Captain," Hexe replied. "But I don't think you made a
special trip just to get my opinion of Esau's political as-
pirations."

Horn sat back, eyeing Hexe like a gambler studying a
racing form. "You're very direct. Just like your grandfa-

ther, Lord Eben. Unlike him, however, you are far more comfortable interacting with, shall we say, the *lower* orders of Golgotham society."

"If that is a polite way of saying that some of my friends and clients are unrulies, then, yes, that is true," Hexe replied.

"The PTU could use someone like you right now. Someone who can use his contacts on the street to keep tabs on the KUP, and give us a heads-up as to what they're planning."

Hexe shifted about uncomfortably, and when he finally spoke, his voice was uncharacteristically stern. "I have made it clear that I find my uncle's misanthropy odious, and consider his little tea party to be a pathetically transparent means of manipulating others in order to grab power. Will I publicly refute him? Yes. Will I fight against what he's trying to do? Most certainly. But I refuse to spy on him, whether for you, the PTU, or the Council.

"Not out of any lingering familial responsibility toward Esau himself, but simply because, despite everything he's done, my mother still loves her brother. If she ever found out I conspired against him—and believe me, she *would* find out—it would break her heart. And that is something I will *never* be party to."

"I understand perfectly, Serenity," Horn said as he levered himself off the couch. "I'll take my leave now. Good night, Ms. Eresby. Have your friend, Lukas, stop by my office in the next day or two, and I'll see that he gets registered and receives a proper license to live in the city."

"Thank you, sir," I said gratefully. "That's very kind of you."

"It's the least I can do for a survivor of the Malandanti's fighting pit."

"I'm sorry I couldn't be of more help to you, Captain," Hexe said as he opened the door. "I trust you understand my reasons for not wanting to be involved in spying on my uncle. I do not intend any disrespect."

"You're a good son, Hexe," Horn replied with a sad smile. "And you're right: It *would* break her heart."

Chapter 18

I love taking showers with the man in my life. Always have, always will. It fosters an intimacy even greater than lovemaking, as it combines the sensuality and vulnerability of naked flesh with the bonding of mutual grooming. It's been my experience that people are at their most honest and real when they're covered in soap.

"You know, my heart nearly stopped when I realized it was you Esau was dangling from the rafters," Hexe said as he shampooed the temporary dye from my hair. "I'm still a little ticked off that you lied to me."

I wiped the soap out of my eyes and glanced over my shoulder. "But you did the exact same thing."

"That's different," he protested.

"Why? Because you're a *man*?"

"No. Don't be silly," he replied. He motioned to the amulet I still wore about my neck. "I lied to protect you. I have magic. I can defend myself. Your lie put you in real danger. That gladeye I gave you is only good against curses. It can't protect you against levitation spells or a fistful of hellfire."

"I realize that now. But I didn't lie to you for the thrill

of it. I realize there is a certain amount of risk that comes with living in Golgotham. I knew that infiltrating Esau's rally was dangerous, but I did it anyway because I believed it was important for me to see with my own two eyes what I was up against. You have to stop treating me like I'm a tourist, Hexe. Believe it or not, I know what the score is."

"But you don't have magic. . . ."

"Neither does Kidron or Giles Gruff, and they seem to get along just fine," I countered. "In fact, I've lived my entire life up to now without magic. Not being able to sling spells and cook up potions shouldn't change how I think or live my life, any more than your inability to sculpt or use a blowtorch should impact yours. I could just as easily get hit by a car while I'm crossing Broadway as be cursed, you know. I just have to keep my eyes open and be aware of my surroundings to make sure neither of those things happens. Granted, tonight wasn't the *greatest* idea I've ever acted on—but now that I know what I'm up against, I won't be making the mistake of letting anyone with a KUP membership pin anywhere near me again."

"I know you must have been terrified."

"It went beyond being scared, Hexe." I shuddered, despite the warmth of the water cascading over my body. "It was degrading. When Esau levitated me, I was not only utterly helpless—I was completely at the mercy of someone else. Someone who I knew saw me as a *thing*, not a person. But what made it worse was the fact the audience laughed like I was an animal being baited for their amusement. Now I know how Jared felt when he was turned into a pig."

"It is very easy for Kymerans to view those without magic as lesser beings," Hexe explained sadly. "It is not a trait of our people I am proud of."

I turned to look at him again. "Is that how *you* see me?"

"Of course not," he replied, carefully wiping away the shampoo trickling down my face before it reached my eyes. "You're right, I can't do what you do with metal, and I am in awe of it. There's a special fire inside of you that manifests itself in your artwork. To me, that is a kind of magic in itself. But, more important, you are the only woman—human or Kymeran—to accept my dedication to the Right Hand Path. And that includes my mother."

"Your mom might not completely understand you, Hexe, but that doesn't mean she doesn't accept you for who you are. Believe me, I know the difference." I sighed as I rinsed the last of the dye from my hair. "This is kind of changing the subject, but why didn't you say something to Captain Horn about Esau's familiar attacking your mother's carriage? I mean, I can understand why you didn't want to act as a spy against your uncle, but why withhold that kind of information?"

"The royal family handles its own," Hexe replied matter-of-factly. "It's been that way since Lord Bexe battled his brother, General Vlad." He leaned into me and wrapped his arms about my waist so that the water from the shower was now pouring over both of us. "I'm sorry you had to experience my people at their worst. It would never have happened if I'd simply told you I was going to the rally. I promise you'll never be treated like that again."

I loved him so much at that exact moment, my heart and eyes filled themselves, and all I could do was smile up at him, because I knew that if I tried to say anything, I would burst into tears. So I reached up and pulled his head down and gave him a long, slow, deep, sensuous kiss that was a mere hint of the far more delicious merger to follow.

Like I said, the shower is a good place for bonding. It's also a great place to get dirty.

A half hour later we were lying in bed together, Beanie tucked between us, stretched out like a pork loin, snoring like the world's cutest buzz saw.

"I must admit, when I bought him, I didn't fully understand the attraction of a pet," Hexe said as he watched Beanie's paws twitch. "But now I can't imagine my life without this little guy."

"Yeah, they'll do that to you." I chuckled as I scratched the dozing puppy behind the ears. Beanie responded by snoring louder and stretching out his little legs even farther in order to take up as much of the bed as doggishly possible.

Hexe raised himself onto his elbow. "What do you think he's chasing in his dream?"

"He's probably pursuing something unobtainable, just like us, but in his case it's a chicken bone or a chocolate chip cookie, instead of world peace."

"If I want to know what Scratch is thinking, I just ask him. It seems strange, not being able to do that with Beanie. I mean, how do I know when he's hungry, or needs to go outside?"

"Don't worry—he'll let you know." I smiled. "All you have to do is pay attention to him and be a good daddy."

"Like I know anything about *that*," he scoffed.

I'd been waiting for Hexe to get around to telling me about his father of his own free will, but I now realized that simply wasn't going to happen. It was up to me to broach the subject.

"Can I ask you something about your dad?"

Hexe glanced at me, his golden eyes seeming to glow in the darkness of the bedroom. "What about him?"

"Is he dead? I mean, you never talk about him. . . ."

"He might be," he replied with a shrug. "To tell you the truth, I don't know who he is. My mother never told me his name, and the rest of her family refused to speak of him."

"Why?" I frowned. "Was the divorce *that* ugly?"

"My parents were never married. But the reason my grandparents and uncle never talked about him around me was because he wasn't a member of the aristocracy."

"How do you know that?"

"Because my hair isn't blue," he said wryly. "There's a reason Kymeran hair is the color it is. Back in ye oldie days—before Kymera sank—there were three distinct castes: the Aristocrats, the Crafters, and the Servitors. The Aristocrats had blue hair and were the ones with the strongest magic. The Crafters had yellow hair and were talented in the creation of talismans, scrying stones, tarot cards, and the like. The Servitors were—well, they were redheaded and served the Aristocrats. And so it went for millennia.

"Then, fifteen thousand years ago, Kymera was drowned by a massive tsunami. Only a hundred Kymerans managed to escape the Deluge on their dragons. My ancestor, Lord Arum, led them to New Kymera, in what would become Eastern Europe. Because there were so few left, the castes were forced to mingle, and that's when green, orange, and purple hair began to appear among my people. Yet the royal family has always remained some shade of blue, at least until I came along

"As far as Esau's concerned, my mother disgraced the family beyond all forgiveness, and it galls him that when she dies, a half-caste will inherit the title of Witch King. Of course, if I'd been born with my mother's blue hair, instead of her golden eyes, he would have automatically become the next in line and reclaimed the title."

"What does the color of your eyes have to do with it?"

"Only the descendants of Arum have golden eyes," he explained. "And only they may claim the throne."

I thought about it for a second, and realized that of all the Kymerans I'd met since moving to Golgotham, only Hexe and his immediate family shared the same distinctive golden eyes.

"I can understand why your uncle and grandparents wouldn't talk about your father. But what about your mother? Haven't you asked Lady Syra about him?"

"Once or twice, when I was a boy," he replied wistfully. "All she would say was that they had loved each other. It upset her so much, I dropped the subject. I do know that it was my grandfather who ordered her to end the relationship. It broke her heart, but she did what was expected of her. Of course, she didn't realize she was pregnant at the time she sent him away. Even if she had, it still would not have changed anything.

"My mother having a child out of wedlock was not a scandal. But when my hair started to grow in, the aristocracy was outraged. The fact she'd had an affair with a Servitor was nowhere near as appalling as her decision to give birth to his child. My people are not famous for their fertility. There are barely a million of us worldwide. The fact that my mother chose to carry me to full term— knowing I was a half-caste—was a slap in the face to the blue hairs.

"My grandfather always felt guilty for what he did to my mother, and he worked hard to replace my father in my life. I love and treasure his memory. But I do not delude myself. If I had been born with my father's eyes, Lord Eben would have placed me with a foster-family of trolls, hidden away where my mother could never have found me. He told me as much, when I was five."

"What a terrible thing to say to a child!" I gasped. Up to this point, I had assumed that Hexe's family, with the exception of dear old Uncle Esau, were far more functional than my own. But now I was starting to see that they had much more in common with the Borgias than the Waltons. "I can't believe he would've done something like that to his own daughter and grandson."

"We witches and warlocks have earned our reputations," Hexe replied with a sad smile, "even among ourselves."

Chapter 19

Though I was exhausted, sleep proved elusive. Whenever I closed my eyes, I saw the faces of the rally audience sneering at me, their laughter echoing in my ears. The one time I did doze off, I started awake with a convulsive jerk, convinced I had been levitating above the bed. After an hour of struggling to fall asleep, I decided to get up. I eased out of bed, careful not to wake Hexe and Beanie, and threw on one of my welding jumpsuits. As long as I couldn't sleep, I might as well get a little work done, right?

I shuffled down the hall, past Lukas's room and the second-floor bathroom, and opened the door to my apartment, flicking on the overhead light. As I entered, I realized that the drapes on the window facing the street were still pulled back. Normally I'm against flashing the neighbors, but since I took up with Hexe, my room had become more studio than living space, although it still housed the majority of my personal belongings.

My drafting table was covered with preliminary sketches and small-scale models of my newest art project, which stood in mid-fabrication beside my workbench. When Boss Marz turned the Dying Gaul, the Thinker, and the Lovers into piles of junk, he didn't just destroy a bunch of magically animated sculptures; he effectively obliterated my life's work. Now I was back to square one, using the bits and pieces I'd scavenged from the salvage yard to build yet another fully articulated found-metal "action figure."

So far my newest creation was little more than a pair of metal legs with piston knees joined to a pair of hips made from the steering knuckles off an old Ford Bronco, with a partial spine composed of various gears. I would have to fabricate the rib cage and sternum from sheet metal, but the skull was going to be made from some spare parts I'd found. I told myself I might as well get a head start (pun intended).

I placed the pair of differential covers I was going to repurpose into a cranium on my workbench and then changed into my boots and leather welding jacket. At the last moment I decided against my full helmet in favor of a pair of protective goggles. I marked the cuts I would be making on the metal with a piece of soapstone, and then checked the gauges on my acetylene torch. Satisfied with the pressure readings, I put on my welding gloves and lifted the striker to the tip of the torch. A second later a small yellow flame leaped into being as the sparks ignited the gas.

As I adjusted the flame on my torch, I got the distinct feeling I was being watched. The back of my neck prickled as the hairs along the nape stood on end, and my arms covered themselves in gooseflesh. I also caught an overpowering scent, far stronger than that of the garlic-like odor of the acetylene gas. With a start, I realized it was brimstone. I turned around, to look out the window, fearful of what I might see, yet unable to look away.

2222

2222

Standing on the ledge on the other side of the glass was a humanoid creature that from the waist down had the legs and hooves of a goat. Large batlike wings grew out of its back, just below the shoulders. It sported curling ram's horns at the temples, and it had three eyes—the extra one located in the middle of its brow—with a piglike snout and the tusks of a boar, from which dripped long, ropy strands of drool.

Seeing my look of terror, the demon grinned and smashed the window as if it was made of spun sugar and balsa wood. It grabbed me, its filthy yellow talons shredding the reinforced leather of my welding jacket like so much tissue paper. I cried out as its apelike hands grabbed my left arm, snapping it like a twig. This seemed to please the demon, as it made a weird, grunting noise like Porky Pig having a giggle. My tormentor's amusement quickly turned to squeals of agony, however, as I shoved the acetylene torch I was holding in my right hand into its face, boiling its third eye like a poached egg.

The creature let go of me so it could clap its hands over the oozing ruin in the middle of its forehead. I moved as far away as the hose attached to the welding tanks would allow; since the acetylene torch was my only weapon, I wasn't about to let go of it. The pain from my broken arm was so intense the edges of my vision were starting to turn gray, but I could not allow myself the luxury of passing out. If I wanted to stay alive, I had to remain on my feet.

Having a third eye reduced to bubbling goo must not be traumatic, at least not for a demon, as this one seemed to shake it off pretty quickly. The creature advanced on me, hurling my half-finished sculpture aside as if it was made out of nothing more than coat hangers and baling wire.

The sight of all my hard work being turned back into scrap metal threw a switch inside me, and suddenly all the pain and fear fled, to be replaced by indignant fury. Terrorizing and trying to kill me was one thing—fucking up my art was something else *entirely*.

"Do you realize how long I've been *working* on that, you chuffer?! Do you know what I had to go through just to get those goddamn parts shipped to this part of *town*? That's *it*! You want to fuck with me, Porky? C'mon—what are you waiting for?" I shouted, making the universal "bring it" motion to the demon with the acetylene torch.

The creature hesitated for a second, surprised by my outburst, and then a nasty smile spread across its face and a malignant glee filled its remaining eyes as it contemplated the fun it would have defiling my fragile human body with its talons and tusks. With an excited squeal it spread its membranous wings and launched itself at me.

As the shadow of the demon fell across me, I did not flinch or look away, but instead tightened my grip on the cutting torch. Even in the face of certain, horrible death, I felt no fear, only a deep resolve peculiar to those who know they are doomed, no matter what. Even if I was armed with a plasma arc welder, I was no match for a hell-spawn. My only consolation came from knowing that if this was how it was going to end, at least I'd be burning some bacon on the way out. Suddenly there was a flash of white light and a squeal like that of a herd of swine trapped in a slaughterhouse as the demon was hurled backward.

Hexe was standing in the doorway, dressed in nothing but a pair of boxers, his right hand held aloft. His eyes glowed like molten gold, and his right palm burned with a white heat so intense I couldn't look at it, even with my welding goggles.

"Get thee hence, foul one!" he commanded, his voice echoing as if he were speaking from the bottom of a well. "Leave this place! You are not welcome here!"

The demon turned on him, growling in defiance. It raised its hand to shield its piggish eyes from the brilliant white light, but did not cower. As it moved toward him, I felt my fear return—but not for myself. The glow surrounding Hexe's right hand grew even brighter, and tendrils of smoke rose from the demon's body. It snarled but continued to advance as if walking into a strong headwind. Its skin grew red and blistered, while sweat poured down Hexe's face and his right arm began to tremble.

As I watched, the right side of the demon's face sloughed away, like the cheese on a pizza, revealing glistening tendons and gleaming bone, and yet it continued to press onward. There came a sudden, condensed flare of light, like the final, defiant flicker of a guttering candle, and Hexe's right arm dropped to his side. With a squeal of bloodthirsty victory, the hellspawn pounced on him, grabbing him by the throat.

I lunged forward to go to his aid, only to be pulled up short by the hoses tethering me to the acetylene/oxygen tanks. I shut off the valves to the cutting torch and grabbed a pair of sheet metal snips from the workbench.

"Leave him alone, asshole!" I screamed as I plunged the shears into the demon's neck. The creature shrieked in pain and let Hexe go. But as I tried to pull the snips free, I was struck by one of the demon's pinions and landed on my broken arm.

The agony was so excruciating I could not suck enough air into my lungs to scream, so all that came out was a groan. Although my life depended on getting back on my feet, every time I moved my left arm I came perilously close to blacking out. The only thing that kept me from doing so was the certainty that if I lost consciousness, I would be torn limb from limb.

There was a thunderous roar that rattled the very walls of the house as Scratch, in his true form, smashed into the demon. Hellspawn and hell-beast rolled about the room, smashing my workbench into kindling as they tore at one another. The demon screamed like a stuck pig as Scratch buried his sabrelike fangs in its left shoulder. With an angry shriek that sounded like a band saw chewing through concrete, the pig-demon jumped out the broken window and soared off into the pre-dawn sky.

I felt a hand touch my cheek, and I opened my eyes to see Hexe kneeling over me. He seemed pale and drawn, and had a ring of bruises around his throat, but was otherwise unharmed. Scratch stood by the window, staring after the escaping fiend. The familiar turned and gave his master a beseeching look.

"He's getting away, boss."

"Go get 'im, tiger," Hexe said.

With a roar of delight, Scratch spread his own dragonlike wings and leaped out the window in pursuit of his enemy.

Now that the danger was over, I could feel myself start to slip into shock. My teeth began to chatter and suddenly everything seemed far away, as if I were looking down the wrong end of a telescope.

"Holy Bast! What happened in here?" Our housemate, Lukas, dressed in a pair of flannel pajama bottoms, was standing in the doorway, staring in disbelief at the wreckage.

"Tate's been attacked," Hexe replied. "Call nine-one-one. Tell them we need an ambulance!"

As Lukas hurried off to call the authorities, I felt myself sinking down, as if something had hold of the back of my head and was trying to drag me through the floor-boards, into endless night. I tightened my grip on Hexe's hand, fearful that should I fall into the void, I might never find my way back again.

"Don't worry, Tate," he whispered as the shadows began to expand. "I'll be with you every step of the way."

And then the darkness rose up and wrapped itself around me.

Chapter 20

The next thing I knew, I was on a gurney, surrounded by noise and movement and unshaded lights. I had no idea how long I'd been out or where I was; all I knew was that Hexe was still standing next to me, holding my hand. He was listening intently while a Kymeran in hospital scrubs spoke to him in an earnest voice. Suddenly a sliver of pain pierced the damp gray fog wrapped around me, and I moaned out loud. I glanced over at my broken arm and saw that it had been placed in a splint.

Hexe bent over and brushed the hair out of my face and kissed me on the forehead. "Everything's going to be okay, baby," he whispered, then let go of my hand and stepped aside so the man dressed in scrubs could take his place.

"Hello, Tate, my name's Dr. Gyre. I'm a boneknitter, and I'm going to be healing your arm now. Before we get started, I have to warn you that what I'm about to do will only take a few seconds—but it *will* hurt. During that time, you can't move or jerk away from me, no matter how much you might want to. Do you understand?"

I nodded yes, even though I didn't have a clue as to

what he was talking about. All I wanted was my arm fixed.

"Good girl," Dr. Gyre said with a smile. Then he put a padded stick in my mouth and clamped his hands just below the wrist and above the elbow of my splinted arm. There was a flash of white light, and my broken arm was healed in less than two minutes.

What did it feel like? Imagine hitting your funny bone with a ball-peen hammer while smashing your hand in a car door—*that's* what it felt like. The truly excruciating part, though, was an intense tingling sensation—part burning, part itching—from inside the bone itself, as if a colony of fire ants armed with tattooing guns was scurrying about underneath my skin. Despite the agony, I did not move, for fear that my arm might come off in his hands.

Just when I thought I would go mad from the pain, Dr. Gyre let go and stepped back, taking the pain with him. The boneknitter plucked the surgical cap from his head, revealing a shock of olive green hair, and used it to wipe away the sweat dripping from his face. He nodded to Hexe, who quickly removed the padded stick from my mouth. I took a deep, shuddering breath, as I blinked the tears from my eyes. Although I was no longer hurting, I was so exhausted I felt like I'd just run the New York City Marathon *and* the Boston Marathon back-to-back.

"She should be good to go later today," Dr. Gyre said. "She's going to need to sleep it off for a few hours, though. I'll have one of our orderlies put her in a recovery room."

"Thank you, Doctor," Hexe said gratefully.

Dr. Gyre pulled aside the curtain behind him, revealing the controlled chaos of what looked to be a typical emergency room—or a veterinary clinic, judging by the pregnant huldra going into labor in the cubicle to the right of me.

"How are you feeling, Tate?" Hexe asked. "Can I get you anything?"

"I'm really thirsty," I replied.

"I'll go get you some water," he said, kissing my forehead. "I'll be right back."

As I waited for Hexe to return with my water, the doors to the ambulance drop-off flew open and a pair of paramedics hustled into the ER pushing a gurney that bore an ipotane wrapped in a thermal blanket. An Amazon in nurse's whites motioned to the empty cubicle to the left of mine.

My eyelids were growing heavier each second, but I wasn't so out of it that I didn't notice the smell of wet horse. I looked over and saw that the gurney the ipotane was lying on was completely soaked, to the point that water was pooling on the floor underneath. The ipotane then groaned and rolled over so that he was facing me. With a start, I realized it was Gus.

"Some merfolk found him in the East River," one of the paramedics said as he handed the patient's chart to the Amazonian nurse. "He was cyanotic when we arrived at the scene, but we managed to revive him."

As if on cue, Gus began to gasp and choke, and the ER staff flew into action. "He's going into cardiac arrest!" the nurse shouted as she began applying CPR to the ipotane's barrel-like chest. "I need a psychic surgeon over here, *stat*!"

Hexe returned with a bottle of water, but by that time I was too tired to do more than take a couple of sips. I wanted to tell him that I knew the person the ER staff were frantically working to save, but I was so exhausted from my own ordeal I could barely squeeze his hand, much less talk. Before I could find out what had happened to Gus, the orderly arrived and pushed my gurney down the hall to the recovery room.

I am on the street in front of the boardinghouse, waiting for my ride. I do not know how long I have been standing there, or where it is I am going. I cannot tell if it is day or night, but I do see that the streets are strangely empty. Suddenly, I become aware of someone calling my name, as if from a great distance.

I look across the street and see Bayard the centaur harnessed to a pony wagon. Quid and Gus are perched on the driver's seat, smiling and waving at me.

"Hurry up, Tate," Quid calls out, "or you're going to be late!"

I trot across the cobblestone street to join my friends. I am relieved to see that they are alive and well. I wonder where I got the crazy idea that they were otherwise. But as I draw closer, the glow of health drains from their faces and their skin turns a pallid, ashy gray.

My eyes must be playing tricks on me, so I rub them and look again, only to have the pony wagon transform into a glass-sided hearse. Quid and Gus are still sitting on the driver's seat, only now they are wearing undertakers' top hats and tails, as is Bayard.

"Aren't you going with us?" Gus asks, water gushing from his mouth.

"There's room for one more," Quid says, gesturing to the interior of the hearse. Save for his trademark fuzzy eyebrows, the favor broker's face is a mass of bruises, and his left eye dangles from its socket by the optic nerve.

"I'm not ready to go," I protest, stepping away from the hearse.

"Neither were we," Bayard replies, turning in his harness to look at me. He is still wearing the earbuds attached

*to his iPod and his mouth is smeared with dried vomit.
"But we went, all the same."*

*Suddenly a shadow falls across me, and I hear a cry
that is a cross between the squawk of a raven and the
squeal of a pig. I look in the sky and see a winged silhou-
ette plummeting toward me. I shield my face by raising
my arms, and when I lower them, I am no longer standing
on the street.*

*I am in a large, shadowy room. I look down and see
that I am standing in the center of a pentacle. I hear the
rustle of feathers and hissing. I turn and see a black
chicken on a nesting box, beside which sits a copper
dragon, steam rising from its nostrils as it watches me
with eyes of flame.*

*There is a flash of lightning and a crash of thunder, il-
luminating the darkness around me. I see a slab, and on it
lies a body covered by a sheet. As I stare in horror, the
cadaver sits up and reaches with a pale, bloodless hand
and slowly pulls at the shroud covering its face. I am
rooted to the spot, unable to look away. I don't know why,
but it is important that I see the corpse's face. Just as the
sheet finally drops away, there is another lightning flash
and . . .*

"Tate? Can you hear me? Are you okay?" Hexe was
bending over me, a concerned look on his face. He
heaved a sigh of relief as I opened my eyes. "It sounded
like you were having a nightmare."

"How long was I asleep?" I asked, looking around. I
was resting in a hospital bed in a small, sparsely decorated room, the walls of which were painted a pale me-
dicinal green. Somewhere along the line I had been
undressed and put in a hospital gown.

"You've been out for a couple of hours," he replied,

arranging my pillows so I could sit up. "How do you feel?"

"A lot better, compared to before." I lifted my splinted arm and stared at it in amazement. "It just seems a little tender—that's all. I'm still really thirsty, though."

"That's a side effect of the accelerated healing," Hexe explained as he poured me a glass of water from a carafe on the bedside table.

I quickly downed the offered glass, eager to quench the persistent dryness at the back of my throat. It was probably just tap water, but as far as my body was concerned it was the ambrosia of the gods.

"Did Scratch catch the demon?" I asked as he refilled my glass.

"I'm afraid not. He lost track of it near Pickman's Slip."

"Did he get hurt?"

"Scratch is fine; don't worry. He's returned to the house and is guarding the home front."

"Merciful God—! Where are you witch doctors hiding my daughter?"

I choked on my water, spitting it back into the glass. A second later my mother appeared in the doorway of the recovery room. She was dressed to the nines, complete with white gloves, as if she had just walked out of a luncheon with the governor. Upon spotting me, she threw her hands up in an exaggerated show of relief and leaned back into the hallway.

"Finally! I found her, Timothy! She's in here!"

My father popped into the doorframe a second later, looking genuinely disconcerted. My dad doesn't like being out of his element, and you couldn't get any further from a boardroom or a yacht club than Golgotham General. The moment he saw me, however, the knot between his eyes unwound and he hurried to my bedside.

Hexe quietly stepped aside so my father could hug me. As always, he smelled of expensive cologne and licorice, his favorite candy.

"How are you feeling, Princess? Are you hurt?"

"I'm fine, Daddy."

"Where am I, a hospital or a barnyard?" My mother sniffed as she ran a white-gloved finger along the foot of the bed. "I just walked in on someone up to their shoulder in a horse's rear end!"

"Hi, Mom. I'm fine. Thank you," I replied drily. "And that wasn't a *horse*; it was a *centaur*."

"To-*may*-tow, to-*mah*-tow; it's still going to haunt me to my dying day," she said with an exaggerated shiver.

"Mom, Dad—don't take this the wrong way, but how did you know I was in the hospital?"

My mother gave one of her trademark short, humorless laughs, and held up the newspaper she was carrying so I could read the headline: ERESBY HEIRESS IN DEMON RAMPAGE.

"You know, it would be nice, for a change, to find out what's going on in your life via some other channel than the tabloid press! Imagine my shock upon reading that my only child had been attacked by a devil of some kind and hospitalized with a broken arm. However, I cannot say I was terribly surprised. I *knew* something like this would eventually happen to you, once you moved downtown!" She scowled and pointed an accusing finger at Hexe. "*You!* This is all *your* fault! If it weren't for *you*, my Timmy wouldn't be hurt!"

"Mom, that's ridiculous!" I protested. "Hexe saved my life!"

My father turned to look at him, seeming to notice Hexe for the first time. His eyebrows rose in surprise at the sight of the bruises that still ringed Hexe's throat. "Is that true, young man? Did you save my daughter's life?"

"I wouldn't go as far as that, sir," Hexe said humbly, bowing his head. "It was my familiar who actually chased away the demon."

"He's being modest, Dad," I interjected. "If it wasn't for him, I'd be dead."

"Don't listen to her, Timothy," my mother warned. "The girl's not in her right mind! The Kymie's slipped her a love potion. I know it in my bones."

"I *beg* your pardon?" Hexe responded indignantly.

"You heard me the *first* time," she replied, refusing to back down. "Political correctness be damned. I know your kind, Kymeran. You've cast a glamour over my daughter to make her your love slave. But if you think you're going to get your six grubby little fingers on her inheritance, you're sadly mistaken!"

"Mother! *Please!*" I snapped in aggravation. You would think by this point in my life, I could no longer be shocked or embarrassed by what comes slithering out of her mouth, but somehow my mother always manages to top herself.

"Don't 'Mother' me, young lady!" She opened the wardrobe next to the bed and began removing my clothes. She glowered in distaste at the shredded remains of my welding jacket and jumpsuit. "Honestly, Timmy—you were wearing *this* when they admitted you?"

"If I hadn't been, I'd be missing an arm," I replied acidly.

"Whatever," she sighed, rolling her eyes. "Just get your things together—we're leaving this dreadful place right this minute. No daughter of mine is going to be poked and prodded by a bunch of rattle-shaking medicine men. We're going straight to Dr. Blumlein's office. I called ahead, so he'll be expecting us."

"I don't *need* your doctor, Mother," I argued. "I'm already healed." To prove my point, I began to free myself from the splint.

"Timmy!" she gasped in alarm. "What are you *doing*?!?"

"See?" I said, ignoring the slight twinge as I flexed my arm. "Nothing's broken."

"Don't get ahead of yourself, my dear," a familiar voice said from the hallway. "That repair to your ulna is still fresh."

My mother spun around as if she'd been stung by a hornet, a look of horrified disbelief on her face.

Lady Syra stood in the door, outfitted in a Dior original that made what my mother was wearing look like she'd scrounged it from Goodwill. The smile on the Witch Queen's face disappeared upon realizing there were others in the room.

"I'm terribly sorry. I didn't know you had company."

"Don't mind us." My father smiled, seemingly oblivious to my mother's reaction to Syra's arrival. "Please come in."

As Lady Syra entered, she paused and looked my mother square in the eye. "Millicent," she said coolly.

My mother's jaw dropped as if the muscles had been severed. "What are *you* doing here?"

"The same thing you are, I daresay," Lady Syra replied. "Checking on the welfare of my child." She then turned to Hexe and kissed his cheek. She shook her head and clucked her tongue upon seeing the marks around his neck. "Look at those bruises!" She opened her designer purse and began rooting about inside it. "I should have some salve that will clear that right up. . . ."

"That's it!" my mother exclaimed, grabbing me by my freshly healed arm. "You're coming home with us! Enough of this playing at being a bohemian artist!"

"I'm not going *anywhere* with you!" I snapped, yanking free of her grip. "When are you going to realize I'm not some 'confused' teenager you can bully into doing what you want anymore? And I'm not 'playing' at anything, Mother! I *am* an artist. This is the life I've chosen, and Hexe is the man I've chosen to live it with. I don't expect you to approve, but I at least hoped you would acknowledge that I'm an adult by now!"

"Ha! A lot you know about being an adult!" she spat angrily. "*Adults* don't run off and leave their families behind so they can do whatever *they* want to do! *Adults* don't get themselves into multiple lawsuits and treat their parents like walking piggy banks! If *this* is how you want to live, and *what* you want to live with—*fine*! Go ahead! Let's see how cool and exciting your lifestyle is without a trust fund to bail you out!"

"You can't do that!" I protested.

"Of *course* we can cut off your trust fund," my mother sneered. "We're the ones who created it!"

"She has a point, Princess," my father said, rubbing the back of his neck. "This has gone on long enough. It was all well and good before things got out of hand. But you could have been killed—you said so yourself. Golgotham is no place for someone like you. As for Hexe ... I'm grateful that he saved your life, but you wouldn't have been in danger in the first place if you weren't involved with him."

"For once your father and I are on the same page. Either you break off your relationship and move back home, or you get your wish and live the life of a *truly* struggling artist," my mother said, with a touch of triumph in her voice. "You've got twenty-four hours to decide which it's going to be."

"I don't need that long to come up with an answer," I replied angrily. "This is my life now, and I'm going to live it in Golgotham, with Hexe."

"We'll see if you still feel the same way once the pain-killers wear off," she said. "The twenty-four-hour dead-line still stands. Now let's get out of here, Timothy." She paused to sniff the sleeve of her silk Yves St. Laurent blouse. "Ugh. Remind me to have Clarence burn our clothes when we get home. This place smells like the livestock exhibition at the state fair."

"Hexe, Syra—I'm *so* sorry about all that!" I said em-phatically after my parents had gone. "I'm *so* embar-rassed for them! *Especially* my mother!"

"You, of all people, shouldn't have to apologize to *me* about rude family members," Lady Syra said with a wry smile. "Your mother may have dropped a bombshell, but at least she didn't set fire to the house like Esau did. However, I *will* say that time certainly hasn't sweetened her disposition, and leave it at that. But, at the risk of sounding like a fuddy-duddy, I agree with your parents, at least in part. Golgotham isn't safe for humans right now—and it's *definitely* not safe for you."

"I'm not leaving," I said with a firm shake of my head. "I'm not going to let bigots chase me from my new home, whether they're Esau and his croggies or my own family. I'm staying put in Golgotham, even if it places me in danger. There's no way I can go back to the life I had before."

"Tate, darling, I applaud the strength of your convictions—truly I do. But you were attacked by a *demon*—and from what Hexe described over the phone, it was probably a Knight of the Infernal Court. A Ky-meran capable of summoning such a fiend is not going to be discouraged simply because Scratch scared off their assassin!" She turned to scowl at her son. "Hon-estly, Hexe, I realize you love the girl, but have you given *any* thought to the danger you've put her in by flaunting your relationship in public? No doubt someone intended that demon as payback for the rally."

"I may be in love, Mother, but I'm not brain-damaged," Hexe retorted. "Of course I know I've turned her into a target for every misanthrope in Golgotham with a chip on his shoulder."

"If she won't leave of her own accord, then you must send her away! You're her landlord, by every hell! Have her evicted! Tear up her lease! Take away her key!"

"I can't do that, Mother," Hexe replied grimly, taking my hand in his. "If Tate leaves Golgotham, I go with her."

"You would exile yourself for a human?" Lady Syra gasped.

Hexe shook his head. "Not for 'a human'—for *her*. The second I laid eyes on Tate, I saw this aura about her head, like a halo or a crown. I knew instantly that this was a woman who held a great power within her, and that she was meant to be part of my life."

A strange look crossed Lady Syra's face, as if something that had been puzzling her was finally solved. "I see," she said quietly. "I understand what you have just told me, but there is still the question of safety. I respect your abilities, Hexe, but you cannot protect her against an infernal courtier. As it is, if it hadn't been for Scratch, both of you would be dead. Courtiers are far cleverer than the typical demon and they learn quickly. When it comes back to finish its task, it will know what to expect, and Scratch won't be able to surprise it. What will you do then?"

There was a polite rap on the door, heralding the arrival of Lieutenant Vivi. She stood smiling on the threshold of the recovery room. "Please forgive the intrusion, Your Highness, but I just stopped by to inform Ms. Eresby that we've apprehended the conjurer responsible for summoning the demon."

"That's great news!" I exclaimed in relief. "How did you track him down?"

"One of our crime scene dowsers located a talisman used in the binding of demons in the wreckage in your apartment. I assume it was dropped during the battle with the familiar. It was identified as the handiwork of a sorceress named Dori, who keeps a stall at the Fly Market."

"Dori?" Hexe frowned. "Are you *sure*?"

"You know her, Serenity?" Vivi asked, regarding him with a cocked eyebrow.

"Yes," Hexe replied, only to immediately correct himself. "That is, I *used* to know her."

"Ah," Vivi said, with a nod of her head. "What about you, Ms. Eresby? Are you familiar with this sorceress as well?"

"She verbally attacked me in public, and then tried to inflict a curse on me."

"When was this?" Lieutenant Vivi asked as she began to make notes on her BlackBerry.

"It was the day of the rally," I explained. "Ask the cashier at the Emerald Spa; he saw the whole thing."

"Dori tried to curse you?" Hexe stared at me in surprised confusion. "Why am I just now hearing about this?"

"Because, compared to being treated like a human yo-yo and beat up by a demon, getting bitched out by your crazy ex-girlfriend didn't really seem that important."

"Well, you no longer have anything to fear from her. She's in custody now, awaiting arraignment in the Tombs."

"Did she admit to summoning the infernal?" Hexe asked.

"Of course not!" the PTU officer said with a dismissive laugh. "She claims it's all a big misunderstanding, just like they always do. Well, I best get back to work—I just thought you'd want to hear the good news in person."

"Thank you, Lieutenant," I said gratefully. "I appreciate you taking the time out of your schedule."

"It's no problem, really," she replied as she headed out the door. "I already had to stop by to take a report on a drowning. An ipotane got drunk and took a long stagger off a short pier early this morning. Take care, now."

"Oh, God—it was real." I groaned. "I hoped I was hallucinating. Poor Gus . . ."

"Wasn't he the ipotane you spoke to in the centaur's funeral procession?" Hexe asked with a frown.

I nodded. "I thought I recognized him in the ER earlier, but I wasn't sure. I didn't know Gus that well, but I liked him. He was so upset over Bayard's death—but I can't imagine him committing suicide."

"It probably was an accident," Hexe said consolingly. "Ipotanes *do* have a reputation for getting so drunk they can't walk straight. They're not as bad as satyrs, mind you, but it's not unheard of for one of them to overindulge and fall into the river."

"I'm sorry to hear about your friend," Lady Syra said as she gathered up her purse, "but I'm relieved they apprehended the responsible party. However, that doesn't mean things are any less dangerous for you. Still, if anyone was to protect you, I can't imagine a worthier bodyguard than my son. We can only hope this unpleasantness with my brother and his political agenda is resolved relatively quickly, and then everything can get back to normal."

"Syra—before you go, do you mind telling me how it is that you happen to know my mother?"

"I'm afraid my answering that would violate privilege," she replied apprehensively.

"What does that mean?"

"It means," the Witch Queen said with a weary smile, "that is a question you should ask your mother— not me."

Chapter 21

Not long after Lady Syra made her exit, I was visited by an older Kymeran gentleman in a white coat with hair the color of celadon who smelled of cedar and bay leaves. Judging from the laminated ID dangling about his neck, he was a hospital administrator.

"Good afternoon, Miss—Eresby," he said, checking the clipboard he was holding. "My name is Dr. Voit. I'm the chief of medicine here at Golgotham General. I just stopped by to get your signature on this release form, and to make sure you've been treated well during your stay."

"Your staff has been very professional and attentive," I assured him, as I signed my name at the bottom of the form. "The hospital where I had my appendectomy could take a few lessons from this place. How much do I owe you?"

"Emergency Room admittances are no charge in Golgotham," he explained.

"Please tell Dr. Gyre I appreciate all he did." Hexe smiled as he shook the doctor's hand.

"I'll be sure to pass that along, Serenity. By the

way—I used to work with your uncle, back in the old days."

"Esau was employed at Golgotham General?" Hexe asked in surprise.

Dr. Voit nodded. "He worked in tandem with Dr. Moot, replacing limbs. Esau created these amazing clockwork arms, and Moot melded them to the patient's nervous system in such a way that some of the patients actually regained the sense of touch! That was a while back, though—before Moot's addiction destroyed his ability to conduct psychic surgery, and long before the incident with poor Nita turned Esau into a cacozealot. Sad business, that."

"Nita?" Hexe frowned.

"Your uncle's wife," Dr. Voit replied matter-of-factly. "She was killed by humans, if memory serves."

"Don't you love it when your family goes for decades without telling you shit like that?" I grunted as Hexe helped me into a cab parked in the hospital's loading zone. Ever since he'd inadvertently discovered an aunt he never knew existed, he had been noticeably pensive, and I decided it was best to draw him out.

"It certainly explains a lot about my uncle," he conceded, gazing up at the looming silhouettes of the World Trade Center in the distance. "It doesn't *excuse* any of his behavior, mind you, but it *does* make it easier to understand."

He paused, then said, "I've known Dori for a long time—we grew up together. I have a hard time imagining her sending forth a demon to do her bidding, much less an infernal courtier."

"I realize you two have a lot of history," I said gingerly, "but I don't think Dori is the same woman you used to know. She's changed, Hexe."

Hexe shook his head. "You don't understand, Tate. I'm not saying she's *above* doing such things. I'm saying she's *incapable* of doing them. I can easily believe Dori would try to inflict a curse on you. But to send a demon after you? *Please!* She's simply not that adept a sorceress!"

"I wouldn't be so quick to write her off," I countered. "Maybe we ought to go talk to her, though, just in case she's gotten a lot stronger than you realize."

"Good idea," he said. "There's something not right about all this, and I mean to find out what it is."

The Golgotham Hall of Justice and Detention Center, better known as the Tombs, was located on the outermost edge of the neighborhood, closer to Manhattan's City Hall and One Police Plaza than Golgotham's seat of government. This was because it basically served as an overglorified drunk tank and relay point for prisoner exchanges between the NYPD and the PTU.

It occupied a full city block, surrounded by Park Row, Ferry, Frankfort, and Horsecart Streets, and had two entrances, depending on who was dropping off or picking up prisoners. The NYPD utilized the entrance on Park Row, while the PTU came and went via the one facing Horsecart Street.

Originally built in the early nineteenth century, the jail got its nickname from its architecture, which at first glance resembled an ancient mausoleum. Built atop vertical piles of gargantuan lashed-together hemlock trunks, it was actually modeled after the Temple of Hathor in the Egyptian city of Dendera, and constructed to appear, from the outside, to be only one story in height. The facade boasted long windows that started just a few feet above the ground and extended almost to the cornice, as well as fanciful pylons, obelisks, winged disks, and lotus flowers. The Egyptian theme was continued by the pair of sphinxes who sat guard on either side of the broad flight of dark stone steps.

Hexe and I hurried past the living sentinels, who watched our approach with the lazy self-assuredness of basking lions, and through a giant, forbidding portico supported by four huge papyrus-stalk columns of polished granite. We then headed down an immense and ominous corridor that led to a large quadrangle, hidden behind the towering outer walls. Inside the greater Detention Center were three lesser prisons, each several stories high: one for men, one for women, and one for humans. Our destination was the women's prison, nicknamed the Charm School.

We were greeted at the entry desk by one of the guards, a female cyclops with blond hair and a blue eye, who carefully patted us down before escorting us to the visitation center. The room where the Charm School's "students" received their visitors was large, sparsely decorated, and outfitted with metal tables and chairs securely bolted to the floor, with a couple of vending machines in the corner, one dispensing snacks like chile-flavored lollipops and ostrich jerky, the other cigarettes.

As we entered, I saw a handful of prisoners in identical bright orange jumpsuits meeting with family members, loved ones, and/or attorneys. To my surprise, I recognized one of the inmates.

"Chory?" I exclaimed. "What are *you* doing here?"

The maenad's cheeks turned bright red as she saw Hexe and me. Her attorney, a huldu in an ill-fitting suit,

turned to glower at us, his bull tail twitching in consternation.

"This is a privileged conversation, if you don't mind."

"It's okay, Horst. They're friends of mine," Chorea
said. "I got busted for D and D, destruction of property,
and violating a restraining order."

"Bloody abdabs, Chorea!"

"I know, I know—it sounds horrible! But I was at
loose ends. I'm out of work until Lafo gets the Calf re-
opened, so I went out barhopping, thinking it would
cheer me up. Everything was okay until I hit Lorelei's
for a nightcap. That's when I ran into Faro. . . ."

"I take it your reunion didn't turn out that well,"
Hexe said drily.

"So I'm told. I don't really remember much of what
happened, to tell you the truth. According to the police
report, I grabbed this sword that had a flaming chicken
stuck on it and chased him around the restaurant. And I
think I may have set fire to a grass hut."

"Oh my! You didn't—I mean, Faro's not—?"

"Don't worry. He's still alive," she replied. "In fact,
we're getting back together! Isn't that right, Horst?"

Chorea's attorney nodded. "My client's husband has
agreed to drop the charges against her and rescind his
restraining order, provided she agrees to attend AA
meetings."

"Faro really *does* love me," Chorea said, beaming. "I
want to make this marriage work, so I've decided to go
on the wagon."

"Good for you," Hexe said sincerely. "I wish you all
the best."

The door on the prisoners' side of the room opened
and Dori entered, accompanied by a brown-eyed cyclopean guard. Stripped of her bangles, scarves, and makeup,
and dressed in a Day-Glo orange jumper, her head now

covered by a do-rag, the haughty sorceress seemed
greatly reduced. Hexe discreetly sniffed the air, and I
saw a flicker of sadness cross his face as he caught the
scent emanating from his ex-girlfriend.

Upon spying Hexe, Dori smiled and a weight seemed
to lift from her shoulders. Then she saw me standing
next to him, and her face closed like an angry fist. "You
bring the nump to see me so she can gloat?" she growled.

"Believe me, I'm as thrilled to be here as you are," I
snapped.

"I just want to talk, Dori," Hexe said reassuringly,
motioning for her to sit down. As she did so, I noticed
for the first time the stainless-steel mesh Chinese finger
traps secured on her right and left "magic" fingers, which
effectively kept her from casting spells while still allowing the use of her hands.

"I don't know what the nump told you," the sorceress
said, glowering in my direction, "but I didn't do it."

"You didn't try to curse her?" Hexe asked, lifting an
eyebrow in surprise.

"Oh, I did *that*, all right!" Dori replied with a nasty
laugh. "But I didn't send a demon after her."

"But they found a binding talisman with your spell
signature on it at the scene," Hexe pointed out.

"So what if they did?" She shrugged. "I sell binders
all the time. That doesn't mean I'm the one that sent the
demon."

"But you were seen arguing with Tate a few hours
before the attack," Hexe countered. "You just admitted
you attempted to inflict a curse on her."

"I was just trying to give her crossed eyes and a
hunched back. That's all!" the sorceress replied with a
dismissive wave of her hand, as if her plans for me were
nothing worse than a wet willie or an Indian rope burn.
"It's not like I was trying to inflict premature aging or

rabies on her! I'll admit to trying to cripple her and ugly her up, but no way did I send a demon to kill your chuffin' concubine."

Hexe sat back, a thoughtful look on his face. "I believe you, Dori."

The muscles in Dori's jaw unclenched, and for a fleeting second I saw something besides anger and hate in her eyes. As much as I disliked her, there was no denying her beauty. No wonder Hexe had been involved with her.

"Wait a second," I protested. "Why are you so quick to accept her word on this?"

"If she was guilty of summoning the demon, she wouldn't have readily admitted to trying to curse you. I don't think she's lying," he explained. "I think she's being framed by someone who is aware of the former relationship between us, as well as her feelings toward you. I'm going to say as much to Captain Horn."

"Thank you, Serenity," Dori replied, bowing her head in ritual gratitude. "That will mean a great deal, coming from you."

"It's the least I can do," Hexe said as he stood up from the table.

"We *were* close once, weren't we?" Dori asked plaintively, reaching out to touch him. The cyclopean guard stepped forward, resting the business end of her billy club on the sorceress's shoulder. Dori quickly pulled back, tucking her hands in her lap.

"Yes," Hexe replied, with a somber nod of his head. "That is true. And if you have suffered because of me, I am sorry. Before I leave, do you remember the last time you sold a binder?"

"There was this young guy with bluish hair, a few days back. He paid cash."

"Do you know his name?"

"No. But he had a KUP pin on his lapel, if that helps."

"You were right, Tate," Hexe said as we left the visitation room. "Dori has changed—you can smell it on her. When she began trafficking in curses I was afraid something like this would happen. The woman that I knew would never inflict a curse on someone who couldn't protect herself. When we first met, she was a cartomancer, designing special tarot decks and doing readings for clients. But the money wasn't good enough, so she decided to branch out. We had a terrible fight about it, and that's when we broke up."

"Does inflicting curses turn the wizards and witches who cast them evil?" I asked.

"Not necessarily. Most Kymerans dabble in both Left and Right disciplines, and as long as they stick to the Lesser Curses, it balances out. But those who deal in the Greater Curses—the ones that are truly malevolent—run the risk of being tainted. To be willing to cast misfortune upon a stranger for no other reason than financial gain requires a certain darkness to begin with. But when you move up to disfigurement and death, what you're doing goes from mischief-making to depraved indifference. The Left Hand Path is as insidious as cancer, and with each additional Greater Curse, the shadow on the heart grows larger."

Upon our return to the entry desk, the blue-eyed Cyclops motioned to Hexe. "You'll need this to leave," she said, handing him a slip of paper. "It's today's exit pass." He glanced at the paper, then stuck it in one of his pockets before continuing out the door.

As we exited the long, shadowy passageway that led from the hidden quadrangle to the street, one of the sphinxes that guarded the portico turned to regard us with a menacing growl, her lambent green eyes glowing in the ever-present gloom. Hexe and I froze as she padded toward us.

From the waist up, save for her pawlike forearms, she appeared to be a beautiful Egyptian princess, complete with vulture cap headdress and a pectoral made of gold, lapis lazuli, and faience, depicting the sun god Horus. From the waist down she was a lioness. To my surprise, the creature spoke with a deceptively sweet voice that belied her razor-sharp claws and needlelike teeth.

> *"With potent, flowery words speak I,*
> *Of something common, vulgar, dry;*
> *I weave webs of pedantic prose,*
> *In effort to befuddle those,*
> *Who think I wile time away,*
> *In lofty things, above all day*
> *The common kind that linger where*
> *Monadic beings live and fare;*
> *Practical I may not be,*
> *But life, it seems, is full of me! What am I?"*

"A riddler," Hexe replied with a knowing smile.

Convinced that we weren't escaped prisoners, the sphinx turned her tawny back on us and resumed her place on the plinth atop the stairs, alongside her mate. As we hurried down to the street, I could feel their twin gazes on my back, eyeing me as lions would a gazelle at the watering hole.

Chapter 22

"So—have you decided what you're going to tell your parents?" Hexe asked quietly as we cabbed home from the Tombs.

"Not only am I going to tell them to go to hell; I'm going to give them road maps and hold the door open for them as they leave!" I replied with a crooked grin. I expected Hexe to laugh, but instead he gave me a serious look.

"Are you *sure* that's what you want to do?"

"No, but it's not like they're giving me a choice," I admitted.

"I hate to sound like my mother, but maybe it *would* be a good idea for you to leave Golgotham for a little while. At least until the matter of the demon is resolved."

"Your mother's a lot nicer about it than mine, but she's definitely not thrilled with us hooking up," I commented. "I wasn't going to mention it in front of her, for fear of providing ammunition for her argument, but Nessie *did* offer to let me crash on her couch."

"Why didn't you say so?" Hexe exclaimed in relief. "Problem solved!"

"I can't impose on her like that, what with the wedding coming up. And I thought you couldn't send me away?"

"I meant everything I said: I can no more tell you to leave than I could cut off my own right hand. But if you go of your own volition—that's different. I'd miss you terribly, but as long as I knew you still loved me, and would come back as soon as it was safe, I could handle it. I realize it would be unpleasant, but at least you'd be safer with your parents than living in Golgotham. It would just be a temporary situation—"

"That's what they all say," I replied with a humorless laugh. "You mentioned the Left Hand Path was insidious—that it corrupts you in slow motion, until you're no longer the person you used to be. Well, the same holds true for my parents. If I pack up my things and head home, I might as well slit my wrists and get it over with. My mother has been trying to drag me back into the fold for years, and this thing with the demon gives her a good excuse to swoop in and try to run my life. You're just icing on the cake, as far as she's concerned. My parents don't like the idea of me being involved with a Kymeran, but they *really* hate the fact that I'm an artist. Believe me, I've seen it before.

"I used to go to high school with this girl named Eleanor. She was an amazing, incredibly talented poet who wrote stuff that could make a statue cry. She had fire inside her—you could see it in her eyes. She went off to Vassar and got a few poems published that got some attention from the *New Yorker*. Everyone said she was going to be this century's Edna St. Vincent Millay. When she graduated from college, she moved to the Village and decided to publish a poetry journal to showcase her work as well as that of her friends.

"One thing led to another, and eventually Eleanor's

so deep in debt she defaults on the mortgage for her loft. That's when her parents told her that if they were going to bail her out, she had to move back in with them. I remember her telling me that it would only be temporary, until she could straighten out her finances and get herself back on her feet. That was a couple of years ago.

"The last time I saw Eleanor, she was no longer 'burning her candle at both ends,' but taking high tea with the rest of the Ladies Who Lunch at the Plaza. She'd gotten married to some dreadful hedge fund manager, who I hear cheats on her every chance he gets, and they'd moved to New Hampshire. Now she just comes into the city to go shopping and attend her mother's charity events. She was surprised and, I think, more than a little embarrassed to see me. When I looked into her eyes, I could tell the fire had been snuffed out. I don't care *how* much safer I'd be sitting in my family's penthouse—I'll be damned if I end up a Bergdorf's zombie."

"I don't think you'll ever be in danger of losing your fire," Hexe replied with a smile, squeezing my hand. "You're a stronger woman than you give yourself credit for, Tate."

"The pits be praised! I've been going crazy waiting for you two to get home!" Scratch yowled, nervously kneading the floor of the foyer with his front paws.

"I'm sorry it took so long, but we had to make a couple of stops after leaving the hospital," Hexe replied. "I'm sure you're *starving*, of course."

"I'm not hungry," the familiar replied.

Hexe stared in disbelief. "*You?* Not hungry? What's the matter? Are you sick?"

"I'm fine. I just can't find Beanie. That's all," Scratch replied with an uncharacteristic hint of worry.

"What?" Hexe and I gasped in unison.

"Did you check the backyard?" I asked, trying to keep the panic out of my voice.

"Of course I checked there—what do I look like, an idiot?" Scratch snapped. "I even searched the maze. I asked the hamadryad, and she says she hasn't seen him all day."

I hurried up the stairs to the second floor, praying that he had simply fallen asleep in the dirty laundry hamper again. "Beanie? C'mere, boy!" I called out. "Mommy's home!" I paused, hoping to hear the velvety flap of his ears as he shook himself awake, followed by the familiar *thumpity-thump* of his paws against the hallway runner as he scampered to greet me, but there was only silence.

"He's not up there!" Scratch shouted after me. "Believe me, I've looked all over the house, and I can't find him *anywhere*! I went downstairs and checked the basement, and I even went up to the third floor, just in case. He's *not* in the house. I think he got out when the PTU crime scene investigators were here. They kept coming in and out. . . ."

I felt the bottom of my stomach fall away as what Scratch said started to sink in. The thought of Beanie being out on the streets, scared and alone, with no one to protect him, was far more distressing to me than the possibility of another demon attack. I hurried back downstairs to join the others in the kitchen.

"Beanie's out there by himself, Hexe," I said breathlessly. "He's just a baby—he's never been mistreated. He doesn't know people can be mean, or that things can hurt him. He's never known anything but love and kindness his whole life. He doesn't even know enough to be scared! What if he runs out in front of a carriage and gets crushed? I've got to go find him! But where do I start?"

"I think I know a way to locate him," Hexe said, ducking into his office.

As I waited for him to find whatever it was he was looking for, Scratch hopped onto the kitchen counter, so that he was eye to eye with me. "I'm sorry, Tate," the familiar said. "This is all my fault. I should have kept watch on him. I would already be out looking for him, but I'm bound to the house until Hexe says otherwise."

"Where's all this concern coming from?" I asked in surprise. "I thought you *hated* Beanie!"

"I don't *hate* him!" Scratch replied indignantly. "I just think I'm *better* than he is."

"This should do the trick," Hexe said, returning to the kitchen with a scrying crystal the size and shape of a small avocado. "It was designed to reveal the exact location of missing persons and misplaced things. And since Beanie falls somewhere between those two categories, I think we have a good chance of finding him with it."

He knelt beside the refrigerator and dunked the odd-shaped crystal into Beanie's water bowl, then held it up to the light. As the water began to dry on its surface, shapes began to move deep within its heart, gradually resolving into distinguishable black-and-white images. My heart leaped at the sight of Beanie running down a narrow, trash-strewn passageway.

"I think I know where he is," Hexe said, turning the scrying crystal around for closer inspection. "That looks like Snuff Alley, behind the Stagger Inn, just off Rutger Street."

"At least he's still alive and in one piece!" I sighed in relief.

"Not for much longer, though," Hexe said grimly, pointing to the living buzz saw of teeth and claws in pursuit of the puppy.

"Bloody abdabs!" I yelped. "What the hell *is* that thing?"

"It's a rat king," Scratch growled, his eyes glowing like lanterns. "I can't *stand* those chuffers!"

As I watched, helpless to intervene, Beanie ducked between a pair of overflowing garbage cans, putting his back against the alley wall, as the mass of writhing rodent flesh advanced upon him with snapping teeth and scuttling claws.

"Come on, let's get him before he's torn to shreds!" I shouted.

As I threw open the front door, Scratch leaped in front of me, blocking our path. "Let me go with you two," the familiar pleaded. "I can get there faster."

Hexe nodded and Scratch jumped over the threshold and with a couple flaps of his wings shot into the air, soaring past the roof of the boardinghouse.

Hexe and I hurried in the direction of Rutger Street, dodging fellow pedestrians as we tried to keep an eye on the hairless cat flying high over our heads. As we crossed Perdition, I spotted a narrow opening between a tenement building and the Stagger Inn, an establishment that catered to the harder drinkers of Golgotham, which was saying something. The passageway was barely wide enough to allow two adults to walk side by side, and was far too narrow to accommodate a centaur, with or without a carriage.

With its rusty fire escapes and clotheslines full of drying laundry hanging overhead, Snuff Alley looked no different than it had a century ago, or the century before that. And judging from the stench coming from the overflowing garbage cans that lined both sides of the alley, that was also the last time the sanitation department had paid a visit.

"I see them!" Scratch called out from his vantage

point high above. "They're twenty yards in, on the left-hand side!"

I charged down Snuff Alley without a thought as to what might be lurking in the shadows. All that mattered at that moment was that my dog was in trouble and needed my help. Then I saw the rat king.

What I had glimpsed in the scrying crystal had been awful enough, but it was nothing compared to seeing the creature in the flesh. It was composed of at least a dozen Norwegian rats, arranged in an outward-facing circle. The long, hairless tails of the individual rodents were tightly braided together, creating the hub of a wheel, of which each rat was a spoke. No matter what direction you looked at it, the rat king was nothing but snarling, snapping heads with razor-sharp teeth and filthy claws, and it was impossible to sneak up on.

"Get away from my dog, you bastards!" I shouted, snatching a discarded bottle from a nearby trash can and chucking it at the writhing mass of fur and fangs.

I expected the rat king to react to my attack the same way a normal rodent would, by scurrying off to the nearest hidey-hole. Instead, the wheel of rats came whirling toward me like a lazy Susan from hell, squealing and gnashing its myriad teeth in anger.

"Let me at 'em!" Scratch snarled, tucking his wings in and dropping from the sky like a hawk going after a rabbit. The familiar nimbly zipped through the maze of crisscrossing laundry lines like a barnstorming stunt pilot and sank his talons into the rat king's knotted tail. The verminous abomination shrieked in alarm, its squeals melding into one voice, as Scratch snatched the creature off the ground.

The familiar flapped up into the air again, the rat king swinging back and forth beneath him like the clapper of a bell. Once Scratch landed atop the roof of a nearby tenement, the screams of the rat king as its individual members met their fate echoed throughout Snuff Alley.

I rushed forward and pushed aside one of the garbage cans, revealing a shivering Beanie. He was covered in filth and badly frightened, but seemed otherwise unharmed. The moment he saw me he jumped up onto his hind legs, waving his little paws in the air. I snatched him up and buried my face in his fur, unmindful of the smell.

"Don't you *ever* scare Mommy like that again!" I scolded the squirming wad of puppy as he licked the relieved tears from my face.

"You can really haul ass—you know that?" Hexe panted as he jogged up to join me. "One second you were standing on the street; the next you were halfway down the alley!"

"I guess my maternal instinct kicked into drive," I replied.

"Overdrive is more like it. Is he okay?"

"You tell me," I said, handing Beanie to him so I could wipe the puppy kisses from my face.

"He seems to be unhurt, but— Hey, that tickles!" Hexe laughed as Beanie started licking his ears by way of greeting. "Phew! He's definitely getting a B-A-T-H when we get home!"

"'And they all lived nauseatingly ever after,'" Scratch said sarcastically as he made a four-point landing, a still writhing length of tail hanging from the corner of his mouth like an errant strand of spaghetti. "Don't everyone thank me at once for saving your stupid dog."

"You know this little guy means a lot to me," I said, kneeling so that I was face-to-face with the familiar. "I owe you one, Scratch."

The winged cat looked at my outstretched hand for a long second, and then stepped forward, butting the top of his head against my palm. His skin was warm and smooth to the touch, like a living chamois cloth.

"Hey, he's *my* pet, too," he purred.

Later that night I lay in bed and stared up at the dragon painted on the ceiling. Hexe was asleep next to me, his tousled purple head resting on my breast. The warmth of his body pressed against mine was comforting after everything we'd recently endured. Despite today easily qualifying as one of the worst of my life, I felt oddly at peace.

All my life I had felt somewhat ... detached ... from my family. I'm not sure whether the fault for that lies with me or my parents. It's not that I don't love them. I do. And I know that they love me, in their own fucked-up way. But when it comes to understanding and accepting one another—that's a different story.

Being an artist isn't the easiest thing in the world. It's more like a genetic disposition than anything I have conscious control over. I can't stop being an artist any more than I can stop being allergic to grapefruit. But my parents have always viewed it as some sort of deliberate act of defiance, done simply to get under their skin. And, to be honest, sometimes it was. But I never set out to be a sculptor simply to piss them off. I've given up on them ever understanding me. And I would be okay with that, if only they could just accept me for what I am.

I'd never experienced much in the way of acceptance, outside of Nessie and Clarence, my family's butler. All my boyfriends before Hexe had certainly fallen short in that regard. Most of them thought my claiming to be an artist was the upper-class version of being a welfare cheat—a way for me to shirk adult responsibilities while giving the finger to my family. In the end, they viewed me no differently than my parents did, really.

But Hexe ... Hexe had accepted me for who and what I was, including my art, right from the start. He'd never once complained about the noise I made when working on my sculptures, or the sparks generated by my welding equipment. And he would be well within his rights to do so, because what I do is sure as fuck loud and dangerous. But he doesn't seem to care. Hell, it seems to make him *happy.*

I glanced down at the foot of the bed, where Beanie, freshly bathed and exhausted from his misadventures, lay sound asleep. He was curled up toes-to-nose and snoring like an adorable little buzz saw. There was a flapping sound and a second later Scratch appeared, perched atop the footboard.

"I just finished the perimeter check," the familiar whispered. "The warding spells Hexe erected are still holding strong. Courtier or not, that demon's not getting back in here."

"Might as well turn in for the night, then," I said, pulling the bedclothes about Hexe and myself. "Good night, Scratch."

"G'night, Tate," the familiar replied as he hopped down onto the foot of the bed next to Beanie, draping his right wing over the sleeping puppy like a mother hen protecting her chick. "See you in the morning."

I'm riding on a cart alongside Gus as Bayard slowly clip-clops through the early-morning fog. I glance up at the sky, in search of the sun, but all I see is gray.

"Where are we going?" I ask, but neither replies.

"I asked them the same question," a strange man's voice says from behind me. "And I got the same response

as you did." I look over my shoulder and see a Kymeran man with apricot-colored hair and a Vandyke beard sitting in the back of the wagon. Although I do not know him, he seems familiar. "Part of me is relieved they won't answer," the stranger says. "I think if they talk to me, it means I'm dead."

"Do I know you?" I ask. "I have the funny feeling we've met before. . . ."

"My name is Jarl," the stranger replies. "I am an alchemist." He gestures to the floor of the wagon, at the copper dragon curled at his feet. The creature regards me with eyes made of flame, steam rising from its nostrils. I do not feel fear or surprise upon seeing the beast, but, instead, a strange sense of connection. Somehow I know the creature will not harm me. Jarl reaches into the pocket of his coat and removes an egg and shows it to the copper dragon, which opens its mouth to receive it.

I turn back around and see a narrow alley before us, barely wide enough for the wagon to pass. There is a bright light at the other end. There is a figure standing at the far end, arms spread as if to block our path.

"This is my last favor!" the figure calls out. I recognize the voice as Quid's, although it sounds as if he's speaking from the bottom of a well. "The girl can go no farther!"

Gus nods his head and turns to speak to Jarl. "Tell her."

A look of dismay flickers across the alchemist's face, as if his worst fears have been confirmed. He glances at me and smiles sadly. "You have to wake up, Tate."

"Why?"

Jarl points at the narrow sliver of sky above our heads. I look up and see the shape of an approaching demon silhouetted against the fog.

*　　*　　*

I came up out of the dream like a swimmer escaping an undertow, gasping and flailing as if my life depended on it. I sat straight up in the bed, my senses strained to their limit. The clock on the bedside table told me it was just before dawn.

"What's wrong?" Hexe yawned as he rubbed the sleep from his eyes.

"Do you hear it?" I whispered.

There was something scratching at the shuttered window over the bed. A few seconds later the sound stopped, only to resume at the secured window in the bathroom.

Hexe threw aside the bedclothes. "It's heading for the roof," he said, pulling on a pair of pants.

Scratch raised his head and sniffed the air, pulling a still-snoring Beanie closer to him with his wing. The familiar's eyes narrowed to gun slits and he began a low, menacing growl as he tracked the sound of the intruder, his ears swiveling like radar dishes.

"Don't worry. I cast the strongest spells of protection possible on all the windows and doors," Hexe assured me.

A rattling sound came from the bedroom fireplace, followed by a tiny spill of displaced soot falling onto the hearth. "What about the chimney?" I asked.

Hexe bounded across the room, his right hand glowing, and fired a bolt of blinding-white magic into the grate. There was a whooshing noise, followed by an all-too-familiar squeal.

"I can't believe I overlooked the chimney," Hexe said, shaking his head in self-reproach. "It's a good thing you woke up when you did, Tate."

"Could that thing really fit down the flue?"

"Demons can make themselves as big or as small, as thick or as thin as necessary," he replied. "That's why it's important to seal every possible means of entry with protective wards, so they don't pour themselves through the keyhole or slip in through the mail slot."

"What do we do now?"

"We wait until cockcrow. If it hasn't fulfilled its mission by then, it must return to its master. And then it will return at the same time tomorrow, and so on, until it either succeeds at its task or is returned to the Infernal Court by whoever summoned it. Now that you know that, are you *still* sure you want to remain in Golgotham?"

I wrapped my arms about him, pressing my head against his bare chest. "If my mother can't scare me into leaving, what chance does a demon have?"

Chapter 23

While Hexe's spells might have been able to keep a demon at bay, they were unable to do the same in regard to my parents, who showed up at the boarding-house bright and early, looking even more ill at ease than they had at the hospital.

"I hope you're satisfied," my mother said as she bulldozed her way across the threshold, my father in tow. "I had to look at some horse's ass all the way over here."

"I must admit, our cabbie had a fine set of hocks on him," my father said appreciatively. "Reminded me of this polo pony I had, back in college—"

"This is neither the time nor the place for you to reminisce about your days on the Harvard polo field, Timothy," my mother said sharply, cutting him off before he could launch into another of his rambling stories. "Good heavens, Timmy—what possessed you to live in such a tacky dump?"

"Sounds like the taxi driver wasn't the only one with a horse's ass, if you ask me."

"Who said that?!?" my mother gasped.

"*I* did," Scratch said, emerging from behind the purple sofa. He eyed my mother as if sizing her up for a takedown. "Wanna make something of it, nump?"

My mother instinctively recoiled, but quickly regained her sense of outrage. "Timmy! Your cat just insulted me to my face!"

"Hang around long enough, and I'll insult the rest of you, too," the familiar sneered. "Oh, and by the way, I'm *not* a cat. And even if I *was* a cat, I wouldn't belong to *her*. No offense, Tate."

"None taken. Mother, this is Scratch—he is Hexe's, um, ah . . ."

"Call him what he is, sweetheart," Hexe said as he came downstairs to join us. I noticed he was freshly groomed and dressed in a dark turtleneck sweater and corduroy pants instead of his normal scruffy jeans and ironic T-shirt. "Scratch is my familiar, Mrs. Eresby. He is both my servant and my friend. Allow me to take this opportunity to welcome both of you to my home. Please, make yourselves comfortable; do sit down."

"That won't be necessary," my mother replied. "We won't be staying long." She looked around the front parlor and scowled. "Where are your things, Timmy? I don't see any suitcases."

"That's because I'm not going anywhere," I replied, taking Hexe's hand. "As I told you yesterday, I'm staying in Golgotham."

Her scowl deepened even further. "Why would you want to live in such a backward place? The streets are full of horse-and-buggies and there are still gaslights on the corner!"

"You consider it 'backward'—I find it charming, and not simply because it's filled with witches and warlocks," I replied.

"Greenport is 'charming.' New Orleans is 'charming.'

Golgotham is a festering sewer filled with the dregs of society."

"You make that sound like it's a bad thing," Scratch wisecracked.

My mother spun on her heel and headed toward the front door. "That's it! I've had enough of this insanity! I refuse to stand here and be insulted by a naked cat!"

"I can go get dressed, if that would make you feel better."

"Scratch! Please be quiet!" Hexe barked in exasperation. "You're *not* helping!"

"I wasn't *trying* to. But since you insist—I will retire from the conversation. Good *day*, madam," the familiar sniffed as he unfurled his wings and flapped away.

"Now that all the talking animals have left the room," my mother said with a sigh of relief, "perhaps we can discuss things in a calm and adult manner."

"How so?" I countered. "There's nothing to discuss, Mother. I'm not leaving Hexe, nor am I moving out of Golgotham."

"Of all the selfish—! Your father and I didn't put you through the finest schools on the East Coast simply for you to throw your future away on some Kymie cursemonger!"

"What *did* you send me to school for, Mother?" I replied hotly. "Oh, that's right—a degree in fine arts! Are you saying you'd rather I be an artist than be in love with a Kymeran? Oh, and for your information: Hexe doesn't deal in curses!"

My mother held up a hand, rolling her eyes in disgust. "*Please!* That's like saying a bank only opens checking accounts and never handles foreclosures!"

"Despite what you might believe, not every Kymeran practices Left Hand magic, Mrs. Eresby," Hexe said, using the long-suffering tone of voice he usually reserved for his more difficult clients. "I do not inflict curses or engage in what is commonly known as 'black magic,' as that would weaken my ability as a healer and worker of white magic."

"Save it for someone who'll believe you, Merlin," my mother sneered. "You talk a good game—I'll grant you that. You clearly have my daughter snowed. But if you think you're going to worm your way into the Eresby family fortune, you're sadly mistaken! And as for *you*, young lady," she said, jabbing a finger at me, "if you want to play haunted house with your boy toy here, you're going to find out just how much fun living together *isn't* when you have to support yourself *and* him on whatever paycheck you can scrounge with that blessed fine arts degree of yours. Because, as of right now, you're cut off *completely* from your trust fund. No more quarterly payments. Nada. Zip. Zilch."

"Mr. and Mrs. Eresby, I can understand why you would be dubious as to my intentions concerning your daughter," Hexe said earnestly. "But I want to assure you I have no interest in her money. I fell in love with Tate long before I learned who she 'really' was. She could be as poor as the lowliest beggar, and I would still feel the same way about her. I love her for *who* she is, not *what* she has."

"Oh, please—don't hand me that 'true love' bullshit," she snorted. "That mother of yours is behind all this!"

"My mother—?" Hexe frowned in bafflement. "What does *she* have to do with any of this?"

"As if you don't know," she replied sourly. "Look, can't you go spin straw into gold, or whatever the hell it is you people do? I would like to be able to speak to my daughter alone, if you don't mind."

"Honey, why don't you show Daddy the garden?" I suggested helpfully. "I'm sure he'll find it interesting."

"You've got a backyard?" my father asked, his eyebrows arching in surprise. "In *this* neighborhood?"

"Appearances can be deceiving in Golgotham, Mr. Eresby," Hexe replied as he led my father to the back door.

"So why did you want Hexe out of the room?" I asked. "Believe me, there's nothing you can say in private that will change my mind." As I turned back to face my mother, I saw her take what looked like a truncated blowpipe from her Hermès handbag. Before I could ask her what she was doing, she put one end to her mouth and suddenly I was enveloped in a thick cloud of white powder.

"What the hell—?!?" I coughed as the fine, chalky substance shot up my nose and filled my mouth. My eyes instantly started to burn and well with tears. Despite being momentarily blinded, I was still able to find my way to the half-bath under the staircase. "What are you chuffin' doing, Mom?" I snapped, splashing water on my face.

"It's okay, Timmy—it's just a love potion counteragent," my mother said reassuringly. "There's nothing to be worried about—you're free now! Quick, run upstairs and get your things before he comes back! Your father and I will make sure you get out of here safely!"

"Holy crap, what is *wrong* with you?" I spat as I wiped the reversing powder from my swollen eyes. "I'm *not* under a spell! Hexe didn't slip me a love potion or cast a come-hither over me! I'm *really* in love with the guy! And it's because he's a *good* man who understands me and accepts me for who I am!"

Instead of looking contrite, my mother merely sighed and shook her head in disappointment. "I should have known this stuff wouldn't work. That's what I get for buying off the Internet. Well, spells4less1965 can kiss their four-star seller recommendation good-bye after I get through with them!"

"Damn it, Mom! Didn't you hear what I just said?"

"Of *course* I did, Timmy." she said, rolling her eyes. "And I might've believed you, if I didn't know his mother."

"Yeah, *about* that . . ." I said, fixing her with a suspicious stare. "Exactly how *do* you know Lady Syra?"

She gave a short, humorless bark of a laugh. "'Lady'? Is *that* what she calls herself now?"

Now it was my turn to roll my eyes. "Mom, where have you been? She's the best-known Kymeran in the country. She has rock stars and billionaires as clients. She's the official astrologer for the president, for crying out loud!"

"I realize your generation is plugged in to the 'information superhighway' like a toaster, but you know I don't read anything outside the society pages."

"For crying out loud! What did you do—buy a love potion from her?"

Instead of making her usual catty remark, my mother abruptly fell silent and dropped her gaze to the floor. While I have seen my mother a good many things in my lifetime, this was the first time I'd ever seen her chagrined.

"Oh. My. God."

Just then my father hurried back into the room, his eyes gleaming with excitement. "Millie! You simply *have* to see the backyard! It's *amazing*! It's at least an acre lot—in *downtown*!"

"I don't care if he's got the gardens of Versailles back there!" she snapped, quickly regaining her composure. "I'm ready to go home, Timothy. There's nothing more we can do here."

My father glanced at me, an uneasy look on his face. "Are you certain about that, Millicent?"

"She says she's made her mind up," my mother replied, tucking her purse firmly under her arm. "I think she's old enough to live with the consequences of her decisions. Don't you?"

My father shrugged and walked to the front door, patiently holding it open for my mother, as he had for as long as I could remember. She paused to cast a final look at me over her shoulder.

"Everyone likes to say 'All you need is love.' But the man who wrote that song was also a multimillionaire. See if you still feel the same way a year or two from now."

I stood on the front stoop and watched my parents hurry back to their waiting cab—my mother walking with a quick, measured stride that indicated she was in no mood to talk to anyone, especially my father. She held her head high, doing her best not to look at the other pedestrians crowding the streets, but there was no disguising her distaste, especially in regard to the centaurs and other half-beasts. Funny, I had never realized she harbored such an abhorrence for farm animals before now. No doubt Clarence would be burning another bundle of designer clothes this evening in the penthouse incinerator.

All my life, my parents had held the family fortune over my head like a golden sword of Damocles. They weren't unique in that, though. All the families in my peer group used money to control their children. And it worked, too. Most of the kids I grew up with viewed Upper-Middle Class as no different than Working Poor—and would do whatever was necessary to keep the trust funds flowing.

Still, I had grown up being told that Not Being Rich was the worst thing that could happen—with the Apocalypse a close second. As the realization that I was on my own without a safety net began to really sink in, I experienced a quick stab of panic, as if someone had slipped a stiletto between my ribs. For the briefest moment I was tempted to chase after my parents and beg their forgiveness like a frightened five-year-old. But then Hexe joined me on the stoop, sliding his arm about my waist, and my self-doubt disappeared as swiftly as it had arrived.

"Are you all right?" he asked gently.

"I'm as okay as I'm ever going to be," I said.

"I kind of like your dad. Your mom, on the other hand, is ... something else," he said diplomatically. "Now I understand why you've been so tolerant of *my* family."

"Every heaven help us next Thanksgiving," I groaned.

"So—how does it feel to be poor?"

"To tell you the truth, it's a little bit scary—but it's also kind of liberating." The Worst Thing That Could Ever Happen had finally occurred, and the ground hadn't swallowed me whole, the sun hadn't fallen out of the sky, and I was pretty sure the oceans hadn't dried up. My parents were determined to teach me a lesson, but I was just as determined to prove that I was capable of making it on my own, whether my bank account had six zeroes or just one.

"Well, you know what they say"—I grinned as I took Hexe by the hand and led him back into the house— "bed is the poor man's opera."

Chapter 24

Later that afternoon, after Hexe and I had staged our own private version of *Salome*, I sat down and studied my checkbook in the cold light of newly acquired penury. The knowledge that once I paid my outstanding bills there would be no further income for the foreseeable future put a damper on my previous high spirits.

There was no way around it—I was going to have to economize. And, as bad luck would have it, Beanie had run out of puppy food. That meant a trek outside of Golgotham to the only pet store I could easily walk to: a trendy, overpriced shop in Tribeca called Baskerville's.

I took the shopping cart out of the hallway closet, threw on my coat, and headed out the door. As I made my way toward Broadway, pulling the cart along behind me on its large back wheels, I found myself thinking about my mother and how she'd reacted when I joked about Lady Syra and the love potion. Now the joke had backfired on me, and it wasn't funny at all.

Nobody wants to imagine their parents "doing it." That's one of those things we all privately agree to ignore—like the amount of insect droppings allowed by law in our food—if we want to enjoy our lives as relatively functional individuals. We have hard evidence that our parents have had sex, since we ourselves exist, but no one wants to give too much contemplation as to exactly *how* that came about. Granted, the unexamined life is not worth living, but there *is* such a thing as Too Much Information.

Yet, despite this willful lacuna, we all want to believe that we were conceived in love. To think that we came into being as the result of a drunken fumble in a backseat and a torn rubber, or a sexual assault, or a calculated power play, diminishes us, as it rewrites our personal mythology from the ground up.

I will admit that I have often wondered why my parents were still together, given that most of their friends were on at least a second spouse, if not in the process of swapping out their third. I had always assumed there had been a time when they were truly in love with one another. But the thought that the only reason I existed was because my mother had sneaked a potion into my father's martini while he wasn't looking was a depressing one.

As I walked past the Emerald Spa, I glimpsed a special afternoon edition of the *Golgotham Gazette* on the newsstand. The headline read: SOA WITCH-BASHING VICTIM DIES OF INJURIES. Accompanying it was a photo of the slain alchemist, Jarl, taken in happier times. A cold finger traced its way between my shoulder blades as I recognized his face as that of the man with the apricot hair I'd seen in my dream earlier that morning, just before the demon tried to get inside the house.

It's funny how not having enough money makes you keenly aware of things you never noticed before. Like the price of dog food, for example. The last time I'd bought Beanie his puppy kibble at Baskerville's, I didn't really notice how much it cost, and I especially didn't notice the price on the large, twenty-pound bags. I just threw it in the cart, along with an armload of cute squeak toys, and took it to the checkout counter. There was no thinking about it; I just *did* it.

Now I found myself spending an inordinate amount of time staring at the price tag, then glancing at the slightly cheaper brands. On the one hand, I wanted to provide the best nutrition possible for Beanie, without detrimental by-products, so he would grow up to be healthy and strong; on the other hand, he's just a dog—how would he know the difference? Hell, he licks his own 'nads. But in the end I did the right thing and loaded the huge bag of expensive kibble into the cart. It made sense that keeping him healthy was a good investment, if it meant not having to make a lot of trips to the vet down the line. And if he got tired of this stuff—tough shit. He could buy something else with his dog dollars.

As I headed to the checkout counter, I glimpsed a familiar figure in the cat food section. It was none other than my downstairs neighbor—and fellow human—Aloysius Manto. He was standing in the middle of the aisle, studying the ingredients of a can of gourmet cat food, his thick reading glasses perched perilously close to the end of his long nose.

Mr. Manto was an oracle who, along with his brace of house cats, lived in the basement apartment of the boardinghouse, amid a jumble of books and magazines that would put most libraries to shame. But instead of being a bibliophile, Mr. Manto practiced a form of divination known as bibliomancy, which involved his taking pages from random books, tearing them into progressively smaller quarters, mixing them together, and then piecing them into prophecy, all while high as a kite. That's how he predicted my using my animated sculptures as an impromptu army in order to free Lukas from Boss Marz's fighting pit.

"Mr. Manto—what are you doing here?"

Instead of pushing his glasses into place, the oracle simply tilted his head farther back so that he could see who had addressed him. He was dressed, as always, in a pair of baggy men's trousers held up by leather suspenders, a frayed cable-knit cardigan, and a dress shirt with a tie so skinny it was anorexic. A dark gray fedora sat atop his head, hiding his balding scalp, so that all that was visible was the fringe of gray-white hair about his ears.

"Hello, my dear—good to see you again," he said in a sepulchral, Midwestern monotone. "As to what I am doing here, I frequent this establishment once a month to buy provisions for my krewe of feline confederates." He turned and dropped the can he had been studying into the shopping cart beside him, where it joined at least a dozen others. "They can be quite insistent when it comes to being fed." He smiled and gestured to the wolf-sized bag of kibble in my own basket. "I am pleased you've been reunited with the errant Beanie."

"How did you know—?" I rolled my eyes and gave my forehead a slap. "Duh."

"I'm afraid I didn't divine that particular bit of information," he said with a chuckle. "I know your puppy ran away because Scratch came knocking at my door in search of him. By the by, I was curious as to whether the rest of the prophecy has come to pass."

"What do you mean 'the rest of it'?" I frowned. "I thought it had already come true. You know, the part about the woman-forged army freeing the beasts."

"You mean '*rise shall a fire-born army forged of*

woman to the bestiarii free,'" the oracle said aloud in a stentorian monotone loud enough to make other shoppers look in our direction. "That was but a portion of what I divined. The rest goes as such: '*Drown will the streets the usurped in blood no mercy for his flesh show. From two will be one turned three. The hand is in the mind.*'" As he recited the remainder of the prophecy, our fellow pet owners began casting sidelong glances at us as if we'd escaped from a loony bin.

"I don't know if it's come true or not," I replied with a shrug. "But I'm pretty sure I'd remember streets full of blood, so I'm going to say it hasn't. But to tell you the truth, I haven't really given it much thought."

"It is the nature of prophecies that one often does not remember or understand them until it is almost too late. That is because Fate resents attempts by mortals to pierce its veil, and is always trying to snatch back its mysteries by clouding the minds of man. But when the time comes, Apollo willing, the words of the prophecy will come to you, and you shall understand their meaning."

As I turned to go, leaving the old oracle to his shopping, a thought suddenly crossed my mind. "Mr. Manto . . . how can you tell the difference between a dream and a vision?"

"That's a good question," he said, tapping his upper lip with a bony forefinger. "In my experience, dreams come from within, and are triggered by something you have experienced or are concerned about. They are the result of your subconscious speaking to you, using symbols that hold special meaning for you, and the outcome of which you control on a certain level. A vision, however, comes from without, and you have no power over when it begins or ends, or the symbolism it uses to communicate its meaning. Dreams are often a rehash of things that have gone before, while visions give insights as to things yet to come, or attempt to reveal knowledge otherwise hidden from you."

"Does it mean anything if I see dead people in these dreams or visions?"

The oracle raised an eyebrow. "Have you lost anyone recently? A family member or close friend, perhaps?"

"I know three people who have died in the last week or so, actually. One of them quite horribly. I barely knew two of them—but, yes, I would call them friends." I then described what I had seen in both of my dreams. When I'd finished, the oracle nodded sagely.

"It makes sense that your friends were capable of talking directly to you the first time, but incapable of speaking in the second," he said. "The longer the dead are departed from the material world, the harder it is for them to speak directly to the living. When they try to do so, it usually comes out garbled. That's why most people have to use a spirit medium to communicate with those who have been deceased for more than a couple of days. Tell me—were you prone to such dreams before you moved to Golgotham?"

"No, never."

"Very interesting. When we first met, I thought perhaps you had a touch of the uncanny in you. Many artistic types do, you know. That's why people like Picasso, Mozart, and Fellini were fascinated by Kymeran culture—it resonated with them. It's also why humans with abilities such as mine—oracles, mediums, dowsers, and the like—have made our homes here. Being surrounded by magic strengthens our gifts. My powers are far stronger here than anywhere else I ever lived, including New Orleans. And that's saying something."

"That's all very interesting, Mr. Manto—but what does it mean?"

"Isn't it obvious, my dear?" the oracle replied, blinking his rheumy eyes in surprise. "You're being warned that whoever murdered your friends is trying to kill you, too."

Chapter 25

"Are you *sure* he wasn't tripping when he told you that?" Hexe said with a frown. He was seated at the desk in his office, poring over an old manuscript for hints on banishing demons.

"No. But would it make any difference if he was? You know him better than I do."

"You're right," he agreed. "Aloysius comes from a long line of oracles, and is exceptionally gifted. That's why my grandfather allowed him to move into the basement, fifty years ago. He said all Witch Kings need an oracle, and there wasn't one better than Mr. Manto. I know my mother still consults with him now and again, as well. If Aloysius says Quid, Gus, and Bayard were murdered, and all by the same person, then it must be true."

"But it doesn't make any sense," I protested, as I flopped down in the chair opposite his desk. "We *know* who killed Quid. Those Sons of Adam assholes beat him to death on YouTube for the whole world to see. But those knuckle-draggers don't seem to have the smarts to do something as subtle as arranging for Bayard's hot shot. And ever since the riot, most Golgothamites have become a lot more sensitive to humans hanging around, so I can't imagine these bozos being able to get close enough to Gus to throw him into the river, no matter *how* drunk he might have been. Plus, why would they go out of their way to take credit for attacking Jarl and Quid, but make Bayard and Gus's deaths look like accidents? It doesn't seem to be their style."

"I agree," Hexe said thoughtfully. "And what do they have to do with the demon? We'd originally assumed it was sent as retaliation for you being a spy. Dori's claims that she sold the binding amulet that the demon dropped to a Kymeran with a KUP pin seem to confirm that suspicion. But if what Mr. Manto says is true . . . I just can't see this Cain fellow paying to have a sorcerer summon something as dangerous—and pricey—as a Knight of the Infernal Court. And even if he *did* do all that, why would he sic it on a fellow human? Last time I checked, the SOA was in the Kymeran-hating business."

"I don't know," I admitted with a sigh. "Maybe Cain knows me—or thinks he does, anyway. I told you that I had a funny feeling I'd seen his face before. Maybe he's someone I went to school with. Or he works for my family in some capacity. But one thing I am certain of—all this has something to do with the favor I paid back to Quid. I never would have met Bayard and Gus otherwise. It's the only thing that makes any sense. But it still doesn't explain Jarl. I'd never spoken to him while he was alive, and the only time I'd seen him in the flesh, his face was pounded to hamburger. So how would I have known what he looked like in my dream if it wasn't a vision?"

"But Jarl *was* attacked by the same people who killed Quid," Hexe pointed out. "That's the only connection we have. What was Jarl doing in your vision?"

"Well, some of it was kind of weird, like a regular dream. Like him feeding eggs to a dragon, for example."

Instead of laughing, Hexe sat up straighter in his seat.

"What's the matter?" I asked. "Does that mean anything?"

"I hope not," he said grimly. "Dragons are the symbol of the royal family. We should visit Jarl's widow, Ruby, and ask her a few questions to find out if there was a connection of any sort between her husband and Quid outside of their being attacked by the same men. We'll need to bring a token of our respect for the departed."

"You mean flowers or a wreath? It's too late in the year for something from the garden, I'm afraid," I pointed out. "But we can stop by a florist's on the way."

"Kymerans don't use flowers to honor the dead," Hexe said, stepping out into the backyard. I watched, perplexed, as he knelt down and dug about in one of the plant beds until he found a walnut-sized piece of rock. "Flowers die. Stone, however, lasts for eternity."

According to the latest edition of the *Golgotham Pages*, a comprehensive listing of the various sorcerers, witches, and other practitioners who offered their skills for sale, Jarl had operated out of his home on Pearl Street, located between Dover and Ferry Streets, near Pickman's Slip. The neighborhood was composed largely of Kymerans and leprechauns, who lived in tightly packed tenement buildings within easy walking distance of the Rookery.

It was already dark by the time we arrived at Jarl's apartment. Hexe pressed the smudged button on one of the call boxes outside the building, and was rewarded a few seconds later by a corresponding buzz from the front door. He swung it open, ushering me ahead of him.

The foyer of the tenement was cramped, with scuffed tile floors and an ornate pressed-tin ceiling that dated back to when whalebone stays were all the rage. Since Jarl's widow lived on the third floor, and there was no elevator, we had to climb the unlighted staircase that penetrated the middle of the building. The steps were clad in marble, which had been worn down in the middle by generations of passing feet.

Each narrow landing had four doors opening onto it, and from behind them could be heard a jumbled mix of muted voices, loud music, and rattling pipes. The smell of Kymeran cooking was so thick you could literally see it coiling about in the uncirculated air like a phantom octopus. As we reached the second floor, we had to squeeze to one side to allow a nymph dressed in a Hooters uniform to hurry down the stairs.

The dead alchemist's apartment was one that looked out onto the street, and was easily identified by the black crepe wreath hung just below the transom. Hexe knocked on the door and a few seconds later we heard the dead bolts being unlocked. The door opened a few inches and I glimpsed Jarl's widow, Ruby, peering out anxiously at us. She looked even sadder than the last time I'd seen her. Her violet-colored eyes widened at the sight of Hexe standing in the hall. She gasped and quickly shut the door again. There was the sound of more unlocking, and then the door swung open.

"You honor our home, Serenity," Ruby said.

The first thing I noticed as I entered the apartment was the bathtub in the kitchen. Wedged between an ancient Kelvinator and an antique woodstove, it was made of cast iron and had claw feet, like the ones in the boardinghouse. A large wooden lid covered the tub, converting it into a tabletop, across which was scattered a collection of beakers, crucibles, mortars, and pestles. The walls of the kitchen were lined with shelves on which stood numerous glass jars containing everything from arsenic to zinc. Just beyond the stove was a pair of pocket doors that sealed the rest of the living space off from the combination kitchen and alchemist's laboratory.

"Madame Ruby, on behalf of the royal family, I would like to extend my sincerest condolences on the loss of your husband," Hexe said softly, handing her the rock from his garden.

"Thank you, Serenity," she whispered, cupping it in her hands as if it were a precious stone.

The pocket doors slowly rumbled open, pushed apart by invisible hands, revealing a large living space that seemed to serve as both parlor and bedroom. The far wall was composed of tall windows that looked out onto Pearl Street. A wind chime fashioned from bits of crystal hung from one of them, advertising Ruby's job as a shaper of scrying stones. One side of the room had been lofted to create a sleeping platform, with an overstuffed divan wedged underneath. On the opposite wall was a modest fireplace set with green tiles. Judging from the other chunks of rock that lined the antique oak mantelpiece, we weren't the first to come pay our respects.

"When is the funeral?" Hexe asked.

"It's scheduled three days from now," she replied. "It would have been sooner, but I couldn't afford the barge to Necropolis until this afternoon. Your uncle was kind enough to step forward and pay the ferryman on my behalf."

"That was . . . considerate of him," Hexe said carefully.

"Please excuse my ignorance," I interjected, "but wasn't Jarl an alchemist? Didn't that mean he could create his own gold?"

"That is a common misunderstanding when it comes to alchemy," Ruby said with a sad smile. "People wonder why most alchemists aren't rich. They don't realize it requires a ton of lead to create a quarter ounce of gold. Besides, Jarl's gift didn't lie in transmutation of base metals. He specialized in producing the rare ingredients used in various potions, and dabbled in panacea and elixir vitae. His clients were other Kymerans—that's why he didn't bother setting up shop in the Rookery."

"Madame Ruby, I am truly sorry to intrude upon you at this time, but it's very important that I ask you a few questions about your husband's business."

"That's all right, Serenity." She smiled wanly. "If not for the aid you and Ms. Eresby rendered that night, Jarl would have died on the street. Ask me whatever questions you need to, and I'll do my best to answer them."

"Did your husband happen to know the favor broker Quid?"

"Yes, they knew each other," Ruby replied, nodding her head. "In fact, Jarl had just repaid his favor to him."

Hexe and I exchanged knowing looks. The connection between the others and the alchemist was finally becoming clear. "How so?"

"Jarl told me he could discharge the favor he owed Quid by drawing up blueprints for a piece of alchemical equipment for one of his clients."

"Did Jarl say anything about what he was working on?"

Ruby shook her head. "You know the code. 'No questions asked; no stories told.'"

"Yes, but that oath died with Quid," Hexe said gently.

"I really don't have much information," she replied. "But I do remember him being uncomfortable about the project. He said there was no sane reason for the device to be the size the client wanted."

"Do you have any idea what sort of apparatus he might have been working on?"

"No, but I *did* accidentally walk in on him while he was at his worktable," she said, gesturing to the covered bathtub. "He rolled the blueprint up, so I couldn't get a good look. But whatever it was, it had a dragon's head."

"That freaky still I built for Quid's client—that *has* to be the thing Jarl designed," I said excitedly as we left the tenement building. "It makes sense. It was made out of copper, and it had a dragon's head and a lion's feet. That's why the dragon I saw in the vision was copper. It still doesn't explain why Jarl was feeding it eggs, though."

"Eggs are a symbol of life, of fertility," Hexe mused aloud, as we headed back in the direction of the boardinghouse. "They also represent creative potential. But the language of visions isn't the same as dreams. What you saw could have any number of interpretations. When we get back to the house, I'll use one of the scrying stones to look into your past. If I can get a glimpse of the 'freaky still' you constructed, maybe I can figure out its purpose, and how it's related to everything that's happened in the last week or so."

"Are you going to call Captain Horn and tell him what we've learned?" I asked.

"He's far more likely to take murder clues revealed in dreams seriously than your average police officer, but I suspect he'll still need something closer to hard evidence to take action," Hexe pointed out. "But at least he will be able to reopen the investigations into Gus and Bayard's deaths. Someone went out of their way to make them seem unrelated, and I want to know why."

As we turned the corner onto Beekman Street, a man suddenly stepped out of a shadowy doorway, blocking our path. He was dressed all in black, from his hoodie jacket to his steel-toed boots. As he raised a lit cigarette to his lips, I could see that his hand had five fingers.

"What do you think you're doing with one of our women, Kymie?" the stranger growled.

"I'm not 'your' woman, asshole!" I snapped. "Who do you think you are to talk to us like that?"

"I am Cain, first among the Sons of Adam," he replied, pushing back the hood to reveal his face. "And my brothers and I plan to teach this Kymie bastard to keep his filthy hands off human women."

As Hexe put himself between me and the terrorist leader, I saw two more figures step out of the shadows behind us. They were dressed identically to Cain, save for the black ski masks hiding their faces, and all I could see were their eyes, which seemed to shine like those of wild animals. As they hefted their weapons, I saw Quid's dried blood smeared along the tips and barrels of the bats.

Hexe spoke in Kymeran, raising his right hand to cast a stasis spell, like the one he'd used during the riot. There was a quick burst of light, like that of a flash camera, but instead of becoming a living statue, Cain merely laughed and blew a plume of cigarette smoke into Hexe's face.

"Better check on lover boy," he sneered. "I don't think he's all there."

I touched Hexe's forearm and he abruptly pitched backward on his heels, right hand still upraised. He was as immobile as a department-store mannequin, and about as easy to maneuver as I lowered him to the pavement.

"What did you do to him, you chuffer?" I demanded, cradling Hexe's head in my lap.

"Nothing that he wasn't trying to do to me first," Cain

chuckled. The amusement quickly disappeared from his face and he grabbed me by the hair, yanking me back onto my feet. "So much for your warlock fuck-buddy. You're going to be partying with *us* now, bitch. We'll show you how *real* men do things." He tightened his grip on my hair until it felt as if my scalp was being torn free of my skull. As Cain brought his face close to mine, I could see his hair was going gray at the temples, although his features seemed oddly smooth and unlined, as if he had never laughed, frowned, or cried throughout his life. In strange counterbalance, his eyes burned with a focused energy composed of equal parts malice, exhilaration, and lust. It was like looking at someone wearing a mask.

"I wanted to taste you from the moment I first saw you," Cain whispered hoarsely. "I could have placed you under a come-hither anytime I wanted, and neither you nor your precious warlock prince would have had a clue. But I did not want to pollute myself through fornication. However, that is not a concern with *this* body. . . ."

Suddenly his mouth was on mine, his tongue plunging down my throat. It was strangely cold, more like a piece of dead meat than a living thing, and it writhed like a slug. Summoning all my strength, I raked the side of his face with my fingernails hard enough to draw blood. He bellowed in pain and let go of my hair. I staggered backward, wiping my mouth in disgust on the back of my arm, only to be punched in the pit of the stomach by one of his ski-masked "brothers." I dropped to my knees, gasping like a landed fish on the bottom of a rowboat.

"I should have expected as much from a chuffing race traitor," Cain growled. Blood seeped from four deep gouges on the right side of his face. "You could have had some fun, but now you're going to get the same as your boyfriend."

He motioned to his confederates, who began to attack Hexe's prone body, still frozen in stasis, kicking him with their steel-toed boots and clubbing him with their bats.

"Leave him alone!" I shouted at his attackers as I struggled back to my feet. I launched myself onto the one closest to me, punching and kicking as hard as I could as I tried to wrench the bat from his hands. He didn't seem to notice me at all until I made a grab for his ski mask, and then he turned and punched me. I shook my head to clear it, spat out a mouthful of blood, and leaped right back in again. The second time I managed to yank the bat out of the bastard's hands.

"Get rid of her!" Cain snapped angrily.

The faceless SOA member lunged at me with the quickness of a cobra strike, grabbing me by the throat. I clawed at his hands, trying to pull his fingers away from my trachea, but his grip was like iron. As he strangled me, I looked into the eyes behind the mask and saw— nothing. There was no hate, no anger, no fear, not even annoyance. Instead his gaze was as blank as that of a cow chewing its cud. Suddenly a beer bottle came flying through the air and bounced off my attacker's head. The SOA member let go of my throat and staggered backward, giving me time to run to the dozen Wee Folk gathered across the street. I was never so happy to see a bunch of pissed-off, drunken leprechauns in my life.

"Oi! Leave the lassie be, nump!" Seamus O'Fae barked as he shouldered his way to the head of the pack. "You bastards picked the wrong neighborhood to pull this shite in!"

Another leprechaun, whom I recognized as Tullamore, stepped forward. "Let me handle this, Seamus! I'll teach these blackguards to come witch-bashing in our neck of Golgotham!" He pointed his shillelagh at

Cain. *"May you feast on hogwash and sleep in filth; may you root with your nose as the farmer till'th!"*

There was another flash of light, and suddenly there was no more Tullamore. In his place was a tiny piglet dressed in a green vest and breeches, frantically running around in circles in the middle of the street, squealing at the top of its lungs.

"The buggers are wearing reflectors, boyos!" Seamus shouted, brandishing his shillelagh. "We're gonna have to settle this *bataireacht* style!"

With voices united in a shared battle cry of *"Faugh a Ballagh!"* the leprechauns rushed to meet their foe. The masked Sons of Adam found themselves suddenly overwhelmed by a swarm of angry redheaded men the size of infants, armed with weighted cudgels. The thugs tried to swat them with their larger baseball bats, but the little men in green were too fast for them.

I was so fascinated by the sight of the Sons of Adam disappearing under a living carpet of leprechauns thumping away with their shillelaghs for all they were worth, I lost track of Cain—until I was struck from behind with a baseball bat.

I rolled over and saw, through a bloodred haze, Cain looming over me. "You should have listened when I told you to leave Golgotham!" he spat as he raised the aluminum bat over his head.

Suddenly the weapon was yanked from his grasp as if pulled by an invisible wire. It flew through the air—to land in Hexe's right hand. He stood slouched against a nearby wall, as bruised and bloodied as a prizefighter. "Get away from her!" he yelled, raising the bat for emphasis. "Don't you *dare* touch her again!"

Faced with an unfrozen Hexe and a small army of hopping-mad leprechauns, Cain turned and fled. His fellow Sons of Adam frantically shook off their diminutive attackers and moved to follow their leader. The first of the two managed to escape fairly quickly, but the second had trouble freeing himself from Seamus O'Fae, who was riding his shoulders piggyback while banging on his skull like a cobbler.

The minute his "brothers" were no longer in sight, the Son of Adam began to wail, more like an animal in pain than any sound a human would make, and run in circles, clawing at his pint-sized tormentor, before dashing in the direction of Pearl Street. Seamus, realizing the terrorist was running into traffic, jumped free seconds before he darted out in front of a Teamster hauling a heavy cart.

The Clydesdale-sized centaur instinctively reared onto his hindquarters, striking at the air with his forelegs. The Son of Adam fell to the cobblestones, his head split open by the Teamster's flailing hooves.

"It was an accident! I swear!" the burly centaur exclaimed as we gathered around the dead body. "He ran right in front of me!"

I turned to Seamus O'Fae, who was dusting himself off. "Thank you," I said, offering my hand to the leprechaun. "I know I didn't get off on the best foot with your people, so I appreciate that you came to my rescue."

"As far as I'm concerned, lassie, yer one of us," Seamus replied as he shook my hand. "Ye've got brass, girl. Everyone knows how Esau toyed with ye at the rally."

"They do?" I winced.

"Aye. And they also know ye didn't pack yer bags and move out of Golgotham the first chance ye got. Not many folk—human or otherwise—would have the guts to burn out the eye of an Infernal Knight, neither. We could use a few more citizens with yer gumption, if ye ask me. Besides, I wasn't going to stand by and let those numps do in a fellow Golgothamite, if I could help it.

"Yer lucky me and my lads happened by when we did. We were on a pub crawl, celebrating the release of our brother, Tullamore. Earlier today I finalized a plea negotiation on his behalf. The felony enchantment charges were dropped down to a D and D, and he was given probation. Speaking of which, I best put him on a leash and get him to a lifter, as his probie is contingent on him abstainin' from turnin' folks into pigs for the next two years!"

"Thank every heaven!" Hexe exclaimed as he threw his arms about me. "Are you all right?"

"Forget me—look what they did to you!" I wailed in dismay at the sight of his blackened left eye and split lower lip. "We need to get you to the hospital!"

"It's nothing I can't tend to myself," he assured me as he knelt beside the fallen Son of Adam. "Right now I'm more interested in getting a good look at this bastard."

I gasped in surprise as Hexe peeled the ski mask away, not because I recognized the dead man as a famous actor or a well-known captain of industry, but because his face was identical to that of Cain, the SOA's leader.

"They must be twins," I marveled as I studied his face. "I guess he wasn't joking when he called his croggies 'brothers.' This one is starting to go gray about the temples, too."

"This one must be Abel, going by the letter *A* scrawled on the tag in his hoodie." Hexe reached down inside the dead man's shirt and tugged, removing an octagonal amulet covered in Kymeran script, the center of which contained a circular mirror. "That explains why they were brazen enough to attack us like they did. Reflector charms boomerang spells back onto whoever cast them. He's got at least a dozen of these things taped around his midsection like a girdle. So much for the Sons of Adam decrying the Kymerans and their magic."

I coughed and covered my nose and mouth with my hand, suddenly aware of an overpowering odor of putrefaction. "God, what is that stink?"

"It's coming from the body." Hexe grimaced in disgust. "It's already starting to bloat."

"How is that possible?"

"It's not ... unless ..." Hexe bent down and quickly unlaced one of Abel's steel-toed boots. When he pulled off the dead man's shoe, I was shocked to see a human-sized chicken's foot growing out of his ankle.

"Of course! It all makes sense now!" Hexe exclaimed.

"It does?" I frowned.

"This isn't a human—it's a homunculus!"

"A hom-knuckle—what?"

"Homunculus—or, rather, homunculi, seeing as how there were three of them. A homunculus is the by-product of *takwin*, a branch of alchemy that specializes in the creation of artificial life. It's a supernatural form of cloning. They're created by taking the sperm from a dead man and placing it inside the unfertilized egg of a black hen, then growing it within a special device called a maternal furnace. The result appears outwardly human, except for the feet."

My eyes lit up as I finally realized where it was I had seen Cain and his twin before. "*That's* where I know this guy from!" I exclaimed. "That's the exact same face as the dead man I saw in the warehouse loft! And I *wondered* what the fuck that chicken was doing hanging around. The reason the other two SOA wore ski masks was to hide the fact they're clones!"

"You mean this chuffin' idiot isn't a nump?" the centaur said with relief. "Praise Zeus! For a minute there, I was afraid my insurance was going to shoot sky-high!"

"Shouldn't we still notify the PTU?" I asked. "I mean, he *is* dead."

"Would you call the police to report a dead dog on the side of the road?" Hexe replied with a shrug. "Besides, in a few more minutes there won't be anything left of him *to* report."

I looked back down at Abel's body and nearly gagged. The dead man's skin had sloughed away, and the underlying muscle and bone were beginning to liquefy. Blood filled his eye sockets and poured from his open mouth and ears, like groundwater rising in a well. As the gore filled the gutter, I felt the hair along my arms and the back of my neck stand on end, and I heard Mr. Manto's sonorous voice echoing in my head.

Drown will the streets the usurped in blood no mercy for his flesh show.

The Teamster was so relieved that he didn't have to file paperwork with his insurance carrier that he offered to drop us off at the boardinghouse. Since neither one of us was in any condition to do a lot of walking, we eagerly accepted the ride.

"Homunculi are things, not living beings in their own right," Hexe continued to explain as the wagon jounced its way along the cobblestone streets. "They don't have minds or souls, and are utterly devoid of morals or conscience. That's why they're usually kept small—normally no larger than a fetus. Having a creature like that the size of a grown man is incredibly dangerous."

"If they're mindless, how is it Cain talks and gives orders?"

"Because it's not Cain who's doing the speaking," he replied. "No doubt their master is manipulating them via telepathy. It's also the reason only one of them speaks—it's difficult enough to control one puppet, much less three. Why spread yourself even thinner by throwing your voice through all of them? That's why Abel went berserk and ran out into the street—his master must have lost control of him during the melee with Seamus and his boys."

"It also explains why Cain spoke as if he knew me," I said uneasily.

"What did he say?"

I blushed as I repeated what Cain had said to me, even though I had nothing to be ashamed about. His words were so ugly, just speaking them was enough to make me shudder in revulsion.

"I'll kill him," Hexe said in a cold, hard voice. There was a grim look on his bruised and battered face I'd never seen before; that of a man on the verge of being pushed one step too far.

"No, you won't," I said firmly, putting my five-fingered hand atop his six-fingered one. "Because that's not the kind of man you are. Besides, we both know who's behind all this."

Hexe nodded, the look in his eyes growing even darker. When he spoke his uncle's name it sounded like a curse.

Chapter 26

The moment we got home, Hexe made a beeline for the kitchen. "I suspected Esau was behind the demon attacks from the start," he said as he took the tiny bottle of katholikon from the shelf over his workbench. "But it never once crossed my mind that he was behind the SOA." He carefully dispensed a dropperful of the foul-tasting panacea into a small glass, then added a dollop of honey and a couple tablespoons of black cherry syrup, finally topping it off with a squirt or two from an old-fashioned seltzer bottle. He turned and handed me the fizzing concoction. "Here—drink this."

I took a deep breath to steel myself and knocked back the potion. Even with the adjustments to render it palatable to human taste buds, it still went down like the cheapest rotgut whiskey. I blinked the tears from my eyes as the katholikon burned its way down my throat and settled in my gut. Within seconds I could feel the pain from my abused muscles and bruised bones fade, as if consumed by the fire burning in my belly. Once the stomach cramps subsided, I looked at myself in the mirror and saw the necklace of bruises around my throat fading out of sight.

"So what do you plan on doing?" I asked as I watched him fix a second glass of the horrid stuff for himself, this time mixing it with Worcestershire sauce and cod liver oil.

"I have to stop him, obviously," he replied, "before he orchestrates a full-scale race war."

"Hexe, you have to tell Captain Horn what you know. This is too big for just you to handle. He's responsible for killing at least four people."

"No, you don't understand," Hexe said with a vehement shake of his head. "The royal family handles its own. Besides, do you realize what would happen if anyone found out about his involvement in this? Esau isn't some Kymeran juggler peddling fast-luck soap and hard-on pills in Witch Alley! He's not only a member of the royal family—he would have been the Witch King if my grandfather hadn't disowned him.

"My family has worked for centuries to put the shadows of the Sufferance behind us, where they belong. If a descendant of Arum is revealed to be framing humans for the murder of Kymerans in order to trigger race riots, can you imagine the repercussions? Plus, if anyone finds out what he's done, it'll destroy my mother's career, as well as my own, not to mention set back human-Kymeran relationships a hundred years."

"'Drown will the streets the usurped in blood no mercy for his flesh show.' That's from Mr. Manto's prophecy," I explained. "I'm starting to understand what it means now. Esau is the 'usurped'—or, at least, that's how he sees himself. And he is determined to make you and your mother pay for his being denied the title of Witch King."

"We've got to destroy the maternal furnace that you fashioned for Esau, as well as the blueprints Jarl created for him," Hexe went on. "Somehow Esau has devised a means of speeding up the gestation time for homunculi. There were only a few days between you finishing work on the maternal furnace and the attack on Jarl. It probably accounts for their rapid aging as well. As soon as these are too old to be of use to him, he'll destroy them and start fresh. As long as he has that artificial womb, he'll have access to an army of mindless drones he can send out to do his bidding.

"Once we take care of destroying the maternal furnace, I can tell my mother what he's done. As justiciar of Golgotham, she has the power to have him arrested under sealed warrant, and as Witch Queen she has the ability to banish him from Golgotham. He'll end up spending the rest of his life in the Tombs or in exile; either way, he'll be out of our hair."

"Well, what are you waiting for?" I asked, pointing to the glass of katholikon. "Drink up. We've got some serious monkey-wrenching ahead of us tonight."

"Not without me you're not."

I looked up to see Scratch perched atop the refrigerator, his eyes glowing like twin stoplights. "How long have you been up there?"

"Long enough to know you two are not setting foot outside this house without me," the familiar replied.

"I appreciate your concern, old friend," Hexe said with a smile. "But I need you to stay behind. Esau has sent an infernal courtier to this house for the last two nights. I have no reason to believe he will stop. I need you here in case the demon gets in, to protect Lukas, Mr. Manto, and Beanie. It is my obligation as their landlord to make sure they come to no harm. Is that understood?"

Scratch scowled. "Yes. But I don't have to like it."

"Are you sure this is the right place?" Hexe whispered as he peered down the darkened alley.

"This is it. It dead-ends at the warehouse," I replied.

We joined hands and stepped into the pitch-black passageway. Hexe led the way, his catlike pupils better suited for such midnight excursions. A couple minutes later I could make out the faint outlines of the cramped courtyard at the back of the warehouse. Suddenly Hexe stepped back, pressing himself against the brick wall, and motioned for me to follow suit. Putting a finger to his lips, he pointed to Esau's familiar, Edgar, perched atop the roof, cleaning his feathers with his jet-black beak.

As I wondered how we could possibly get past the creature without it alerting its master, I heard a familiar squealing noise overhead, followed by the scrambling of numerous claws across shingles. Edgar gave an abrupt caw of delight and spread his ebony wings, flapping off in pursuit of a juicy rat king running across the rooftops of Pickman's Slip.

Hexe and I didn't waste any time exploiting our good luck. We hurried across the courtyard and were relieved to find the loading dock unlocked. The interior of the building was almost as dark as it was outside, but it didn't take me long to locate the stairway that led to the next story. As we reached the second floor, Hexe gasped in surprise upon seeing the metal arms lining the hallway. Although the glow from the witchfire torches dyed everything blue, and made our teeth and the whites of our eyes glow like irradiated pearls, it at least provided enough illumination for us to see where we were going.

As we opened the door at the end of the hallway, we were rewarded by the sight of the maternal furnace, sitting right where I had left it. Its stylized dragon's head stared blindly up at the warehouse's roof, its jaws frozen in midroar. I glimpsed steam curling from its nostrils, and when I looked down I saw a smudge pot, like those used in citrus groves during the winter, parked between its taloned feet, warming its copper belly.

"It looks like Esau's not wasting any time," Hexe grunted. "He's already incubating replacements."

He pulled a handkerchief from his pocket and opened the hatch of the turnip-shaped body. There was a rush of steam, followed by the smell of composting plant matter. I looked inside the hollow container and saw a huge mound of rotting lawn clippings, discarded coffee grounds, and less-identifiable organic debris the size of an alligator's nest.

Suddenly there was movement deep within the mass, like a sleeper stirring underneath a blanket. A pallid human arm emerged from the pile of decomposing vegetation, like a grub burrowing out of a rotten stump. I stared in disbelief as a milk white, unfinished *thing* writhed out of the hatchway, only to flop onto the floor like a sack of wet laundry.

From the waist up it appeared to be a fully grown adult male, save that it was completely bald and missing both its eyebrows and eyelashes. Its legs were fused together, so that it resembled an albino tadpole, and at the very end of its "tail" was a single chicken's foot, the toes of which clawed feebly at the floorboards like a newly hatched peep learning to scratch.

The abomination lifted its head and gave voice to a single, wordless cry, before collapsing dead. Within seconds of expiring, the homunculus's body began to decompose, just like its older brother's had earlier that night.

"Born of corruption, to corruption they return," Hexe said grimly. "At least we've located the maternal furnace. Now all we have to do is find the blueprints."

"I think I know where he keeps them."

As I cautiously peered around the doorjamb into the room across the hall, it seemed no different than when

I'd last seen it. The stuffed giraffe was still there, as was the black hen sitting in its cage and the pentacle on the floor. Then my eyes adjusted to the gloom, and I saw that the body on the slab had been removed and in its place stood a large cage, like those used to transport dangerous animals.

"It smells like the monkey house at the zoo," Hexe whispered under his breath.

As we neared the cage, I saw a couple of shadowy figures crouched in one corner, eating from a metal trough. One of them turned to look at us with a quick, birdlike movement of his head. It was Cain—or perhaps his identical "brother," Seth, as it was impossible to tell one homunculus from the other now. He was completely naked, his lower body smeared with filth, especially his scaly bird feet.

Despite Cain's hair being liberally shot through with gray, his face remained as smooth and unlined as a mask, no doubt because he had not lived long enough to actually break it in. There was no recognition in the SOA leader's pale gray eyes; instead they seemed as clear as freshly washed windows, and completely unclouded by thought. The homunculus returned to his feeding, shoving a handful of writhing something into his mouth.

"Ugh! What are they eating?" I grimaced.

"Probably the traditionally approved diet for homunculi: live earthworms and lavender seeds," Hexe replied.

A squirt of bile scorched the back of my throat. "I think I'm going to be sick."

"You can puke later," Hexe chided as he rifled through an antique rolltop desk covered in a drift of yellowed newspaper and old parchment. "Right now we have to find those blueprints and destroy them."

A couple of minutes into our search, we stopped upon

hearing a pair of male voices, raised in argument, in the hallway. Hexe grabbed my hand and together we scrambled into the deep shadows of the loft. Seconds after we hid behind a large wooden packing crate in the farthest corner, the door swung open and Esau, with Edgar perched on his left shoulder, entered the room, followed closely by his KPU lieutenant, Skal. Esau had his usual imperious look on his face, but judging from the younger wizard's haggard appearance and the massive pit stains on his shirt, Skal had not eaten, slept, or bathed since the night of the rally.

"This is it, Esau—I'm through with this crazy scheme of yours! Seeing that the centaur colt scored an overdose of ketamine was one thing, and making sure the ipotane got drunk and fell off the pier was simple enough. But I should have known better than to get mixed up with this demon shite! I only agreed to help you in the first place because you promised Dori would make the perfect frame for the nump bitch's death. Well, the nump bitch is still alive, Esau, and now Dori is talking to the PTU!

"My mother was sent to the Tombs to take her testimony. She *saw* me buying the binding talisman when Dori breathed on the scrying stone. Mom just called ten minutes ago to inform me that she's through covering for me. She says I have two options: either turn myself in or never set foot in Golgotham again."

Esau gave his second-in-command a withering glance. "You're as mother-haunted as my wretched excuse for a nephew. When you first came to me, you had fire in your belly. You wanted revolution, and you wanted it *now*! I told you how we could bring it about, and you swore to it in blood, if you remember." The necromancer reached into his breast pocket and withdrew a small parchment scroll bound with a red satin ribbon, holding it up so Skal could see it. "Are you reneging on that oath?"

The young wizard's face went pale. "Of course not. I'm not the kind to go back on my word, Esau. You know I'm as dedicated to the cause as you are. But what are we going to do? The Paranormal Threat Unit has traced the demon attack back to us."

"I'm afraid you're mistaken, my friend," Esau replied with a humorless smile. "The PTU has traced it back to *you*."

The scroll Esau held abruptly burst into flame. Skal opened his mouth to scream, but all that came out was a jet of blue fire. Twin tongues of flame shot from his eye sockets, then his ears, as if someone had poured gasoline into a jack-o'-lantern. Skal dropped to the floor as the fire burned him from the inside out, his arms and legs drawing into his body as the intense heat shrank his tissue and muscles.

I covered my mouth in horror, for fear I might give away our position, and quickly looked away. Skal was a loathsome person, and responsible, by his own admission, for the death of two of my friends—but nobody deserved to die such a death.

When I looked again, Esau was nudging the smoldering remains with the tip of his shoe, nodding his head in apparent satisfaction. His familiar, Edgar, spread his wings and cawed raucously, as if laughing.

"Take this traitor's body and dump it in the deepest trench in the ocean," Esau commanded, giving the charred corpse a final, dismissive kick. "Let Skua think her precious son has fled Golgotham rather than face the GoBOO's so-called justice. I will make a show of disavowing his 'extremism' at the next rally, to throw the hounds off my scent."

Edgar obediently hopped down from Esau's shoulder, taking on his demon-bird aspect in order to better carry out his master's bidding. Sinking his talons deep into what was left of Skal's body, the familiar clattered its toothed bill in farewell, then, with a single beat of its monstrous wings, flew out through the open skylight.

"Well, that settles *that* little problem," Esau announced to the empty air, wiping his hands against his lapels. The necromancer walked over to the cage containing the remaining homunculi and leaned against its bars, studying his handiwork. "Now if only you morons could tell me what happened to Abel." Seth and Cain barely glanced up as he spoke, preferring to shovel their meal of earthworms and lavender seeds into their mouths. Esau scowled and picked up an instrument from his nearby workbench. "Look at me when I'm talking, you misbegotten idiot!" he snapped as he thrust the electric cattle prod into the side of one of the homunculi.

The creature shrieked in pain and surprise, but instead of striking out at its tormentor, fell instead upon its companion, who returned the attack with equal vehemence. Esau stood and watched the two roll about on the floor of the cage as they fought tooth and nail, a cruel smirk on his face. After a couple of minutes the homunculi ceased their fighting, whether out of exhaustion or boredom, and returned to their feeding trough.

"You're no different than the nump who fathered you," Esau sneered, his voice dripping with disdain. "Reacting to all uncomfortable stimuli with brute aggression; striking out at the closest thing at hand, regardless of the role it played. Your lust and hunger control you, just as they do your father's race. My mistake was in allowing your base nature to inflame my own. That was sloppy of me."

Putting aside the cattle prod, he reached inside his shirt and pulled out an amulet affixed to a long golden chain. He wrapped his left hand about it and made a noise like a farmer calling hogs: *"Sooo-ie!"*

There was a ripple in the air of the loft, like that of heat rising from a sidewalk, accompanied by the strong smell of brimstone, and the pig-faced demon that had attacked me appeared before the necromancer. The demon knelt on one knee before Esau, raising its claws in ritual supplication. "Master, I implore you," the demon begged in a deep, grunting voice. "Release me from your service. I cannot recover from the wounds dealt me by the warlock prince and his human bitch in this realm." The infernal gestured to its mangled, melted face and missing eye. "Every moment I spend on this plane of existence is agony to me. I must return to my home, so I may bathe in the brimstone pits and make myself whole once more. I only ask this of you so I may serve you better."

"You must think I'm as empty-headed as those things over there," Esau said with a dry laugh, pointing to the homunculi in their cage. "I have set you to a task, and you have failed at it twice. You fail a third time and you are bound to my will for eternity. I'm not about to let you off the hook. You'll suffer your wounds until you bring her to me—is that understood? "

"Perfectly, Master," the demon replied, disappearing as suddenly as it had first appeared—

Only to materialize at my side.

Chapter 27

I screamed as the demon tore me from Hexe's arms and, in a single bound, leaped the length of the room, to land before Esau.

"The girl is yours," the infernal said, hurling me at the wizard's feet. "Now return me to my home, as you promised."

"I'll free you when I am good and ready," Esau snarled at the demon.

The necromancer grabbed me by the wrist and yanked me to my feet. I tried to break free of his grasp, but his hold was as strong as iron. "I would advise you not to struggle, my dear," he hissed, as he bent my newly healed arm behind my back. "I know how all too easy it is to permanently damage a limb." I bit my lower lip, determined not to give him the satisfaction of hearing me cry out in pain.

"*Hexe!*" Esau's voice shook the walls like a thunderclap. "So you finally put everything together, eh? Well, it certainly took you long enough. Show yourself, boy! There's no point in pretending to hide now."

"Let her go, Uncle," Hexe said as he stepped out into

the open. "You have no reason to kill Tate now. She's no threat to you."

"That may be true," the necromancer replied. "But what she represents threatens all of Golgotham."

Hexe shook his head in disgust. "You're a chuffing hypocrite, you know that? You've done more to harm Golgotham than a dozen real estate developers ever could."

"That beating my proxies gave you must have rattled your brains," Esau said with a derisive laugh. "There is nothing I would not do to protect Golgotham's sovereignty and safeguard it from those who would pollute and weaken it."

"Including killing and terrorizing your fellow citizens?"

"The deaths of Quid and Jarl were regrettable. I had hoped their murders would result in Golgotham sealing its borders and becoming a human-free zone, but the populace wasn't ready for such radical change. Still, your friends' blood will not have been spilled in vain. The Unification Party is strong, and continues to grow. Come the next election, I will replace that stooge Lash as mayor of Golgotham. I will see to it that Quid and Jarl are treated as martyrs, and raise statues in their honor."

"And what about Gus and Bayard? Will you raise statues to them as well?" Hexe asked sarcastically. "Or are only Kymerans worthy to be recognized as martyrs?"

"What are a couple of five-fingered half-beasts of burden compared to the new era I will bring forth?" Esau replied with a shrug. "Their ancestors swore fealty to my forefathers, and by rights their lives were mine to do with as I saw fit. Their spirits will be appeased knowing their deaths were necessary to bring Golgotham's savior to power and keep our borders safe from the real estate developers and the fast-food chains."

I turned to glare at my captor in disgust. "You orchestrated all this death and suffering, simply to put yourself in politics and keep McDonald's and Starbucks out of Golgotham?"

"Trust a nump to see it in such a limited fashion!" Esau growled, giving my pinned arm an extra crank for daring to speak out. "The Kymeran people deserve better than a few cramped city blocks, selling cheap magic to disgruntled office workers and cheating husbands. For years the city of New York has slowly encroached on our sovereign territory; it is time we finally pushed back to extend our borders. Until we dedicate ourselves to recapturing the glory that was Kymera, we will never be free of human oppression!"

"Kymera was drowned by the Indian Ocean millennia ago, and what you're planning will destroy Golgotham just as surely as the tsunami!" Hexe countered. "I thought perhaps you were merely bitter and power-hungry, but you truly *are* mad if you think I will allow you to destroy the treaty and declare war on New York City!"

"What makes you think you'll live that long?" Esau laughed as the door to the homunculi's cage swung open of its own accord and Seth and Cain came bounding toward Hexe.

He raised his right hand and one of the brothers fell to the floor, as rigid as a department store mannequin, while his twin remained unaffected. Screeching at the top of his lungs like an angry baboon, the freed homunculus delivered a vicious roundhouse blow to Hexe's head.

"I've wanted to do that ever since you were five years old," Esau laughed via his proxy. "Your mother shamed our blood by bringing you into this world, and it's high time I took you out of it!"

Hexe backpedaled, trying to put distance between himself and the homunculus. The creature lunged at him, coming in low like a grappler. But this time Hexe was ready for him, freezing him in midtakedown.

Esau cursed as he was forced to relinquish control of his living puppet and turned to the demon crouched beside him. "Kill him!"

The infernal gave a frightened squeal and shook its head, as it still wore the wounds from the last time it had crossed Hexe's path. The necromancer held up the amulet with his free hand and shook it at the reluctant hellspawn.

"By this seal, I *command* you to do as I say!" he shouted angrily. "Kill him—and once you've finished tearing him limb from limb, I want you to take his head and show it to his mother before you kill *her*. Then, and *only* then, will I set you free!"

The demon snarled and grudgingly bowed his head in acceptance of his task, his remaining two eyes filled with a hate as hot as boiling lead. The infernal spun about to face Hexe, and with a single leap cleared half the space between them.

As the demon advanced on him, Hexe raised his right hand to his forehead, palm outward, shielding his third eye. A beam of white light shot forth from its center, where the lines of Heart, Fate, Head, and Life intersect, bathing the hellish courtier in its radiance. The demon's bellow of pain was so loud it shook the dust from the rafters and left my ears ringing. Now I understood the demon's reluctance to obey Esau's command. The wounds it had suffered the last time it confronted Hexe had weakened it considerably. Huge blisters rose across the demon's torso, causing the skin to fall away like handfuls of wet paper. It turned to look at Esau, stretching out a claw in supplication as the flesh was stripped from its body, begging to be released from its torment, but the necromancer merely stared ahead, his face as unreadable as a statue's.

There was a sudden movement behind Hexe, as Seth and Cain, now freed from their stasis spells, grabbed him from either side, pinning his arms behind his back. The white light winked out as if turned off at the switch. As Hexe struggled to extricate himself, the demon got back onto its crooked hind legs, tossed back its head and made a noise that passed for laughter among the damned.

The hellspawn stepped forward and grabbed Hexe by the throat, holding his head so that he could not look away, and pried his jaws apart with one of its talons. It then placed its face scant inches from his and took a deep, deep breath, so that its chest swelled out like a blacksmith's bellows, slowly sucking the air from Hexe's lungs into its own. I watched in horror as Hexe gasped for breath, his eyes starting from his head as his face began to turn blue. His body bucked and twisted mightily, but he was unable to break free from the homunculi's grasp.

"Your lover is doomed," Esau whispered in my ear. "And it is all because of you. If you had never set foot in Golgotham, none of this would be happening. Jarl, Quid, Skal . . . all of them would still be alive."

The only man I'd ever truly loved was dying right before my eyes, and I was powerless to stop it. But what could I do? I wasn't a sorceress, or a ninja, or a badass street fighter. I had no power in the day-to-day world, much less one full of wizards and demons. I desperately wished I had my cutting torch—at least I'd leave Esau with something to remember me by.

Suddenly there was a loud, high-pitched hissing sound, like a cross between an angry snake and a steam radiator springing a leak, and a loud thud that shook the entire building like a mortar round. The demon stopped to turn and stare at the door, sniffing the air suspiciously. There was a heavy thumping sound from the other side, as if a rhino was galloping full throttle down the hallway, then a tremendous crash as a copper dragon smashed its way through the door.

It was completely unlike any dragon I'd ever seen pictures of, with a squat, turnip-shaped body balanced on three sturdy legs, with lion's paws for feet, and a long, snakelike neck. With a start, I realized I wasn't looking at a true dragon, but the maternal furnace I had constructed from Jarl's blueprints brought to life, just as my old sculptures had been animated by Hexe's magic.

The copper dragon opened its jaws, releasing a plume of steam, and then snapped them closed onto one of the homunculi. It whipped its serpentlike neck back and forth, worrying the artificial humanoid like a terrier does a rat.

Esau cried out, his shriek melding with that of the homunculus as the copper dragon broke its spine, and abruptly let go of my arm. I quickly grabbed the talisman hanging from his neck and yanked as hard as I could, breaking the golden chain. As I ran toward Hexe, the copper dragon slammed its tanklike body against the remaining homunculus, crushing him into a paste against the brick wall of the warehouse.

I looked around the chaos, trying to find Hexe, only to spot him doubled up on the floor, desperately trying to suck air back into his lungs. As I made to rush to his side, my path was blocked by the Infernal Knight, its wings spread and talons bared. I did not flinch or scream, but instead held up the talisman for it to see. The demon's snarl disappeared and it bowed its head in acknowledgment.

"What do you command of me, Mistress?" the infernal asked.

"Go to hell. And take that chuffer with you when you leave," I said, pointing to Esau.

The demon squealed in glee, its remaining eyes lighting up with an unholy fire. It leaped straight up and over me, like Jack jumping over the candlestick, and landed beside its erstwhile master, grabbing him by the hair.

"Let go of me!" Esau shouted as the demon dragged him to the middle of the pentacle. "Don't you know who I am? I'm the Witch King! In the name of the Left Hand, I command you to release me!"

The demon laughed and a tongue of hellfire sprang into being at the topmost vertex of the pentacle and then raced down its edges, until the entire pentagram was ablaze. Esau cried out in fear and tried to break free of the infernal's grasp as the floor beneath his feet began to bubble like a tar pit, but the demon held him tight, all the while continuing to laugh.

I helped Hexe back onto his feet, and together we watched as Esau was pulled inexorably downward into the bowels of whatever hell awaited him, alternately begging for mercy and cursing us. Once the duo had disappeared beneath its surface, the hellfire extinguished itself and the floor returned to its previous solid state.

"Is he dead?" I whispered.

Hexe shook his head. "No. But he's going to wish he was."

I glanced over at the copper dragon, which stood nearby. It had reverted to its previous inanimate state, with only a few dents and an unsightly bloodstain or two as proof of its brief, miraculous life.

"How did you manage to animate that thing?" I asked. "I thought that required a specific ritual?"

"This isn't my magic," he replied. I could tell by the way he was squinting that he was trying to decipher the signature on the spell, which would identify whoever had enchanted the piece of alchemical equipment.

"Well, whose is it, then?"

His golden eyes widened in surprise. "It's yours."

Chapter 28

"Welcome back to the Two-Headed Calf!" Chorea smiled as she greeted us from the newly installed hostess station. Although she still wore a wreath of ivy in her dark hair, the maenad was no longer dressed in the diaphanous chiton and leopard skin of her cult. Instead, she wore a contemporary, if equally revealing, cocktail dress and high-heeled shoes.

"How's the AA going, Chory?" I asked.

"One day at a time. I'm making my meetings, and I haven't had a drink in three weeks," she said proudly. "Just ask Faro." She pointed to her husband, who waved at us from his seat at the horseshoe-shaped bar, hoisting a glass of club soda in salute.

"I'm glad everything is working out for the two of you." Hexe smiled and gave her a peck on the cheek.

After a month of remodeling to repair the damage from the riot, the Two-Headed Calf was ready for business. While the official grand reopening was scheduled for the coming weekend, tonight was what Lafo called a "special pre-reopening" for his friends, family, and long-time customers.

I scanned the downstairs bar area, trying to discern what changes had been made to Golgotham's oldest dining establishment. Outside of new tables and chairs and a couple of brass ceiling fixtures to replace the ones that had been destroyed, the only real difference was that the small stage at the back of the room was now noticeably bigger, with a professional lighting system and mixing board safely ensconced in its own booth.

"Thanks for showing up, guys!" Lafo said, throwing his arms about us in welcome. The Calf's chief cook, bartender, and bottle washer was dressed in a raspberry sherbet–colored zoot suit and had braided his long red beard in honor of the occasion. "It really means a lot to me."

"I'm just glad you're back in business," Hexe told him.

"Not half as glad as I am!" Lafo said with a chuckle. "Getting trashed in the riot was a huge pain in the ass, but there was a silver lining to it. Since I had to shut down to remodel the downstairs, I decided to go ahead and upgrade the kitchen and make some improvements to the dining room upstairs. It's already paying off— Talisman has booked their record release party here, and the *Herald* is sending a reporter to cover the official reopening this weekend."

"Congratulations! That's wonderful news!"

A beeping sound started coming from somewhere inside the restaurateur's voluminous jacket. "Excuse me, please," he said as he deactivated the timer on his smartphone. "I need to get the seal flipper pie out of the oven!"

As Lafo hurried off to the kitchen on the second floor, I saw Captain Horn sitting in one of the booths, talking to Lady Syra. She must have said something funny, because his poker face suddenly split into a grin.

There was something oddly familiar about the way he laughed, but I could not exactly put my finger on it. The moment the PTU officer spotted Hexe, he instantly regained his usual sober composure.

"Ms. Eresby, Serenity," he said, rising to greet us. "I trust you are no longer plagued by demons, now that Skal has fled Golgotham?"

"Haven't seen a hair on its demonic chinny-chin-chin in weeks, Captain," I replied.

"Good. I want to assure you that we *will* find Skal, and eventually bring him to justice. After all, he's not just wanted for the attack on you—he's also the prime suspect in the disappearance of Esau. I was just talking to your mother, Hexe—as Esau's next of kin, she went through your uncle's accounts and informs me that a good deal of money is missing from the KUP coffers. No doubt Esau caught Skal embezzling and the young punk did something to him. I don't care if his mother works for the GoBOO; I never *did* trust that kid."

"Are you *sure* you'll be able to catch him, Captain?" Lady Syra asked. "Granted, Esau and I have not been close for some time, but he *is* my brother."

"Don't worry, Your Highness. There are only so many Kymeran enclaves scattered about the world. He's bound to show up in one of them. It's just a matter of time. As soon as I can spare a couple of agents from the SOA Task Force, I'll be sending them down to Faubourg Cauchemar in New Orleans, and overseas to Limehouse and the Pigalle, to look for him. Well, I think I'm going to hit the bar. . . ." The PTU officer took a couple of steps, then turned back around, as if he had just remembered something. "Oh! Speaking of the SOA, Serenity— one of my officers busted a leprechaun on a D and D who claims he saw you chase a human in a ski mask out into Pearl Street, where he was trampled by a Teamster. You wouldn't know anything about that, would you?"

"It's certainly news to me, Captain," Hexe replied.

"I thought as much," Horn grunted. "No doubt my informant was mistaken—not to mention three sheets to the wind. I would have known if a dead human dressed like a member of the SOA showed up in our morgue. It's still my job to ask questions. No offense, Serenity."

"None taken, Captain. Like you said, it's your job."

"I really *do* hate lying to him," Lady Syra sighed as I slid into the booth opposite her. "But Esau didn't leave us much of a choice, did he? Once things calm down, I'll let certain members of the GoBOO and the PTU in on the secret. But make no mistake: If the humans ever learn about what he was doing, we really *will* have a race war on our hands."

"What about Skal's mother? Shouldn't we at least tell *her* the truth?" I asked, looking across the room at Skua, who was busy talking to Seamus O'Fae. Now that Esau had disappeared from the political scene, the leprechaun leader had declared his interest in running for mayor. All of Golgotham's previous mayors had been Kymeran, but who knows? Times change. He's got my vote, at least.

"Better she wonder if he's an embezzler and a likely murderer than to remove all doubt," Lady Syra replied. "Besides, it would destroy her career and livelihood just as surely as it would our own."

"You're right," I said with a sigh. "I just can't help feeling sorry for her. Skal was a piece of shit, but his mother still loved him, even though she was no longer willing to shield him. But she doesn't know what really happened to him, just like Bayard's family will never know."

"Speaking of which, I saw to it that the 'missing funds' from the KUP treasury were redistributed between the young centaur's herd and Jarl's widow," Lady Syra reported. "Anonymously, of course."

"What about Gus?" I asked.

"Since he was a Teamster, the union paid for his funeral and the ferryman," she explained. "But I made sure he will have a proper monument in Necropolis. I did the same for Quid. Hopefully it will be enough to put their spirits to rest."

"What about Esau?" I asked uneasily. "Do you think he'll ever come back?"

"That is always a possibility," the Witch Queen conceded. "After all, he's not really dead—just trapped in another dimension. A really *unpleasant* one at that, from what you described." She clucked her tongue in reproach. "He should have known better than to antagonize a demon, especially a Knight of the Infernal Court. They don't forget insults, no matter how slight."

"Do you miss him?"

Lady Syra glanced up at me, surprised by the question. "Yes, I guess I do. But I've been missing my brother for a long, long time. The Esau you cast into the hell he so richly deserved was not the one I grew up with. Ever since he lost poor Nita, he was never the same. . . ."

"Yeah, about that," Hexe said, clearing his throat. "How is it that no one in the family ever mentioned Esau's wife when I was growing up? It probably wouldn't have changed how he treated me, but at least I would have had a better understanding of why he was such a miserable bastard."

Lady Syra took a deep breath and let it out in a long, sad sigh. "It all happened so long ago, sweetie, years before you were born. Nita was a lovely woman, in both body and spirit. She was also a healer, by the way, and worked alongside Esau on his projects. He loved her so terribly, terribly much. When the psychic surgeons pronounced her brain-dead after what happened, he went quite mad for a while. That's when Father decided to make me the Heir Apparent, of course. Esau recovered somewhat, after that, but he had become an adherent to the Left Hand Path, and we learned it was better never to mention Nita's name around him. After a while, we stopped talking about her altogether. It was far less stressful that way." Syra straightened up and clapped her hands, as if to dispel the old memories. "But enough about such sad things!" she exclaimed. "Let's talk about something more cheerful! So, my dear, I hear you've been left destitute!"

"Mom!" Hexe groaned in embarrassment.

"It's okay, baby." I laughed. "It's no big secret that my parents cut off my trust fund. I've landed a job working metal at Chiron's blacksmith shop. It's hard work, but I think I'm starting to get used to it."

"It's good to know that you can still make the rent," she said with a chuckle. "But look at it this way—you may have lost a fortune, but you've gained magical powers! It might not be a win-win, but at least you've come out even."

"Mr. Manto has this theory that my living in Golgotham, surrounded by magic, has triggered some latent 'uncanny' trait," I explained. "He says I am touched by Hephaestus, the Blacksmith of the Gods, and that's why I have the power to bring anything I create out of metal to life. Maybe he's right. After all, the first Eresby who came to this country was the son of a blacksmith."

"I always thought that Cyber-Panther of yours had a special spark," Hexe said. "The other sculptures were merely animate, but it seemed to possess something resembling awareness."

"Well, if your parents are foolish enough to cast you aside, then you're more than welcome here." Lady Syra smiled, reaching across the booth and giving my hand a squeeze.

I opened my mouth, but the tightness at the back of my throat made it impossible for me to speak. So I simply smiled, blinking back the tears that threatened to spill from my eyes, and squeezed her hand in return.

"So, you're giving us your blessing? I thought you were worried about the ramifications of the next Witch King taking a human as his consort?" Hexe said.

"That was before you told me you saw a corona about her head," she replied, her manner suddenly quite serious. "What you described is known as the Crown of Adon. It is a phenomenon that appears only to heirs to the throne and, even then, not to all of them.

"As you know, Adon was the ancient Kymeran goddess of love, mother to the first Witch King and protectress of the royal family. According to the Scroll of the Dragon Oracle, when a Witch King or Witch Queen is in the presence of the one the goddess has chosen for them, the Crown of Adon appears above their head as you described it—but only they, and they alone, can see it.

"Sadly, not every heir to the throne receives this vision. My father did not see a halo above my mother's head, nor did my grandfather see one above my grandmother's, and so forth, going back for centuries. Because so many of our ancestors have been denied this vision, the Crown of Adon has been labeled 'apocryphal.' But I know it is real, because I saw it shine above your father's head the first time I laid eyes on him—and I still see it every time I look at him. Basically, what I'm trying to say is that you two are meant to be together, and no one, Kymeran or human, should keep you apart. Now, if you don't mind, I think I will go take my own advice." With that, Lady Syra slid out of the booth and made her way to the bar, where she slid her hand through the crook of Captain Horn's arm.

"My dad's a *cop*?" Hexe gasped in disbelief.

"Your mother looks very happy," I said, reaching over and pushing his jaw shut.

"Yes, she does," he agreed, slipping an arm about my shoulders. "And, for once, I think I understand how she feels. I believe this calls for a drink, don't you?" He laughed, motioning for one of the waitresses to come take our order.

The waitress, a buxom nymph dressed in a short skirt and a tight-fitting T-shirt bearing the Two-Headed Calf's logo, hurried forward.

"Hi, my name is Eurydice. I'll be your server tonight. Would you like to see our new menus?" she asked, handing us a pair of laminated trifolds.

Hexe frowned. "New menus?"

"Lafo decided he wanted to experiment with ethnic food," the nymph said with a shrug. "To each his own, I guess."

I opened up the menu, glossing over the familiar descriptions for Pig's Face and Cabbage, Five Kinds of Snake Soup, and Fried Clams Sundae, wondering what could possibly be considered "ethnic food" in a Kymeran restaurant. I got my answer as my gaze dropped to the bottom. I blinked in surprise, my contentment now tempered by a touch of dismay.

Funny how a single word like "cheeseburger" can change everything.

Golgotham Glossary

Abdabs: The frights/terrors; any number of creatures known for harassing/frightening humans. Used in Kymeran slang to connote annoyance, as in "Bloody abdabs!"

Ambi: Someone who practices both Right and Left Hand disciplines.

Bastet: A shape-shifting race taking the form of different big cats, such as tiger, lion, and panther. Also known as the Children of Bast.

Cacozealot: Someone suffering from misdirected zeal; an extremist devoted to the Left Hand Path.

Centauride: A female centaur; also known as a centauress.

Charmer: A wizard who creates charms for a living.

Chuff/Chuffing/Chuffed: Euphemism for sexual intercourse.

Come-hither: A spell that calls a man or woman against his or her will, often during sleep or in an altered state of consciousness. Because of this, the subjects of come-hithers rarely have any memory of what happened to them once the spell is lifted. This spell is a favorite of date rapists and stalkers.

Client: Humans who pay to consult Kymeran witches and warlocks for any number of reasons.

Croggy: A subordinate or acolyte.

Crossed: Also known as cursed, afflicted, hexed, jinxed.

Dexter/Dexie: Someone who practices Right Hand magic, such as lifting curses and curing ailments. Right Hand magic is protective/defensive, as opposed to Left Hand magic, which is malicious/offensive.

Dowser: A psychic who specializes in finding lost things or locating fresh water.

Fecker: A contemptible person.

Gladeye: The opposite of the Evil Eye. A charm that casts good fortune and success, especially in love and business, and protects against curses.

Hamadryad: A shy, seldom-seen nature-spirit who lives inside one particular tree, such as an oak, birch, ash, or sycamore. Because of the urban nature of New York City, only a handful of hamadryads live in Golgotham.

Heavy Lifter: One who can lift malignant curses.

Hedger: Short for "hedgewitch" or "hedge doctor"; a wizard specializing in herbal treatments of various illnesses.

Huldra: Female member of the huldrefolk, one of the supernatural races living in Golgotham. They resemble beautiful young women, except for the cow tails growing from the base of their spines. The males of their kind, known as huldu, appear as handsome men, except for the tails of bulls growing from the base of their spines.

Inflicted: The state of having an illness or spate of misfortune supernatural in origin.

Inflictions: A number of spiteful/socially embarrassing medical illnesses and physical conditions that are the result of supernatural agents. These curses mimic genuine physical and mental illnesses, such as cancer or schizophrenia, and require a diagnosis by a Kymeran healer. If the illness is natural in origin, the client is referred to a doctor. Also referred to as afflictions.

Ipotane: One of the supernatural races found in Golgotham. Humans from the waist up, they are horses from the waist down. Unlike centaurs, they have only two legs. They are often mistaken for satyrs, much to their disgust.

Juggler: Someone who is known as a competent practitioner of both Right and Left Hand magic.

Lifter: A witch or warlock who specializes in lifting curses.

Ligature: Magical binding using knotted cords that prevents someone from physically doing something.

Maenads: One of the supernatural races living in Golgotham. Maenads are female followers of Dionysius, the Greek god of wine. They go into ecstatic frenzies during which they lose all self-control and engage in sexual orgies, ritualistically hunt down wild animals (and occasionally men and children), tear them to pieces, and devour the raw flesh.

Misanthrope: An antihuman bigot.

Munted: Extremely drunk or otherwise intoxicated.

Nump: A fool. A derogatory racial slur directed at humans.

Peddler: Short for "charm peddler"—a wizard who specializes in selling charmed objects for commercial gain.

Pissing Contest: A magic battle between drunken wizards.

PTU: Short for Paranormal Threat Unit, a separate branch of the NYPD in charge of policing Golgotham and responding to paranormal/supernatural events throughout the triborough area.

Pusher: Short for "potion pusher"—a wizard who specializes in selling love potions, untraceable poisons, etc., for commercial gain.

Satyr: One of the supernatural races living in Golgotham. Satyrs are humans from the waist up; goats from the waist down. They also sport horns on their heads. They are notorious for being prone to gambling, drinking, and kidnapping beautiful women. Female satyrs are called fauns.

Slinging Blind: Casting spells without regard to safety, usually due to panic or intoxication.

Talent: A natural magic ability, applying both to humans and Kymerans.

Widdershins: The direction in which a curse must be turned in order to undo it.

The Witch Finders: An elite medieval military group composed of both Christian and Islamic knights and soldiers during the Unholy War. Famous for severing the extra 'magic' fingers of Kymerans.